JO
DUFFY

AZURE SKIES

MALICE

Copyright © 2016 Jon Duffy

Jon Duffy asserts the moral right to be identified as the author of this work

All rights reserved

All characters in this publication are fictitious and any resemblance to real persons, living or dead, is purely coincidental

Published by Jon Duffy

Printed by CreateSpace
Available on Kindle and from Amazon.com

ISBN: 1523452382
ISBN-13: 978-1523452385

Dedicated to my parents BOB and
ADELE DUFFY for reasons too
numerous to fit on to a single page.

1

A distant groan caught at his tongue, preventing words from emerging. His hand was instantly upon his gun, removing it quickly and carefully from its holster. Willow too seemed to have heard the sound and was turning nervously, the large hunting knife drawn from his belt and held firmly in his hand.

The Malice seemed to be thicker now, closing in on them as they circled in the snow, their senses sharpened, muscles tensed. Willow's nervousness was evident, his breathing uneven as his body seemed to visibly shake under the pressure of the situation. Using his experience to control his breathing and remain alert, the old man gazed deeply into the Malice, searching for the slightest sign of movement. He knew something was there, stalking them through the mist. A growl emerged as if from thin air, echoing around them, making it impossible to identify the location of the source.

'Where is it?' The panic in Willow's voice was evident, his eyes wild and petrified as he turned rapidly.

Focus. Listen carefully. Not just where, but how many? The Death Cheater's eyes scanned the surrounding area. A few ramshackle old buildings with plenty of dark corners to hide in, but very little protection and easy to get trapped within. Aside from that there were no obvious clues of what lay beyond, obscured beneath the Malice and behind the blanket of falling snow. For now there was little choice but to hold their ground and hope that the danger passed.

Both men's eyes fell upon the dark figure slowly forming before them as it emerged from the Malice. The creature's blood red eyes seemed to penetrate their very souls as it released another menacing growl, slowly approaching the Dead Men with hungry arms outstretched.

The snow crunched lightly as the creature's deformed feet pressed down upon the white blanket, leaving a trail of midnight black blood in its wake. A few remnants of clothing remained, clinging to the blackened skin covered by deep blue veins through which the Malice seemed to visibly course, though the heart which lay within its shallow chest had long since surrendered. Decay seemed to hang in the air as the creature's scent caught the wind, deadly breath emerging from its gaping mouth of rotten teeth. What once had been a man was now a hollow, evil shell, intent only upon death, destruction and feeding.

They get uglier every time, thought the Death Cheater, tightening his grip on his weapon. It was not the first time he had come face to face with one of these creatures, nor was it the first time he had felt a sense of hopelessness tug at him in the face of such a fearsome monster. But as before, he buried it deep within himself and refused to acknowledge it. *This won't be the last time either.* Thinking clearly now, he felt the familiar calm set in as he raised his weapon and took aim at the demon.

As he pulled the trigger, a simple statement repeated continuously in his mind as he thought back on the event which had led them to this moment.

This is all your fault...

* * *

The glass glistened captivatingly in the palm of the old man's gloved hand, catching the light as it gleamed down from his torch and creating rainbows within itself. His cold fingers turned it slowly, observing its unorthodox shape and texture. There was no doubt in his mind that in a land of ice, he had found something truly unique.

The small decrepit house had seemed as promising as any of the other weathered remains of society that constituted the long abandoned village. In the back of his mind, the old man knew that the place had once had a name, but it no longer mattered. It existed simply as a source of food and equipment for the society which lay huddled beneath the planet's surface, hibernating in a permanent waking nightmare, attempting to ride out the abnormal elements which had claimed the surface as their own. The ice and the snow were surmountable; the Malice was not.

In spite of himself, the old man found himself grinning as he pocketed the glass and lifted himself from his knees, feeling his ageing frame creak and click beneath him under the strain. Unable to suppress the grunt which escaped from his lips, he felt the eyes of his young companion burn into him. He was suddenly thankful for the mask which covered his face, disguising his pained expression.

'Don't see too many people with Malice Gear,' mused the younger man, his curiosity tempered only by his respect for the apparent wealth and experience of the older man. The old man grinned, looking down at his apparel. It was true that Malice Gear was largely an exclusive privilege afforded only to the rich and powerful, a suit designed to allow ultimate freedom of movement whilst protecting completely against both the elements and the Malice. It was common knowledge that the majority of mercenaries would not live to see old age due to one of these two factors, protected purely by the rag tag pieces of material they could shape to cover their mouth and nose. The Malice would still seep through and enter their bodies, destroying them slowly from the inside. It was little wonder that they were commonly referred to as Dead Men.

'A small gift for some work I did up in Pelera,' explained the old man, opening a nearby crate which may have at one time contained food. It was empty save for a small puddle of the miasmic Malice which quickly grew as the surrounding smog seeped into the fresh space, the base of the crate quickly hidden beneath the thick purple hued mist.

The young man laughed incredulously, the sound muffled by the thick scarf wrapped around his mouth. 'Nobody can afford to just give away Malice Gear. Do you have any idea how valuable those things are? People would slit your throat just to take it off your corpse.'

'Would *you*?' The question hung in the air, as thick and deadly as the Malice itself. The young man immediately ceased laughing and stared at his colleague. The old man tensed his muscles within the suit, his eyes locked upon the younger man. He knew the youngster was right; the Malice Gear was easily worth more than his life, a fact he had learned to come to terms with since he had first been awarded the precious gift. Sleeping with one eye open had become common practise, the lack of sleep a small price to pay for his safety.

He doesn't have it in him, thought the old man, his eyes locked upon the increasingly unnerved looking younger man, whose flitting gaze fell briefly upon the weapon holstered at the old man's side.

'I'm no Raider,' fumed the younger man, dragging his eyes away from the blackness of the old man's featureless face hidden behind the mask. 'I was just making conversation.'

The old man remained focused upon the younger man a few moments longer before returning to his task. 'What's your name, kid?'

Silence followed for a few moments as the younger man seemed to ponder the question. 'The name's Willow,' he eventually answered, before turning furiously as the old man chuckled quietly beside him. 'You got a problem with that, old man?'

So quick to lose his temper, mused the old man, shaking his head slowly. *The kid doesn't stand a chance.* 'No problem at all.' He noted the young man clench his fist, but continued to search through the remains of the house, determined not to return empty-handed. *I can't afford to, not right now.*

'I heard you're the Death Cheater. That right?'

My reputation precedes me... The old man smiled wearily. 'You found anything yet?' he asked, avoiding the question.

'There's nothing here. Nothing of use anyway.' Willow turned and moved across to the doorway, his heavy boots echoing loudly on the creaking wooden floorboards. 'We should head back, the Malice is starting to get thicker.'

The old man frowned silently. He knew Willow was right, but without the reward from this task, he would be forced to choose between parting with something or sleeping rough for a third night in a row. The merchants at The Bunker would doubtlessly offer him a meagre price for any possession he would be willing to part with, far less than its actual worth. He held no grudge against them; they were simply trying to survive in their own way.

Moving across to the window of the house, he raised his gloved hands to the frame and pushed upward. The window shuddered, but the frost held firm against the pressure.

'What are you doing?' asked Willow impatiently.

'They will come here. We need to cover our tracks as much as possible.'

'The demons?' Willow's voice sounded strained.

Heaving with all his might, the Death Cheater finally felt the frost relinquish its grip on the base of the window and the frame flew upwards, a blast of icy air hitting his face as it surged into the house. He blinked behind his mask, but through squinted eyes he spotted something. He paused, certain that his eyes were playing tricks on him.

That's... impossible...

The old man's mind struggled to grasp what he had just seen. He knew it was impossible, yet even as he attempted to confirm that fact his mind began to drift backwards, bringing forth visions he had tried to forget for so many years. *A trick of the Malice,* he told himself repeatedly, searching for an explanation. There were many stories of people suffering hallucinatory experiences upon the surface, seeing shapes and hearing sounds which seemed to emerge from the Malice itself. *That was before they went mad…*

Willow's hand upon his shoulder shook him from his trance, yet he still felt detached from what was occurring around him. He was aware of the younger man talking to him, though the sound was distant and vague. He felt as though his head had been submerged in water, that all he could see was the blurry outline of what he had glimpsed through the blizzard.

Pushing past Willow, he rushed out of the door, plunging himself into the snow. For a moment he was blind, only able to identify the white blur of the snow amongst the purple of the thickening Malice. He was aware of a sense of delirium setting in and fought to maintain control of his thoughts, but the vision remained seared in his mind, crying out for an explanation as it disappeared into the darkness. The heavy snowfall slowed his progress as he chased the fleeing mirage, hands stretched out before him, waving frantically at the Malice as it impeded his progress. It felt almost as though he were wading through water, the Malice seeming to thicken and push back against him tauntingly. Further and further he drifted into the unknown, the sight eternally floating at the edge of his vision. With every attempt to focus the image, it blurred further into obscurity.

Then as quickly as it had appeared, it vanished.

The old man skidded to a halt, his breathing hard and laboured as he desperately scanned the environment for sight of the vision. Madness clawed at his mind as all around him the remains of buildings loomed over him, ready to collapse and consume him into their forgotten darkness.

So this is how it ends, he thought as a brief moment of clarity washed over him, closing his eyes and awaiting the inevitable fall into oblivion. Everybody knew what happened when the Malice eventually poisoned the flesh, having corrupted the soul which would never find peace. The descent into madness was unpredictable, influenced by factors beyond common understanding, but ultimately the poison would have the same impact upon all its victims. It felt oddly peaceful. *It's about time. I've been waiting for this.*

The strong hand fell upon his shoulder without warning. In his mind, the old man felt the warm embrace of death grudgingly release him as he escaped from its grasp, floating upwards towards the devastatingly cold world he thought he had finally escaped from.

He was alive. Rage coursed through his veins. The Malice seemed to have turned a bloody red. In a flash he had unsheathed his gun, his finger ready and waiting upon the trigger as he spun.

Willow stared back at him, his expression an odd mix of fear and acceptance as the barrel of the Death Cheater's gun rested impatiently against the young man's forehead. Silence embraced the scene, save for the deep desperate breaths of anguish as they escaped the old man's shaking frame.

'The Malice...' Willow's voice trembled slightly as he remained frozen to the spot. 'Don't let it take you.'

Madness. Malice poisoning.

As though awakening from a dream, the old man glanced around. His breathing slowly became steady as his eyes finally focused once more. The madness that had gripped him so tightly seemed to fade, the shadows which had loomed over him melting away in the snow. A wave of embarrassment flooded through his frame as he slowly lowered his weapon, taking a deep breath to allow himself a moment to collect his thoughts.

'I saw... I thought I saw...' he started, searching for the words. None came that could explain his behaviour. 'We need to get back to the Citadel,' he said, ignoring the frustrated expression upon Willow's face and setting off at a determined pace.

'You were screaming,' Willow said awkwardly, jogging to catch up with the old man's stride. 'I thought the Malice must have taken you for a moment.'

It almost did. He could not recall screaming, but the tightness in his throat seemed to suggest Willow was not lying.

When the old man refused to respond, Willow broke the silence. 'Who's Rosa?'

The Death Cheater's heart jumped at the name. 'It's not important.'

The younger man clutched hold of his arm and spun him around, halting him in his tracks. 'I just risked my life saving you. Anybody else would have left you for dead. I think I at least deserve to know what happened to you.'

The old man smiled behind his mask. He had never really cared for working with other Dead Men; it was a young man's profession due to their notoriously short life span, and he had outgrown the need for companionship. But the young man still clutching hold of his sleeve seemed the genuine sort. And there was no doubting that he had just pulled him back from the edge of madness.

He opened his mouth to respond when a disturbing sound emerged from the Malice...

* * *

The bullet surged from the chamber and buried itself into the shoulder of the demon, but the monster's charge was not halted. Gritting his teeth, the old man threw himself out of the demon's path, landing heavily in the snow. Before he could pick himself up, it was bearing down upon him once more, the bloodlust in its eyes evident even through the thick Malice. Taking aim once more, the gun chamber emptied another bullet into the demon's body. But the monster was already upon him, its drool slobbering across the old man's mask as he fought back with failing strength.

Willow's blade cut through the Malice and barely slowed as it entered the demon's flesh, the monster releasing a cry of anguish and rolling away from the old man. It writhed with a venomous howl, spreading further black decay upon the crystal white snow before falling silent as Willow's blade surged effortlessly into its skull. The old man rolled over and stared mournfully at the eternal dark clouds overhead. Strangely, he felt equally resentful as he did thankful towards Willow. He attempted to shake the uncharacteristically bitter thought from his head. *You've just got to accept that you're getting too old for this.*

'Not too bad, eh?' grinned Willow, lifting his boot and delivering a swift stomp to the fallen demon's head. 'It's okay, you can thank me later.' Wandering over, he offered his hand to the old man to help him up. Reluctantly, the Death Cheater accepted.

He spotted the danger over Willow's shoulder before he had a chance to speak.

The second demon had approached silently, taking advantage of the distraction caused by its fallen kin which it had practically trampled over in its pursuit of fresh meat. It was upon Willow in a heartbeat, plunging its rancid teeth into his neck and knocking the young man to the floor. The old man stumbled back and fumbled with his weapon, hearing Willow's cry of despair. His fingers would not obey, as though they had been numbed by some unseen force. The demon's fangs tore through Willow's flesh as the young man screamed in agony. It was a sound that would haunt the Death Cheater forever, though it lasted just seconds as the demon tore at Willow's tongue, silencing his final anguish.

Satisfied that its first victim had been subdued, the demon turned menacingly towards the old man, who continued to fumble with his weapon. With an unusual sensation of exhaustion, he fired towards the demon, the bullet vanishing into the Malice harmlessly. Still the demon came closer, hunting its prey with complete focus. Stumbling backwards, the old man frowned at his own lack of coordination. He had taken down many demons before, some more challenging than others, but he had never felt such helplessness before. It crippled him, his cold tired limbs refusing to cooperate as he retreated from the creature. Unable to tear his eyes away from the approaching demon, he tripped and fell backwards heavily, the impact knocking the wind out of him. The demon pounced. Closing his eyes, he hoped it would be over quickly.

An explosive sound cut the air, but the old man made no move. *Perhaps I'm already dead?* he wondered as he waited in the darkness behind his closed eyelids. He had expected a floating sensation, but the ground was very much still beneath his prone body. Nearby, he heard the familiar crunch of footsteps on snow.

'You're a lucky son of a bitch, you know that?'

Lucky? Slowly forcing his eyes open, the old man found himself staring up at the dark clouds of the Eternal Storm. Lifting himself to a sitting position, his eyes fell upon the demon. A single bullet had penetrated the back of its head, brain and pitch black blood now flowing out, staining the pure white of the snow. Crouched beside the demon, a figure dressed in Malice Gear examined his kill, tugging the body this way and that as though evaluating the creature. Cradled in his arms balanced an impressive rifle.

Turning his gaze to his left, the Death Cheater's eyes fell upon Willow's body. An immense feeling of guilt surged up from the pit of his stomach as he watched the young man's soul slowly emerge from the body. It was a sight he had seen a hundred times before, yet it always inspired a sense of awe in the old man; the Echo, a simple ball of light, rippling as though it were a droplet of water suspended in midair, slowly dancing away from the flesh frame which had contained it before disappearing into the Malice. It floated at the edge of his vision, a brief spot of colour in the otherwise dull and lifeless backdrop of the surface. And then it was gone.

At length the figure stood and looked towards the Death Cheater, who still had not moved. 'You hurt?' The figure didn't seem particularly interested in receiving an answer as he observed the old man.

Lucky is definitely the right word, mused the old man as he silently eased his body back to life. Spotting his gun in the snow a short distance away, he began to move towards it.

'Hold it right there.' The figure's voice was authoritative. Even with his back to the stranger the Death Cheater knew the rifle was drawn and aimed in his direction. Turning slowly, he watched stoically as the figure approached him and aimed the barrel of his weapon at the crest that adorned the old man's Malice Gear. 'How did you come about owning this suit?' The old man allowed his eyes to focus upon the stranger's Malice Gear, noting an identical crest to his own.

Instantly feeling relaxed, he boldly pointed towards the matching crest on the stranger's Malice Gear. 'The Broxhart crest. That would make you one of the sons of Ruskin Broxhart, correct?' The old man grinned behind his mask as he saw the figure lower his weapon in recognition. 'And last I heard, only young master Haswell was crazy enough to venture up here to the surface.'

The other figure laughed. 'And there's only one man I know who would have the balls to still call me Haswell.' He extended a hand towards the old man who gripped it warmly. 'It's been a long time Madock.'

2

Madock Leocadia was known by the underground society as the Death Cheater; his age and experience were unparalleled amongst those in his profession, the majority of whom never lived to see their thirtieth birthday. Madock was still going strong with his fifty-first birthday quickly approaching. His lifestyle and profession had taken their toll on his appearance though, the numerous scars and wounds of battles across his body each telling their own story. His long flowing hair had maintained its length, but not its youth as black had faded to weathered grey. The change had not bothered him vastly; Madock preferring to believe it symbolised his experience and wisdom.

With Haswell's help he had buried Willow's body in the snow. He felt it was the least he could do for the young mercenary who had died trying to protect him. The body would not fall victim to scavengers, be they demon or Raider. There were no tears spilled for his loss though; death was simply an aspect of life for those who chose to earn their living on the surface of the planet. Madock had discovered as he gazed down upon the spot where the body lay that he could not recall the last day he had endured without experiencing a death of some description. It had simply been something he accepted, but today the realisation sickened him.

The Citadel was a welcoming sight as it slowly emerged from the Malice, looming above the shattered remains of civilisation which littered its base. The building had once been the focal point of the city of Tsau, towering over a wide array of buildings and bustling streets back before the Eternal Storm and the Malice drove the population underground. Now it mournfully gazed down upon wreckage and abandoned lives. Madock could recall his father speaking of visiting the city as a young child, in the days before humanity had fled to the underground tunnels. It had been a glorious testament to their society back then, both a technological mecca and a haven for religious enlightenment, second only to the capital Gair far to the south. Gair had survived the transition to the new world, but at the cost of its power and dominance, which now lay firmly with nearby Pelera. These days fresh water was the most valuable commodity, and thanks to the Enki cenote the Broxhart family had risen to become the most powerful family, converting Pelera into the power capital of the new world.

Madock slowed as Haswell approached the mighty oak doors to the Citadel, banging his fist against the door. A small slit opened, revealing a pair of suspicious eyes which briefly examined the two men before disappearing from sight once more. During the pause that followed, Madock's eyes fell upon the vast chimney emerging from the ground beside the Citadel. Clouds of fumes soared up through the hole, quickly fading from their original black hue as they dissipated into the Malice; the product of the underground generators which were providing the settlement below with the light, oxygen and power it required to function.

With a deep creaking noise which filled the silent air, the Citadel doors slowly swung open to reveal the innards of the Citadel. Guards stood to attention as they passed, clearly recognising the Broxhart crest upon their suits as they made their way into the building.

Breathing a sigh of relief, Haswell raised his hands to his mask and removed it, revealing a face that Madock instantly recognised as the child he had met all those years ago, now matured into the young man who stood before him. His mouth retained the same boisterous grin he had seen upon the young boy, while cerulean eyes still sparkled with excitement and mischief. His once curly blonde hair had been shaved close, a style Madock recognised as being indicative of those in the young man's profession. Demon hunters were regarded by many as the deadliest warriors of their society and enjoyed almost god-like status, touted by many as the heroes and champions of humanity.

'How many years has it been, Madock?' asked Haswell as they strolled through the dimly lit Citadel, the fluttering candles casting dancing shadows across the ancient stone walls. 'Feels like it must be, what, thirteen years or so?'

Madock smiled and nodded as he removed his own mask, listening to their footsteps echo against the stone floor. 'Fourteen, I think. You were just a young lad when I last saw you.' He turned and briefly studied the tall, sturdy man beside him. 'You grew up.'

'And you got old!' Haswell laughed, a rich deep sound which shattered the reverential quiet of the Citadel.

Madock shook his head, but found it hard to deny the smile that tugged at the corners of his mouth. Haswell had always been outspoken and straight talking as a child. It seemed that time had done little to change that. In many ways, Madock was glad to discover that some things remained constant other than the Eternal Storm.

'Are you... You're Haze Broxhart, aren't you?' The question was posed by an excitable guard patrolling the entry to the lift that disappeared into the planet's core, leading towards the settlement beneath their feet. Haswell grinned and nodded silently at the guard. Madock suppressed a tired yawn and waited patiently as the guard searched his pockets urgently. Glancing around nervously, the guard handed Haswell a thin sheet of paper and a weathered pen. 'Please could I have your autograph? My son would be thrilled.' Smiling grandly, Haswell took the pen and scribbled roughly onto the paper before handing it back to the guard who gratefully folded the precious piece of paper into his pocket and waved them onto the lift.

With a shudder, the lift slowly began to descend into the darkness, lit only briefly by intermittent lights which marked the distance as they slowly lost sight of the surface.

'Haze?' questioned Madock without turning to look at his companion.

Haswell folded his arms in the darkness. 'I prefer it.'

'Your father wouldn't be pleased if he knew.'

'He knows.' A brief flash of light allowed Madock to see the smile upon Haswell's face. 'And he isn't.'

The lift slowed as it approached the end of its descent, settling against the rocky base of the cavern. Stepping from the small metal frame, Madock and Haswell entered the underground settlement known simply as The Bunker.

The Bunker had existed long before humanity began its exodus into the underground tunnels. Carved out beneath the base of the Citadel, The Bunker had originally been used as a place of safety for the people of Tsau during some long forgotten war, hence the name which it had kept from that point onwards. The vast underground cave was maintained through a wide number of generators which provided light and oxygen to the people dwelling beneath the ground, and supported by water flowing from the Enki cenote to the north in Pelera. As humanity began to flee underground to escape the ever increasing Malice, The Bunker had presented itself as an ideal location. Pledging its allegiance to the Broxharts of Pelera in return for support and access to the precious drinking water had allowed it to flourish, particularly due to its ideal location within reach of several other underground settlements.

Hard to believe this place was once an epicentre for religion, thought Madock solemnly as they trudged through the settlement. In stark contrast to the surface above their heads, the underground settlement teemed with activity.

Wooden buildings lined dusty stone streets, the jagged walls surrounding the settlement echoing the sounds of life to amplify the volume to an almost intrusive level. Madock preferred the smaller, quieter settlements but he could not deny the allure of the bright lights mounted everywhere, powered by the various buzzing generators which provided a constant humming ambience to the atmosphere. The air was humid and smelled of sweat, the result of the sheer number of people wandering the confines of the settlement; what little fresh air that could be pumped in was quickly overwhelmed. The Bunker had become widely regarded as the easiest settlement to lose what little wealth an individual possessed. Merchants lined the streets with a wide variety of goods available at extortionate prices, ready to tempt naïve buyers into parting with their coins and possessions. Brothels and bars made up more than half the settlement's structures, leading the hopeless and the desperate to part with their possessions in return for the chance to forget about their problems, however briefly. Madock tended to avoid The Bunker as much as possible, but it was common knowledge amongst Dead Men that the best paying jobs were to be found there. Only this time, there was no payment waiting for him.

'So, a demon hunter eh?' started Madock, his hands buried in his pockets subconsciously fumbling with the glass he had found earlier. 'I can't imagine your father approves of that either.'

Haswell seemed not to hear the question as he glanced towards a quiet tavern to their right. 'How about a drink?' he asked. Noting Madock's awkward expression, he added, 'I'm buying.'

The Death Cheater nodded thankfully and followed Haswell into the dimly lit tavern.

The tavern was far from welcoming as the two men entered, the scent of cheap alcohol, sweat and vomit hanging heavily in the cramped space. A number of deadened eyes turned to observe them, but only the bartender held his gaze as they approached the rotting wooden bar.

'Two mugs of whatever tastes the least like piss,' stated Haswell, digging a silver coin from the pocket of his suit and setting it spinning on the bar. 'Oh,' he added, grabbing hold of the bartender's wrist, 'And if you can serve it in clean mugs, that would be great.'

Cursing under his breath, the bartender scooped up the silver coin and set about pouring the drinks. Glancing over the bar, Madock noticed that the liquid emerging from the tap was a foamy brown substance that at one point may have passed for drinkable. He was not about to complain though; a free drink was a free drink.

'How is your father?'

'Not now.' Haswell's tone was serious. The bartender slammed the two mugs of questionable liquid down in front of them, the contents spilling over the sides. The demon hunter shot the man a sarcastic grin. 'Keep the change.'

Leading Madock over to a quiet table in the corner of the tavern, he placed the two mugs upon the uneven wooden table and sat with his back to the wall. The placement seemed to be deliberate, perhaps a hunter's intuition to have full sight of his surroundings. Madock sat down carefully opposite him, gripping the mug and taking an experimental sip. The liquid was warm, but much to his surprise, drinkable. Placing it down upon the table, he fixed his piercing green eyes upon Haswell expectantly.

'I'm heading to Elysium,' Haswell explained flatly, not meeting Madock's gaze as the Death Cheater's eyes widened in surprise.

Elysium was an isolated settlement located in the far south, and Madock knew only what he had heard in rumours. The settlement was accessible only by braving the planet's surface across the southern ice fields, and therefore details were vague and unconfirmed. There were rumours of a religious sect which resided exclusively within the settlement, whilst others claimed Elysium was somehow overgrown with plant life in spite of being buried deep in the planet's crust. Madock believed neither.

'I didn't take you for being a Harbinger as well as a demon hunter,' said the old man, his eyes still locked upon Haswell. 'And I know that you're not stupid enough to do it for fame and fortune. Seems you have enough of that anyway...' He raised the mug once more to his lips.

'My father... he's dying.' Haswell seemed barely able to say the words, reaching for his own mug and drinking deeply from it to distract himself from the confession.

Madock's mug hovered by his lips as he struggled to take in what he had just heard. *Ruskin Broxhart? Dying?* 'The Malice?'

Haswell shook his head, finally meeting Madock's gaze. 'Old age.'

'And you hope to find the cure to old age in Elysium?' Madock had heard rumours of the supposed healing powers the settlement possessed. Even if this were true, the old man doubted it could control the inevitable decay of old age.

'Is it that crazy? We don't really know anything about Elysium, there could be anything there,' said Haswell, placing his mug down firmly on the table.

'And there could be *nothing* there,' pointed out Madock. 'All we hear about Elysium are rumours and children's tales of plants and magic. Nobody has ever seen Elysium and returned to talk about it and you know why? Because there's nothing there, nothing but ice and death.'

'You're wrong Madock.' Haswell's voice was firm. 'The Harbingers wouldn't go on pilgrimages there if it didn't exist.' In spite of his tone, Madock could hear the desperation behind the words.

'Wouldn't they?' Madock let the question hang in the air between them as Haswell allowed his attention to drift around the bar, eager to avoid considering the answer. Beneath his strong, determined face, Madock recognised the same scared boy he had watched attend public ceremonies with his father and family. He recognised the sadness in the eyes, just as he had when watching over the boy at his grandfather's funeral. He had been there for the boy then, and he suddenly realised that in many ways Haswell needed him just as badly now.

'How long have you known?' asked Madock, softening his tone.

'A messenger found me in Silverbridge a few days ago. I've been heading back north ever since, but…' Haswell paused uncomfortably. 'I just feel it would be a better use of my time to try and do something to help him. That's why I thought Elysium…' He trailed off.

Madock's response was blunt. 'You're worried he's already dead.'

Haswell's eyes flared, though whether with anger or guilt Madock could not tell. The two men sat in silence for a moment, lost in thought as they both reflected on their memories of a man who had been so important in both of their lives.

The image that formed in Madock's mind was of a boisterous, cheerful man who had never allowed the pressure of leadership to weigh down his thirst for life and fundamental belief in balance and fairness. From the depths of his mind a memory conjured itself, painting the image of himself as a young man walking side by side with Ruskin through the streets of Pelera with the children scurrying a short distance ahead to meet the various citizens who had gathered to greet the royal procession. There had been guards, of course, though they were limited in number and largely focused on monitoring the children rather than Ruskin himself. It had been common knowledge that he detested being supervised like a child, and preferred to wander around the Peleran settlement with only those he deemed necessary to secure his safety. Madock had been counted amongst that number.

The memory was becoming clearer the longer he considered it. They had been discussing the children's futures, a topic Ruskin had often steered their conversations towards.

'If they grow up to be anything like their old man, they'll want to be out there having adventures rather than stuck down here,' he had predicted boldly. 'Sometimes I miss the freedom you Dead Men have.'

'It's not freedom Ruskin,' Madock had replied solemnly. 'There's nothing up there anymore. But there is something down here.' He had allowed his gaze to drink in the scenery around him, recreated firmly within his memory. 'This is what's really worth fighting for.'

Ruskin had laughed heartily at that. 'Perhaps you should be the one upon the throne, my friend. You certainly have a way with words.'

Their conversation had been cut short by a cry from ahead. Haswell had tripped while trying to walk along the top of a crumbling wall, landing heavily as he had crashed to the floor and bursting into floods of tears. Several of the guards had rushed to his aid, while his brother and sister looked on with concerned expressions.

Madock had looked to Ruskin seeking guidance on how to proceed, but Ruskin had held him back from getting involved. 'He'll learn from this experience,' he said confidently, watching his son pick himself up from the floor. 'And he'll learn to recover from far worse in the future.' He turned and fixed Madock with his emerald eyes. 'And should there ever come a time when he needs somebody to pick him up in the future, I expect that you'll be the one to do it.'

The memory started to fade, replaced by flames as an unwelcome thought screamed for attention.

That was just a few weeks before the explosion.

Madock jolted, glancing around quickly at the bar to remind himself of his current surroundings. Haswell was still sat opposite him, apparently as lost in thought as he himself had been moments before.

Drowning the last of his drink, Madock stood and pushed his chair back firmly. Haswell looked up, startled from his daydream and watching the old man curiously.

'Drink up, kid. We're going to see your father.'

3

Lord Ruskin Broxhart was dying.

It was a secret truth, contained within the walls of the Broxhart manor overlooking the Enki cenote and the settlement that thrived upon its flowing waters. If knowledge of their Lord's ill health were to spread throughout the tunnels, there was a distinct possibility of panic infecting the population, its effect as potentially dangerous as the Malice that lurked overhead. There would of course be a successor, but these were dangerous days; the absence of an authority figure for any length of time was an open invitation to any power hungry usurper. The Broxhart family were widely respected and supported, but there would always be those who would abandon loyalty in a heartbeat for the chance of power. Especially with the Enki cenote up for grabs.

Kerrin paced back and forth impatiently as he awaited the medic's latest report on his father's health. Though he prayed for good news, he knew that it was simply a question of how much further his father had sunk towards the darkness of death. In many ways it would be a welcome release for the old man; the previous week had been the hardest, as he became a frail shadow of the powerful figure he had once been. Yet his spirit prevailed. Even now Kerrin could hear the Lord of Pelera berating the Harbinger from behind the closed doors that led to his bedroom. It tugged at the corners of Kerrin's mouth without ever forming a full smile. It had been a long time since he last smiled.

Only one question threatened to displace his concern for his father's health. It was becoming an increasingly important question as Ruskin descended further into the darkness. It was a question he had asked before, yet never with as much concern or desperation.

Where was his brother?

Haswell Broxhart's decision to leave the safety of Pelera to pursue a life as a demon hunter had not been received well by anybody other than his brother and, more importantly, his father. Kerrin had supported his brother's dream, albeit purely due to the fact that it meant he would see less of him. They had never been that close, a fact that had been reflected in their almost polar opposite public images. His brother was regarded as the successful athletic child, the natural successor to the leadership of Pelera and immensely popular with the people. This had gone some way to explaining his desire to join the demon hunters, arguably the greatest form of celebrity status known to society in this period known as the Dark Days. Kerrin knew his brother well enough to know that he thrived on attention and respect.

In direct comparison Kerrin believed he had been sidelined as the quiet, insignificant brother, yet he was content in this role; it removed any pressure as nobody realistically viewed him as a successor to the Peleran throne, though he had just as much claim to it as his brother. It had allowed him to observe his family's position and responsibilities almost as a spectator, an outsider to the whole affair. The people rarely compared the merits of the brothers as potential future rulers. Some didn't even recognise them as twins anymore.

Since he had left almost a year ago, Haswell had not been seen in Pelera, though there had been rumours of sightings in the nearby settlements at Mikara and Tirneth. Kerrin doubted any of these were true; his brother already had the love of the Peleran people and the northern folk at large. Therefore it was far more likely that he was exploring the southern regions beyond Silverbridge in search of further adoration. Unfortunately, Haswell's departure had raised eyebrows but also questions as to who would inherit the leadership of the Peleran tunnels in the future. Many maintained that Haswell would return like a saviour to assume the role, whilst others had cast suspicious eyes towards Kerrin's capabilities. He had avoided the topic as much as possible, busying himself until public interest faded or switched to other more pressing issues. The question of inheritance had been purely speculation back then, but now the moment had arrived, even if the masses were not aware of it yet.

    The doors to Lord Broxhart's chamber were flung open as the Harbinger departed, Ruskin's powerful voice forming a wave that escorted the shaken man from the room. There was no doubting that Kerrin's father had maintained his own unique sense of humour to the end, his booming voice insisting that the Harbinger's "magic show" had brought him little amusement. Ruskin Broxhart had never had much time for the Harbingers and their religious beliefs, in spite of their proven healing ability. "Whatever doesn't kill you makes you stronger." That had always been his father's approach.

    The Harbinger waited nervously by the doors until Ruskin's aide joined them in the corridor, walking calmly from the room. Closing the doors to the chamber behind him, he dismissed the healer with a raised hand and turned to address Kerrin.

    Marcus Ortiz was a wiry old man, yet he was as wise as he was awkward to behold. His long limbs moved with a complete lack of grace, his quick eyes constantly darting around within his narrow skull. Marcus had been by Ruskin's side since Kerrin's father began his reign, and nothing had changed even as the Lord became entirely bedridden. He smiled weakly at Kerrin as Ruskin continued to laugh and rant within his chamber at the remaining medics, though the sound was soon replaced by another fit of coughing.

'How is he?' asked Kerrin, escorting Marcus down the corridor until the coughing faded into obscurity in their wake.

'Fading, I'm afraid. But his spirit remains… spirited.' Marcus forced a smile, which quickly faded as he noted the stern look upon Kerrin's face.

'How much longer can he last?'

'Difficult to say,' conceded the aide. 'His mind could stand the test of time, but his body is failing. A month perhaps? I would hesitate to offer you any more comfort than that.'

Kerrin sighed, but continued his determined stride as Marcus kept pace alongside. 'Any word on my brother?'

'Our scouts are still out searching for Master Haswell, but the surface is wide and fraught with dangers. They can only cover so much ground at any one time.'

Kerrin scowled. 'Surely the demon hunters must have some sort of organization? Some form of headquarters or communication links?'

Marcus smiled softly. It was a smile he had used since Kerrin was a child, and the Lord's son knew exactly what it meant: *You know nothing of the real world* was what that smile said. Kerrin hated it but said nothing. 'The demon hunters are as brave as they are scattered,' explained Marcus. 'Though they follow the same oath, they often act independently, as is their nature. I'm afraid that if we wish to locate your brother, we must do it with our eyes alone.' He paused, aware of Kerrin's frustration. 'They may even have reached him by now and be escorting him back as we speak.' He fell silent, sensing that the attempt at comforting words was falling on deaf ears.

The stone hallways of the Broxhart manor bustled with activity, yet the two of them moved softly as though they were alone under the watchful eyes of the marble statues of Kerrin's ancestors which lined the walls. In the days before the darkness destroyed the surface, the settlement in which their people now survived had existed beneath the original city. When the Malice had begun to spread, his grandfather had ushered his people underground to safety. But before this building had been converted to the living quarters of the Broxhart family to rule over their new subterranean lands, the manor had been a mausoleum. Generations of his family lay buried within its stone walls, great rulers of the past who had protected both the people of Pelera and the Enki cenote itself, regarded by many as a spiritual epicentre due to the tendency for Echoes to congregate above its waters. Exactly why the souls of the dead would choose to gather in that location was unclear, but the dancing orbs of light brought great comfort to those who travelled to witness them. That in itself was worth protecting.

Together they reached the enormous wooden doors that led to the great hall at the centre of the manor. The ancient oak had been carved to proudly display the names of those who lay within the crypt, dating far back into generations who had ruled Pelera long before the Dark Days. In truth, nobody could remember who, if anybody, had ruled Pelera before the Broxharts. Despite his pride as his eyes drank in the illustrious names of his ancestors, Kerrin wondered how long it would be till his father's name was added to the monument.

'Have you seen my sister today?' he asked in an effort to distract himself from the thought.

Marcus paused and removed his glasses, cleaning them on his sleeve as he attempted to avoid the question. It was a familiar tactic as old as the condescending smile. Kerrin waited patiently, determined to draw a response from the old man. At length he provided it.

'Lady Calipse is where she has been for the last three days,' Marcus admitted, returning his glasses to their rightful place upon his narrow head. 'She fears that your father's Echo will soon depart his body and make its journey to the Enki cenote.' He paused for effect, fixing the young man with a sympathetic gaze. 'She wants to be the first person to greet him there.'

* * *

Kerrin allowed his eyes to scan the water's edge in search of his sister. Aside from the Enki cenote, there was another reason Pelera was seen as such an important settlement. They floated before him, majestic and terrifying in equal measure: the Echoes.

Life in the underground tunnels was full of mysteries and dangers. The Echoes represented both. They had existed for as long as humanity could remember, escaping the human frame once life had left the body, carrying with them the memories of the deceased. Rising from the body in the form of a colourful rippling orb of light, they simply drifted away into the unknown. For reasons that had never been clear to Kerrin, they seemed to congregate at the Enki cenote before continuing their journey, though no-one had ever been able to track their ultimate destination.

They drifted everywhere beneath the surface, often alone but occasionally in large clusters creating a startling carnival of lights within the underground darkness. Predominantly they followed the flow of water from the Enki cenote as it worked its way southwards. Although largely passive, the Echoes seemed to possess a collective consciousness, and when startled or angered were known to react violently.

The inevitable end for all human life, thought Kerrin. *I wonder if he will end up here soon?* Frowning, he shook the thought from his mind and edged his way down the wet rocks to the edge of the water.

He should have known he would find her by the Enki cenote. Calipse was always here, and since their father's decline into ill health she had spent longer and longer gazing at the dancing Echoes which floated above the rippling surface of the water. His concerns once more reared their heads as he scanned the edge of the Enki cenote seeking his sister. Whilst the Echoes were known to bring peace and tranquility to those who observed them, there were also cases of those who become obsessed with watching the dancing lights. There were those who would sit and watch them, oblivious to their surroundings or the needs of their own bodies, wasting away as their thoughts became obsessions. The Echoes would become like a drug to them, and like most drugs it would erode at their very life force. They were known as Echo Gazers. Kerrin could only pray that his sister sought only peace as she watched them.

Reluctant to allow his own gaze to linger on the Echoes for too long, he turned and instead drank in the spectacle of the Peleran settlement around him.

The settlement was predominantly occupied by the vast Enki cenote, from which many believed a magnificent tree had once surged to the surface above. There was plenty of evidence to support this theory. High above the settlement the hole from which the Tree may have emerged remained, once framing a beautiful landscape of skies and stars in the days before the Eternal Storm. Now only Malice was visible. Nobody knew why the Malice did not flow through the hole into the settlement. As long as it remained that way, nobody questioned it.

Emerging from the Enki cenote there flowed the numerous rivers, weaving between the houses of the Peleran settlement. They were simple buildings but numerous, constructed of wood and sometimes even carved from the rock face itself. Long ago when the exodus from the surface began, the Peleran people had united to create a life for themselves in their new subterranean home. This spirit had endured, allowing the people to adapt with surprising speed and through the following years life underground had become the norm. There was nobody left who remembered the old world, but the stories continued to be passed down of how people lived on the surface, surrounded by towering buildings, forests, streams and mountains, all of which existed under beautiful changing skies.

The Pelera settlement was a mass of bridges, connecting the fragmented sections of the community over the flowing waters which allowed them to flourish underground. The bridges were narrow but maintained with a great degree of care and attention to avoid any part of the settlement from becoming isolated or cut off from the main population.

The Enki cenote flowed throughout the entire settlement before following tunnels which disappeared into the darkness, supplying water to the surrounding settlements as it followed the slope of the land southwards. It was this that had allowed Pelera to rise to become the most powerful settlement, with the surroundings settlements pledging allegiance to the Broxhart family and trading livestock and goods in return for access to the life-sustaining water which flowed down into their settlements.

As he reached the bottom of his descent, the water splashing just a few metres from his feet, Kerrin turned and realised why he had been unable to spot his sister from the higher vantage point.

She was tucked into an alcove in the rocks a short distance way, largely hidden from sight and seemingly lost in thought. Her eyes were locked on the orbs of light which danced above the water, and just for a moment Kerrin's heart sank into his stomach. To his instant relief, she turned her eyes towards him and smiled, beckoning him towards her calmly.

Moving uneasily over the shifting wet rock, Kerrin carefully made his way over to his sister. Opening his mouth to speak he was silenced by Calipse, as she turned to him and raised a delicate finger to her mouth. Something in her innocent eyes calmed him, and nodding his assent, Kerrin settled himself beside her. They sat in silence, Kerrin unable to gauge his sister's mood or how best to start a conversation. He had always found small talk unbearable, and actively avoided social situations as much as possible in order to avoid awkward silences. In his mind, it was no wonder the people preferred his brother, a man who seemed able to talk about anything and everything, particularly if the subject was himself.

At length, Calipse sighed. 'Do you think dad will like it here?'

Kerrin shuffled awkwardly. 'Don't talk like that.'

'Like what?' asked Calipse calmly. 'Kerrin, I know how bad dad is. I just want to know he's going to be happy when it's over. You understand that, right?'

Kerrin remained silent, unsure how to answer. His sister's calm logic unnerved him. Though he hated to admit it, he would have preferred her to be distraught; at least that way he could have played the role of the supportive older brother. Instead, her peaceful acceptance of the situation had left him feeling almost as though she was comforting him instead.

'There's still no sign of Haswell,' he mumbled, eager to change the subject.

Calipse smiled, though the expression was tinged with sadness. 'It's so like him to be late. I just hope he doesn't leave it to the last second like he always does.' She turned and fixed Kerrin with her deep green eyes. 'Do you remember the last time all three of us were down here together? I thought you were going to hit Haswell for sure…' She leaned back, clearly picturing the scene in her mind. 'I don't think he was expecting that reaction from you. Normally you don't let him get to you like that.'

Kerrin knew exactly what she was talking about. It had been the day that Haswell had left Pelera to become a demon hunter. Kerrin hadn't cared. Though Haswell was his twin, he had never felt close to him. His leaving wouldn't have significantly impacted on the amount of time they spent together.

'He was just... so arrogant...' muttered Kerrin.

Calipse nodded and hugged her knees. 'I don't know why he said all those things,' she admitted. Kerrin knew that Calipse loved both of her brothers and would avoid choosing a side in any of the arguments which had occurred between them. 'I guess he was just looking for a reaction out of you. Anything really.' She glanced at Kerrin. 'Just to check that you really did feel something. Any emotion. Even anger.'

Kerrin turned his attention back to the flowing water to avoid his sister's eyes.

Is that how they see me? Emotionless?

Together they sat in silence and watched the orbs of light drift before them.

4

As the Citadel doors swung shut behind them, the two men in matching Malice Gear exchanged a glance before stepping forward into the blizzard once more. Side by side, the Dead Man and the demon hunter pressed onward through the towering relics of the old city, leaving hidden footprints in the snow beneath the swirling purple Malice which seemed to snatch at their ankles, attempting to halt their progress as the two men walked in silence. Madock was comfortable with the quiet, but his colleague's silence was uncharacteristic of the young man.

Haswell had been a confident child. Whilst his twin brother Kerrin had been quietly introverted and his younger sister Calipse had demonstrated peaceful calmness to most situations, Haswell had been a whirlwind of vocalised emotions. He would cry, shout and laugh with equal enthusiasm, seemingly overwhelmed by the power of each emotion and occasionally unable to limit its impact. One thing he had never been as a boy was quiet, and Madock suspected that the same was true of the young man he had grown into. As such, his reluctance to talk was unnerving.

'We should aim for Mikara,' said Madock, testing his partner's resolve to remain silent.

'Tirneth is closer,' replied Haswell absently, adjusting the rifle which hung over his shoulder. 'We don't need to take stupid risks. There's plenty of time.'

'Is there?' asked Madock. Haswell refused to answer but instead quickened his pace to move ahead of the Dead Man, who broke into a jog to match the young man's stride.

'And the Haswell I remember was always taking stupid risks,' Madock continued, attempting to hide his shortness of breath. 'Climbing the walls, jumping the rivers... Marcus always blamed me for not keeping a close enough eye on you. I have to admit, I did feel guilty the first few times you hurt yourself, but your father just laughed. "It's character building," he'd say to me. He said that you'd learn not to do something so stupid again. Or better yet, you'd go back and try again, learn from your mistakes...'

'What's your point Madock?' asked Haswell, struggling to suppress the frustration in his voice.

Madock stopped in his tracks, forcing Haswell to stop and turn towards him. Although both of their faces were hidden behind their masks, Madock could sense Haswell's eyes focused on him expectantly. 'I don't know what's going to happen. Maybe we'll make it in time, maybe we won't. All I know is that this is a risk worth taking to say goodbye to a great man.'

Haswell continued to stare at him, his expression a mystery behind the mask, but Madock sensed that his message had hit home. At length, Haswell turned and gazed skyward, inhaling deeply and allowing his whole frame to straighten.

As he spoke, Madock heard the sad resignation in his voice, but also the renewed determination. 'Then let's go say goodbye.'

The buildings around them became smaller and more isolated as they pressed onwards until eventually they passed the outskirts of the old city and found themselves out in the open elements surrounded by nothing but snow, Malice and the faint landmarks of the old roads which linked the long abandoned villages, town and cities of the surface.

In spite of his insistence that time was an important factor in their travels north to Pelera, Madock was glad that they had rested in the Bunker the night before. Haswell's wealth had enabled them to sleep in relative comfort, solving Madock's concern about what he could have parted with to afford the bed. His worldly possessions were dwindling faster than he cared for, leaving only essential and sentimental artifacts left to barter with. At one point he had considered sacrificing the fascinating glass he had found in the house yesterday, but he could not bring himself to part with such a unique object. Even now it remained tucked securely into the pocket of his Malice Gear, his gloved fingers occasionally seeking it out to rub his fingers against its smooth surface. He had seen many things before in his time, yet this was something new, and the mystery intrigued him.

Haswell had grown increasingly chatty as they followed the remnants of an old road both had travelled many times before, knowing that it would lead them towards the settlement of Mikara. In particular, he seemed keen to regale Madock with stories of his accomplishments since leaving the safety of Pelera to become a demon hunter. Madock was more than happy to listen. It distracted him from the memories of what he had seen yesterday through the blizzard, the vision that had driven him to the edge of madness. The vision that may well have been responsible for Willow's death.

It had been years since he had thought about her. Back after it had first happened he had believed he'd seen her everywhere, a face in the crowd or a shadow disappearing into the darkness. He had been unable to let go for so long that he had almost killed himself in the process of chasing a ghost. But he had believed those days were behind him.

'There must have been about seven of them...' Haswell continued to tell his story, oblivious as to whether the Death Cheater was listening or not. 'An ugly horde, a swarm of them. I knew I had to make every shot count.' He mimed raising his rifle to his shoulder, taking aim at an invisible foe as their boots crunched into the snow, eating up the miles to their destination.

'Bang! One went down. Bang! Another.' Haswell swung the imaginary rifle from side to side, clearly thrilled to be reliving the moment. 'I turned and...'

He paused as Madock grabbed hold of his arm to silence him. Pointing ahead, Madock's gloved finger directed the demon hunter towards the figure he had spotted lying prone at the side of the road a short distance ahead. Haswell instantly straightened and replaced his imaginary rifle with the real one, holding it confidently with the barrel trained on the figure on the ground.

Carefully removing his own gun from its holster, Madock took the lead as he moved carefully forward, his feet barely making a sound as he quietly approached the figure. It had taken him longer than he cared to admit to spot the stranger who had largely been concealed by the thick Malice lingering above the ground. But as they had moved closer, improving their vision through the poisonous mist, he had identified the figure lying there.

In the quiet, both Haswell and Madock became aware of the rasping breath that was emerging from the fallen stranger. As they drew closer, Madock also instinctively raised his weapon and trained it on the stranger. The Malice grew thinner, revealing more details about the stranger.

The woman was in a bad way. Her clothes had been torn and many bleeding wounds were allowing ruby blood to seep into the snow around her. A tattered scarf, presumably used at one point as a rudimentary form of protection against the Malice, lay cast aside nearby. Her eyes were wide open, though whether she could see them or not was unclear. The only sound that emerged from her mouth was the uneven rattling breathing that they had heard earlier. As they stood over her, her eyes seemed to register their presence momentarily. With obvious physical effort, she whispered urgently through the laboured breathing.

'Help me...'

Madock crouched to observe the woman carefully. She attempted to raise her hand to him in a pleading gesture, but the simple act exhausted her and the hand fell uselessly to the snow beneath her.

Be cold, Madock reminded himself. *Be careful.*

Allowing his eyes to scan the woman's body, his eyes fell on a makeshift blood soaked bandage tied around her right leg. The skin around it seemed a darker colour than the rest of the leg. Moving his hands towards the bandage, he began to carefully untie it. He hoped it would simply be a case of replacing it with a fresh bandage, but he had to be certain.

As he began to remove the bandage, the woman struggled helplessly.

'No... don't...' she gasped through pained breaths.

Madock removed the bandage. His heart sank. Beneath where the bandage had been lay familiar black veins which coursed around a bloody wound. He stood silently and allowed the bandage to fall uselessly to the ground beside him.

Malice poisoning. It was exactly as he had feared.

Haswell had noticed the infection too and was questioning the woman as to how she had contracted the disease. She refused to answer, her pleading eyes focused upon Madock as she struggled to sit up.

'Please... help me...' she repeated.

Madock holstered his gun and exhaled deeply. There was nothing they could do about the infection. Malice poisoning was effectively a death sentence. Once the Malice was in the bloodstream, it would spread and infect every organ and limb until eventually the victim became one of them. Another demon seeking only death and destruction.

Madock turned towards Haswell and pulled him aside to speak privately. The woman was in no danger of disappearing, and the wound seemed fresh enough to suggest that she wouldn't succumb to the poisoning at that moment.

'Perhaps the Harbingers?' suggested Madock, aware of how helpless he sounded.

Haswell shook his head. 'All they can do is slow the poison. Face it, Madock, she's finished.'

Madock knew the demon hunter was right. The woman was already living on borrowed time, and attempting to move her to a settlement would simply endanger their own lives. It was a dilemma he had been faced with before, and though he prayed every time that the outcome would be different, the realist in him knew it would always end the same way.

'We need to take care of this,' continued Haswell. 'We can't let her become one of those things.'

Madock sighed and nodded, resigning himself to the inevitable. Haswell sensed his mood and rested his hand on the old man's shoulder.

'I'll take care of it.'

Together they turned to face the fallen woman. She stared up at them with wide, frightened eyes. Whether she had heard their conversation Madock couldn't tell, but hidden behind the panicked expression he thought he could identify a hint of acceptance. It didn't help him feel any better about what was about to happen.

Haswell raised his rifle and aimed at the woman's head.

'Wait!' The woman gasped with startling strength. Haswell paused. With a great deal of effort, the woman tore her eyes away from the barrel of the gun to fix her pleading gaze on Madock. 'I want... I want to.... do it myself...'

Madock stared at her, dumbfounded by the request. Haswell glanced at his companion questioningly.

The wind swirled around them, the snow and Malice blurring the rest of the world into obscurity. Right now, there were just the three of them, and one decision to make.

Wouldn't you want the same in her situation? Madock reflected reluctantly on the woman's request. There was every chance she was delirious, but ultimately her fate was already sealed. Wouldn't it be a greater mercy to allow her to control the ending to her story?

Hesitantly, Madock removed his gun from its holster.

'You can't be serious Madock?' questioned Haswell urgently. 'What if she turns that thing on us?'

'Keep your gun on her,' replied Madock calmly as he took the woman's weak hand and carefully placed his weapon into it, tightening the cold fingers around it. 'If she tries anything, you end it for her.' He held the woman's gaze unflinchingly and spoke softly to her. 'We're giving you this option. Don't waste it.'

In spite of the pain, the woman managed a weak smile as she allowed Madock to position her hand next to her head, the barrel of the gun resting against the side of her temple.

'Can you manage?' asked Madock gently as he straightened to kneel beside her.

She nodded, her chest moving rapidly as she struggled to catch her breath. 'Yes... Thank you...'

Taking her other hand, Madock squeezed the cold flesh reassuringly. Then rising slowly, he stepped backwards. Haswell remained focused, his rifle trained on the woman, though Madock knew there was no need. Her strength was failing her fast. She would never be able to move the weapon, let alone train it on either of them before Haswell took her out. She only had enough strength left for one act.

As the snow fell silently around them, the woman pulled the trigger.

5

The gunshot was still echoing in Madock's mind as they approached the outskirts of Mikara. They had made good time in spite of the unfortunate encounter on the road, and the darkness of night was only just beginning to set in. He was silently relieved. Having suggested gambling on reaching Mikara instead of the much more conveniently located Tirneth, he knew his exhausted feet were a small price to pay for ensuring that they would reach Pelera sooner. Even better, with the exception of the woman who now lay buried beneath the snow, they had met with no other obstacles on their route.

'How are you holding up, old timer?' asked Haswell, adjusting the rifle on his shoulder.

'Told you we'd make it,' replied Madock, not even attempting to disguise his shortness of breath. It had been years since he had attempted such a long distance in a single journey, but the pain in his chest was balanced by his pride in the achievement.

Mikara was a small settlement, nestled between skeletal trees and largely hidden beneath large drifts of snow. It had once been a farming village, providing a wide array of crops for the surrounding towns and cities. In order to achieve the required output, a large underground network of cellars and tunnels had been constructed beneath the village to house the wide range of products ready to be shipped across the lands. This had formed an ideal shelter during the early days of the Malice, and over time had been expanded and developed to allow a small but determined collection of survivors to create a settlement. Under the protection of Pelera and with continued access to the Enki cenote, it had become an ideal point for travellers to stop at when moving in and out of Pelera.

Tracking through the snow drifts which concealed the remains of many of the buildings, the two men headed straight for the manor which provided secure access to the settlement below. It had belonged to the richest family in the village, though they had disappeared during the early days of the Malice. The people had embraced the opportunity and moved underground, willing to face the consequences of their actions if the family returned. They never did.

'That's odd…' mumbled Haswell as they approached the building. 'There should be Peleran guards protecting the door.'

Madock nodded, having noticed their absence as well. He had travelled to Mikara many times before, and there had always been a security presence at the manor entrance. He tried to dismiss the bad feeling that was brewing in the back of his mind, but he knew better than to ignore it. They often turned out to be well-founded.

Approaching the door, Madock's fears were further confirmed as they noted that it was unlocked, banging softly as it swung back and forth in the breeze. Without saying a word, both men drew their weapons. Pushing open the door with his gloved hand, Madock surveyed the scene within the manor. The candles were still flickering within their lanterns, casting light around the hallway which led to the stairs down to the settlement below. In Madock's experience, there should have been two further guards patrolling the hallway. Just as with the exterior, there was no sign of anybody.

'Demons?' whispered Madock questioningly as they stealthily moved through the hallway towards the stairs.

Haswell shook his head. 'There'd be more mess than this.'

The stairway was as well-lit as the hallway, as though suggesting that nothing was out of the ordinary at all. Their footsteps were soft as they carefully made their way downstairs, ears straining for any noise. Nothing but silence met them.

We should have been able to hear them by now, thought Madock solemnly. The settlement, although small, had always been alive with noise in his previous visits. The silence meant nothing but bad news ahead.

Turning the corner at the bottom of the stairs, the low ceiling rose suddenly as they entered the main chamber of the settlement. Madock lowered his weapon and swallowed hard. Haswell emerged into the chamber from behind him, coming to a complete stand still as he stood beside the Death Cheater. Together, they silently took in the scene of devastation.

The bodies were scattered everywhere. There was no need for either of them to go and check on the fallen; it was clear even from this distance that none of them were alive. Many lay face down in the dirt whilst some stared up at the stone ceiling supported by the ancient timber beams, their mouths hanging open as if to scream some final words before the breath had been robbed from their lungs.

Madock moved forwards carefully, his every movement echoing loudly in the silence. Steeling himself, he knelt beside a nearby victim, an older man with receding grey hair who gazed up at him without ever seeing him. Casting his eye over the corpse, Madock frowned in confusion. There was no obvious indication of what had killed him. There were no wounds, no signs of Malice poisoning, not a drop of blood around the body.

Perhaps a heart attack? Madock stretched out his hand and closed the old man's eyes. *I can only hope...* He knew it was unlikely, and that there was only one way to be sure. Standing, he glanced around to identify another victim to examine. There were plenty to choose from, but his heart shuddered as his eyes fell upon a young boy face down in the dirt. Taking a deep breath, he moved purposefully towards the body. As he walked, he glanced back towards his companion. Haswell remained rooted to the spot, though he had taken the positive step of scanning the darker corners of the chamber with his rifle, his senses alert to any potential danger which may be lurking in the shadows. It reassured Madock.

The boy seemed so small as Madock crouched down beside him. Placing his hands beneath the boy's shoulder, he gently rolled him over onto his back. He was glad to see that his eyes were already closed; he wasn't sure he could have coped with seeing his young dead eyes staring up at him. A quick glance over his body confirmed Madock's worst suspicions. Just as with the old man, there seemed no obvious cause of death.

They can't all have just dropped dead…

Somewhere in the darkness, something stirred. Madock and Haswell both heard the noise, their weapons instantly trained on the location of the sound. A tense silence followed. Madock trained every ounce of his focus on the darkness. Though his heart was pounding alarmingly quickly, he felt as though they had frozen in time as they waited.

He couldn't say how long they had stood there in silence, but eventually it became clear that they would have to either move forward or retreat. Haswell raised his rifle to his shoulder and nodded at Madock reassuringly. Together, they started to move further into the darkness.

Madock was unsure what to expect, and in many ways did not want to find out what awaited them a short distance off as a further shuffling noise echoed off the buildings around them. Instead, he focused on his foot placement. However, the task of having to carefully step between the corpses did little to alleviate his concerns.

As they turned the corner, both men stopped as they spotted the source of the noises.

The girl was hunched over a fallen woman with her back to them. She seemed lost in thought and blissfully unaware as she cradled the woman's head in her arms and rocked gently. Though the sound was very soft, Madock thought he could hear the girl humming gently as she swayed.

Haswell glanced at Madock, then gently coughed to gain the girl's attention. At first she offered no response, continuing to rock back and forth. Haswell coughed again, a little louder this time. Again, there was no response. Casting an uncertain glance at Madock, Haswell bent down and picked up a small pebble from the floor. Aiming carefully, he threw the pebble so that it clattered to the floor near the girl without ever being likely to hit her. As the stone crashed against the floor, the girl shrieked in surprise, crouching protectively over the woman and turning her head towards the source of the noise.

For a moment Madock's heart seemed to sink to his stomach as he saw the girl's face. A sense of terrifying déjà vu swept over him. She was a distance off, but Madock's eyes had already decided what they could see.

'Rosa?' he mumbled awkwardly before he could swallow the words. Luckily neither Haswell nor the frightened girl seemed to hear, and Madock thankfully shook his head to clear his thoughts.

She's dead Madock. She's been dead for a long time. This has to stop.

The girl fixed her eyes on the two men. 'Are you here to stop the monster?'

Haswell seemed uncertain how to respond, so Madock stepped in. 'That's right, we're here to stop the monster,' he replied reassuringly. 'We need you to tell us all about it. Can you do that?'

The girl glanced down at the woman's head in her arms, seemingly uncertain as to whether to answer. Gathering her courage, she spoke. 'Mum says I shouldn't talk to strangers.'

'Very sensible,' replied Madock, taking a further hesitant step towards the girl. For a moment, she tensed as if to run, but something kept her rooted to the ground. Whether it was fear, curiosity or respect, Madock was glad that she had stayed where she was; attempting to locate her again in the darkness and death of the settlement seemed a far from appealing prospect. 'Is that your mum there? Is she okay?'

The girl shuffled awkwardly, glancing between the two men. Tears were flowing down her dirty cheeks and words seemed to have frozen in her throat. In spite of his better judgement, Madock lowered his weapon, making a grand gesture of placing it back into its holster. The girl seemed to relax slightly, though when she turned to face Haswell, the demon hunter gave no indication that he would follow Madock's lead.

Turning her attention back to Madock, she rubbed her arm self-consciously. 'The monster… It did this…' she whispered quietly.

Madock took a further step towards the girl and crouched down to put himself on her eye level. 'What did it look like?'

The girl frowned, as though attempting to recall an image of the creature responsible for the chaos around them. 'Mum told me to hide in my room. She said not to come out till they came to get me…'

'How long ago was this?' asked Madock.

The girl looked up, as though working this out in her head like a mental calculation. 'I'm not sure,' she admitted at last before turning back to the woman on the ground in front of her. 'Mum? How long ago was the monster here?'

Madock looked at the girl's mother. She was clearly dead, though just like every other body he had encountered so far there seemed no obvious cause of death. For whatever reason, the girl either couldn't see or wouldn't accept the fact that the woman in her arms was dead. Madock decided not to pursue that matter at that moment.

'So you were hiding in your room...' prompted Madock gently.

'Yeah, but... I could hear the people screaming,' she continued, the tears flowing more freely now. 'I looked out the window and I saw it. It was... It kept...'

Madock instinctively placed a hand on the girl's arm to reassure her. She nodded, acknowledging the gesture as she took a deep breath and pressed on. 'It looked like a man, but then it looked like a woman.'

'So you weren't sure if it was a man or a woman?' said Madock.

The girl shook her head firmly. 'No, it was both. Not at the same time. It kept changing what it looked like. It had lots and lots of faces. I think that's why nobody knew what to do.' She whimpered and brushed angrily at the tears streaming down her cheeks. 'It didn't kill them. Well, not normally. It kind of... sucked their Echo out of them. I don't know how... Then the people just kind of fell over.' She paused and glanced around. 'Everybody else is dead, aren't they?'

Madock stood and turned to Haswell, who still had his gun held firmly in his hands. 'We can't leave her here,' said the Death Cheater firmly.

Haswell seemed reluctant to lower his guard. His response was blunt. 'She might be the thing that did this.'

Madock was startled by the demon hunter's accusation, but after a moment of reflection he realised it was well-founded. The facts were difficult to understand right now, but what was clear was that after all the death that had occurred here, the girl was the only thing left behind. However, whether she was a survivor or in some way responsible for the tragedy, Madock's original statement also held true: they couldn't leave her here. If she was a survivor, it would be beyond cruel to leave her here on her own. If she was some kind of monster, they needed to deal with her.

The girl seemed uncertain how to respond. 'I... I didn't do anything...' she pleaded. 'I just hid in my room like I was told. Tell them mum!' She rocked her mother gently. As always, there was no answer, though the girl seemed to ignore this. 'You're from Pelera, right?'

Madock paused. 'Pelera?'

The girl nodded and pointed at the crest upon the old man's Malice Gear. 'That's the Peleran symbol, right? I recognise it from the guards' outfits and when we went there last year.' Desperately, she caught hold of Madock's sleeve. 'Please take us there! My mum needs help, she isn't well.'

Madock avoided her gaze by watching Haswell carefully. The younger man seemed to come to the same conclusion as Madock and slowly, reluctantly lowered his weapon.

'I guess I get to be the hero all over again,' he joked, forcing a smile back onto his face. It wasn't difficult to see through.

The girl seemed unclear as to whether she was being rescued or not, and looked at Madock questioningly.

You've gone soft in your old age thought Madock as he removed his mask and smiled at the girl. As she stared back at him curiously, he felt convinced that she was simply a victim, a scared child forced to watch horrors unfold before her eyes. *I hope Rosa didn't...*

His smile waivered, then re-established itself. It wouldn't be easy to say what he had to say next. It made him feel sick, but he knew it was their only option.

'We're going to get you out of here,' he promised, 'But we can't leave right now. It's night time up there, and very dangerous.'

The girl nodded, though Madock was uncertain whether she had understood. He pressed on. 'We need to stay here tonight.'

'I understand,' replied the girl, surprisingly calmly.

She must be in shock, thought Madock. Her inability to recognise that her mother was dead seemed to support that theory.

'That means we need to sleep in one of these buildings,' explained Madock.

The girl seemed to ponder this quietly for a moment. She turned and stared at her mum for a long time, leaning in close to the body and whispering quietly. At first Madock wondered if perhaps she had finally come to grips with the reality of her situation and was saying goodbye to her mother. However, when she turned and smiled up at him, her words sent a chill down Madock's spine. 'Mum says you can stay at our house.'

6

'We can't leave her out there...'

The two men stood, arms folded, watching from the doorway of the house the stubborn girl who remained crouched over her mother's corpse. She had seemed shocked at Haswell's refusal to help move her mother into the house, staring at him with wild, confused eyes.

'But she needs help,' she had pleaded with them. 'We can't leave her lying in the dirt. It won't help her get better.'

Madock had been tempted to address the issue at that point, mulling over a tactful way to speak to the girl, to make her see the reality of the situation.

Haswell had been neither tactful nor patient.

'She's dead.'

The bluntness of his words had startled both the girl and Madock. It had occurred to the Death Cheater at that moment that Haswell was still not coping very well with his father's ill health, though he had attempted to conceal it beneath his traditional confident personality. Now though, dealing with the imminent death of his father, his emotional turmoil was resurfacing in ugly forms.

The girl had stared at him with increasing hatred until finally she had shouted defiantly at the demon hunter with venom. 'She's not dead!'

Those had been the last words she had said to either of them. Whether she was sulking or simply coming to terms with the truth, she had remained crouched over her mother staring into her unseeing eyes.

'You really think she might be the one that did all this?' asked Madock.

Haswell sighed and shrugged. It was clear he felt bad about upsetting the girl, but his own stubbornness was preventing him from dealing with the issue. 'I've seen a lot of weird things in this world, Madock, but...' He paused. 'I'd be surprised. Still, we need to get to the bottom of whatever happened here. If the girl's telling the truth, there's some sort of shape shifting creature out there sucking the souls out of living people. That's worse than any demon I've ever dealt with.'

I've certainly never heard of anything like it before, thought Madock. He couldn't bring himself to believe that the girl was responsible, leaving only two possibilities: her innocent mind had concocted some elaborate story involving an imaginary monster, or...

'We need to be careful,' Madock mused aloud. 'We don't know what we're dealing with.' He glanced around the small room behind them, the main living space of the girl's house. It was rather plain, with little in the way of decoration or furniture, but it would serve them perfectly well as a place to make camp till the morning. The sofas would provide a degree of comfort and the walls felt protective circling around the room. But no matter how strong the walls seemed, the idea that the monster responsible for the devastation throughout the settlement might still be lurking in the shadows was unnerving. Haswell had suggested sweeping the entire settlement, but Madock knew that with just the two of them it would have been a pointless endeavour. Plus they had the girl to think about now.

'You should say something to her,' suggested Haswell awkwardly.

'Why me? You're the one who hurt her feelings,' pointed out Madock, turning his attention back to his companion.

'Exactly. She won't listen to me, but she'll listen to you.'

Madock sighed and placed a hand on the young man's shoulders as he stepped through the doorway and approached the girl. He sensed Haswell would benefit from some time alone with his thoughts, giving him a chance to sort his mind out. He hoped the demon hunter would be able to focus on reaching his father before it was too late to say goodbye.

Kneeling down beside the girl, Madock made a show of grunting with effort. He was surprised to find that it wasn't entirely forced.

'I'm Madock,' he said, trying to meet the girl's eyes. They remained focused on the woman lying on the floor in front of them.

'I'm... Lottie,' she replied eventually, all the while stroking her mother's hair.

Madock smiled gently. 'Thank you for letting us stay in your house, Lottie,' he started, pausing to watch for any reaction. When none came, he pressed on. 'We're going to take you to Pelera, where it's safe. But... your mother won't be coming with us.'

Lottie looked up, angry tears already filling her eyes. 'Why not?'

Madock held his nerve. 'What do you think is wrong with your mother?'

The girl paused, her eyes scanning her mother's body. 'I... I don't know. She... must just be scared. She has talked to me, she has!'

The passion in her eyes convinced Madock that Lottie felt she was telling the truth. Perhaps she really had heard her mother's voice in her head. He couldn't blame her for being traumatised. But he knew he had to make her see the truth.

Raising his fingers to his neck, he found his pulse. 'Try this, see if you can feel your heartbeat.' The girl copied his example, then nodded as she discovered the pulse, tapping out the rhythm with her other hand. 'That's your heart pumping blood around your body. Now, try and find your mother's.'

The girl removed the fingers from her neck and began placing it on different spots on her mother's neck. She frowned as she struggled to find the non-existent pulse. Growing increasingly frustrated, she lay her head on her mother's chest, listening for a heartbeat. Madock knew she would hear nothing.

'Do you know what this means?' asked Madock, making his tone as gentle as possible. Lottie stared at him, shaking her head as though unwilling to accept the truth that was dawning upon her.

'No... I don't want to...' she whimpered, gazing at him desperately for some other explanation. At that moment, she reminded Madock more than ever of his daughter. He remembered a time when they had travelled as a family to Pelera, just before he began working for the Broxharts. He had taken her to the edge of the Enki cenote to watch the Echoes dance, and encouraged her to take a sip from the water. She had stared at him with the same unhappy, desperate eyes...

'I'm sorry, Lottie...'

The tears flowed, an unstoppable explosion of emotion completely overwhelming her small body as she hugged her mother tightly. Madock waited patiently. If there was one thing the Death Cheater knew how to do, it was wait.

* * *

Morning came with no other clue than the changing hours. Underground, time had little meaning, making the need for clocks all the more important to maintain a sense of regularity. As the clock in Lottie's house ticked round to eight, Madock stepped out into the corpse-littered streets of the Mikara.

He and Haswell had taken it in shifts to keep watch, wary of the unseen and unknown threat which may have been lurking in the darkness, but much to his relief the night had passed without incident. Lottie had joined them eventually inside the house, though both Madock and Haswell had watched over her from the doorway until she had made her decision. She had not spoken to either of them, but neither had she returned to her mother's corpse. It was almost as if she had lost the ability to communicate having suffered such a powerful outburst of emotion.

Haswell joined him, stretching his tired joints.

'She still hasn't said anything,' said Madock.

Haswell grunted. Clearly the lack of sleep from keeping watch had done little to improve his mood. 'Are we really taking her with us?'

Madock fixed the demon hunter with a piercing stare. Haswell struggled to meet it and sighed in exasperation.

'Don't worry, we'll still get back to Pelera in time,' said the Death Cheater reassuringly. Haswell seemed uncertain how to respond, so instead placed the mask of Malice Gear over his head and wandered off silently.

Sighing, Madock turned back towards the house and waited patiently for Lottie to emerge.

Finally she appeared, clutching a small shoulder bag tightly, with her eyes glued to the floor. Madock felt guilty for having brought her to her senses, but he knew it had been necessary.

'Are you ready?' he asked.

Lottie didn't respond instantly, but then slowly she opened her shoulder bag and silently removed a delicate embroidered sheet. Holding it high above her head to make sure it wouldn't drag in the dirt, she carried it across to where her mother lay. With almost ceremonial grace, she spread the sheet carefully over the woman, covering her from head to toe.

Madock watched in silent admiration as Lottie quietly stood over her mother's body. He could not say how long the two of them stood there, but eventually Lottie wandered over to him.

'I'm ready,' she said, her voice quiet and broken.
Madock nodded. 'Let's go then.'

* * *

They left Mikara in silence, each one of them lost in thought. The storm was swirling viciously as they stepped into the cold embrace of the surface. Though Madock was used to the conditions, it always took his breath away whenever he took his first few steps, crunching his boots through the Malice-laden snow.

It must be even worse for her, he thought.

They had managed to outfit Lottie with thick clothing they had found in her home. A scarf formed a makeshift barrier across her face against the elements and the Malice, though Madock knew they would provide little protection over an extended period of time. He hoped their journey to Pelera would not last long.

Madock had been disappointed to find that the underground tunnels leading to Pelera had been blocked, perhaps as a result of the chaos that had occurred or even deliberately caused by whatever had been responsible for all the dead bodies littering the settlement. The tunnels would have offered a much quicker route to Pelera, as well as being marginally safer than exposing Lottie to the Malice on the surface. Now they were left with no choice but to confront that reality.

The dark skies overhead growled threateningly as driving snow threatened to blind them and drive them off the path. Madock was experienced enough to cope with these factors, having walked under this darkness countless times before, often in even worse conditions. He recalled one journey in his youth, a time when he had still worked in unison with other Dead Men; they had set out from the

Bunker heading south towards Silverbridge. The storm had been particularly unkind that day, lashing them with freezing rain and plummeting the temperature far below the endurance of many. Without the protection of the Malice Gear which he would not come to own for several years, Madock could clearly remember making peace with losing a number of his fingers, such was the intensity of the frost. As if sensing an opportunity for chaos, the Malice had also ravaged them, thickening to the point that it became almost a sludge which tugged at their tired legs. Many of his colleagues had fallen into its clutches during that journey, but not him. The Death Cheater was destined to live on.

Haswell, Madock and Lottie had been travelling for several hours when Haswell suddenly stopped, raising his hand to signal the others to follow his lead. As they glanced around through the driving snow and Malice, Madock felt his senses heighten. Instinctively he placed one hand on his weapon and drew Lottie behind him with the other. He had not sensed anything around them, but he knew better than to question Haswell's judgement. The young man had become a legendary demon hunter, and that status had been acquired through experience and success. If he felt something was out there, it was almost guaranteed there would be.

Haswell turned and almost silently fell to a crouching position, raising his rifle and aiming into the midst of the darkness. Madock focused on the supposed target, but was embarrassed to admit he still could not register a threat. Silently cursing his own failing senses, he copied Haswell in sinking to a lower position and indicated for Lottie to do the same.

Then suddenly it appeared, seemingly forming from the Malice itself; a demon, quietly growling and staggering aimlessly through the snow. It's blackened, decayed skin seemed to drip from the creatures bones. At some point its leg had been broken, though whether this was before or after its transformation into a monster was unclear. Regardless, it now limped onwards leaving an unsteady trail in the deep snow behind it.

It would be no challenge for a demon hunter to track it, though Madock. *It's a wonder it hasn't been taken care of already.*

Haswell braced himself, ready to fire the weapon that would end the creature's miserable existence. Madock waited patiently for the gun shot that would announce the act, but none came. Instead, Haswell was lifting himself to his feet and retreating unsteadily. With a sinking feeling in his stomach, Madock squinted through the darkness.

The shadows emerged almost simultaneously. As though deliberately taunting them, the storm eased for just a moment, allowing Madock a clearer view of his surroundings. The scenery was not appealing. There were more demons in this one place than he had ever seen before, all of them quietly shuffling through the snow following the creature in front of them, blind to anything else around it.

A horde.... He had heard stories of these vast waves of demons, yet he had dismissed them as little more than demon hunter exaggeration. In all his years he had never encountered more than a cluster of demons, four at the most in a group together. They had no means of communication that he was aware of, so the concept of them moving as a collective seemed unlikely. Yet here they were now; vast, united and terrifying.

A quick glance around revealed no obvious hiding place, and attacking the horde seemed a guaranteed way to become one of its number. Haswell seemed to have recovered from his initial shock and was indicating at them urgently to lie down in the snow, presumably to try and avoid being spotted.

It seemed their only option.

Turning and grabbing Lottie by the shoulders, he saw the frightened look in her eyes. The scarf around her face seemed devastatingly thin as it flapped around in the breeze.

'Down,' he instructed, as loudly as he dared. The demons weren't known for their hearing, but this was hardly the time to be testing that theory. 'Silent.'

Lottie nodded and instantly lay down, almost disappearing into the Malice. Though it worried him, it also convinced him that Haswell's plan might actually work. Turning around, he hoped that the demon hunter must also be following his own advice as he was nowhere to be seen. As stealthily as he could, the old man lowered himself to the ground, watching as the Malice enveloped him and obscured his vision.

Now there was only the sound of the shuffling demons. And they was drawing closer.

7

She didn't trust the man. She also didn't understand why her father had summoned them all there to meet him. What she *did* know was that something didn't feel right.

'I hope you have good reason for disturbing my father.' Her brother Blake spat the words at the stranger, clearly equally confused at the sudden meeting but far more willing to express his frustration. He had been confrontational since they had all been drawn together and seemed in a mood to direct his anger at the small man who stood silently before them.

'I assure you, I would not dare to approach the ruler of Gair with a merely trivial offer,' the stranger replied awkwardly. He was a short fidgety man who struggled to hold eye contact with anything other than the floor. Constantly wringing his hands together, he seemed like a wild scavenging animal; scanning for danger, focused only upon his own survival and gain. The very idea that he might have something to offer their father seemed entirely absurd, and once again she questioned the purpose of his presence. She would have labelled him nothing but a mere Raider, but his eyes seemed too intelligent, his body too weak to survive as one of those vultures.

'My father is a busy man, have your say and be done.' Her brother's tone was fierce, ushering the man forward impatiently. His shoes shuffled against the stone floor of the Gairen throne room as the four figures watched him with a mixture of curiosity and confusion. Whilst she and her brother stood either side of her father, who had remained strangely silent thus far, the fourth remained in the background, quietly observing as he always tended to.

The stranger tried to make eye contact with her, but something in those unfamiliar eyes made her feel very uncomfortable. Instead, she turned to look at her father upon his throne.

Bayne Airenguarde looked a tired man. In truth, he had often seemed that way to his daughter, yet it broke her heart every time to see him so exhausted in his duties to his city, his people and most of all his family. His offspring did as much as they could to keep out of his way in an effort to relieve his stress. Blake kept himself to himself, often disappearing for days at a time to pursue his own errands. Many regarded him as a form of enforcer for their father. Indeed, Blake had gained a fearful reputation, though she hoped most of what she had heard was simply propaganda and exaggeration. She had heard it said that he had a network of informants not just within the protected walls of Gair but stretching across the southern settlements, reaching as far north as the Bunker. However far her brother's influence spread, she knew he was respected and feared in equal measure within the confines of her home town.

For her own part, she attempted to make herself as useful as possible, aiming never to disturb her father unless absolutely necessary. She could deal capably with most minor issues that were presented by the people of Gair, her warm and approachable personality making her popular amongst the people. On the occasions when she did require her father's authority she knew she would find him in one of three places: in counsel with the Harbingers, studying in the library or, most frequently, by her mother's bedside.

Starr Airenguarde knew the condition her mother suffered with: Malice poisoning. Ever since the day of Starr's birth, her mother had been bedridden, and her father had only left her side for short periods to deal with issues of office. She had seen her mother only on a handful of occasions throughout her life, thus it did not pain her that she regarded the woman largely as a stranger. During each visit it had been clear that her mother had seen her in much the same way. The Malice burned at Emi's mind, and it seemed that her mother's eyes beheld her with a complete lack of recognition. She could not say she had given up on her mother as she did not know the woman; in her mind she was just a ghost, clinging to life. If not for the Harbingers, her Echo would have risen from the broken shell many years ago. It amazed her that her mother had survived this long. What little she had read or heard about Malice poisoning suggested that the mind was the first victim of its taint, though usually this occurred within a matter of days, if not hours. Her mother had been existing within this phase for twenty years. She could only assume that beneath the twisted remains of her mother's mind, her will to live possessed incredible strength. She may not have truly known her mother, but she respected her willpower.

    The strange man was before her father's throne now, still wringing his hands nervously. 'Lord Airenguarde, we have much to discuss, yet...' He paused awkwardly, his eyes switching to the young man who stood in the corner, the fourth member of their committee who remained largely shrouded in shadow 'I would feel more comfortable if the Necromancer were not here.'

    All eyes switched to the young man and the dancing orb of light by his side as he emerged from the darkness.

    Gray had been Lord Airenguarde's ward for many years now, though the circumstances of his arrival into their family's life remained something of a mystery to Starr. From the moment she had met him, a young boy hiding nervously behind her father as he was introduced to her and Blake, she had known he was different. His pale face and fair hair had seemed strange to her, especially when compared to her own coal black hair. Whilst she and her brother had been confident and happy, the new boy had carried himself with an air of introverted sorrow. Yet far more alien to her than any of this was the dancing orb of light that gravitated around the boy.

Necromancer was a dirty word these days, but it had not always been that way. Since first learning of the boy's true nature, Starr had endeavoured to learn as much as possible about his mysterious people. The Necromancers were known for their ability to interact with the Echoes of the dead, and were instantly identifiable by their own glowing Echo floating beside them to allow foreign Echoes to enter their bodies. By doing so, the Necromancers could recall the memories of the departed, a highly desirable and widely sought skill. They had been regarded as drifting nomads, establishing camps across the land and seeking the wisdom of the Echoes.

The Sheol Disaster changed everything.

'Gray is my ward, and has as much right to be here as anybody else,' replied Bayne firmly from his throne. 'I suggest you put your prejudice to one side or take your business elsewhere.'

The stranger frowned, clearly uncomfortable with the situation. He seemed to silently assess Lord Airenguarde's words for a few moments before electing to continue in spite of the Necromancer's presence. 'My name is Merle Enrick. I am a scientist, of sorts.'

'Of sorts?' questioned Blake. Starr knew her brother's patience was wearing thin with the man.

'I... retired several years ago. The work I was involved in proved rather unpopular and I felt it immoral to continue offering my assistance to such a project.'

'My father is not interested in your life story,' interrupted Blake, folding his arms. 'I suggest you get to the point before I have you dragged from here and thrown in the cells for wasting our time.'

'That's enough, Blake,' their father sighed, raising his hand to call for calm. He directed his attention back to the scientist. 'My son has a temper, though his point remains valid Mr Enrick. Please do not waste our time unnecessarily.'

The scientist coughed to clear his throat as he collected his thoughts. 'I believe that I can offer you a means of harnessing this world's most reliable form of renewable energy; a means to restore not only this city but also the surface of the planet. In short, my lord, I can offer you the chance to become a very powerful man.'

Bayne straightened slightly in his throne, whilst Blake's glare threatened to waiver into a look of interest. For her own part, Starr's curiosity was almost unbearable. She had read much about the dwindling energy supplies and the search for alternative sources of energy, though to her limited knowledge nothing had been identified. The world was forced to continue to use electricity, generated by burning the precious fossil fuels which had served them so well for generations but now were in immensely short supply. Yet the stranger before them claimed to not only have knowledge of such an energy source, but that it could dispel the miasma of the Malice and restore the surface. It seemed almost impossible to believe, but she was eager to hear more in spite of her reservations about the scientist.

'You have my attention. What energy source do you speak of?' asked Bayne.

Enrick seemed almost to brim over with pride. 'I believe it is possible to convert the Malice itself into energy.'

Bayne sank back into his seat, clearly disappointed. 'Mr. Enrick, I have had my best scientific minds working on replacement energy sources. They too considered Malice, but found it impossible to harness its power. It is simply too dangerous and too unstable.' He fixed the scientist with a stern glare. 'Do you believe yourself to be superior to my entire scientific division?'

If he had believed Enrick would wither under the strength of his accusation, he was to be disappointed. If anything, the scientist seemed to stand firmer, straightening his back as much as possible. It did little to add to his height, but it did present an increased air of confidence.

'My lord, I would never dream of making such a claim. That does not, however, prevent me from being right. I *can* turn Malice into a power source.'

'But how?' Starr heard herself say the words, curiosity taking control of her tongue before measured reason could resist it. It seemed so unreal, so inconceivable that this strange little man could possess such knowledge that could change the world.

Enrick's eyes met hers. They unnerved her, sending a chill through her entire being. She still did not trust him, but she confessed that she longed to hear the answer to her question.

'I possess the blueprints for a modified Echo Filter. It should easily contain and manipulate the Malice into an energy source we can control.' Enrick crossed his arms, as though his point had been proven and he had nothing more to say.

Silence engulfed the room, but a dangerous flicker of deep red light reflected the tension. It emanated from the Necromancer's Echo.

'What madness is this?' Gray's voice was tense, the Necromancer's body seething with rage. Starr had never seen him react to anything like this before, and it worried her. The term "Echo Filter" was one she had heard before, so she knew the exact cause of Gray's anger. She remained silent.

Gray continued, his voice wavering as though struggling to suppress the fury behind it. 'The Echo Filter is dangerous. It caused the Sheol Disaster.'

'Wrong!' The scientist's voice blasted out suddenly, taking them all by surprise. The man had not seemed capable of producing such an authoritative sound, which now threatened to crack his calm demeanour. Even Enrick seemed startled at his own rage, and took a moment to gather himself. 'You're wrong,' he repeated, his voice calm once more. 'The Necromancers were to blame for the Sheol Disaster. We all know it, even if your kind does not wish to accept it. The Echo Filter technology is sound, and I have modified it to be even more successful. There is no doubt in my mind that this technology will change the world.'

'It's already changed the world, for the worse!' argued Gray, his Echo continuing to burn dangerously like a rippling drop of blood floating in the air. Starr found it immensely unsettling, yet she was unable to tear her eyes away from it. 'Thanks to that machine, my people have been hunted and forced to flee these lands. It has no place in this city or any other!'

Bayne raised his hand. 'Enough, Gray.'

The young Necromancer seemed to panic, aware of the possibility that Lord Airenguarde may well be considering the scientist's offer. Starr could understand why her father would be interested. The potential to own a new energy source that could restore the surface would make their family very powerful, easily more so than the Broxharts of Pelera. It had been a long time since their family had held such power.

'My lord, you cannot...' Gray begged weakly, trailing off as Bayne raised his hand once more. Starr knew her father had heard all he needed to. The only question was what he would elect to do.

Lord Airenguarde sighed at length, avoiding eye contact with anybody else in the room as he considered the issue. Starr knew her father would not make this decision lightly, that all of the factors and variables would currently be running through his mind. He was notoriously overcautious, yet she believed her father would find the promise of such power difficult to resist.

Gray desperately attempted a different approach. 'Perhaps we should discuss this with the Harbingers?'

'I cannot bring this matter before the Harbinger council,' replied Bayne, frowning. 'They will have their greedy fingers all over it before I can even take control of the situation.' He watched Enrick carefully, but the scientist merely remained silent and held his gaze. Starr had to admit that the man's confidence in his project was startling, transforming him from the nervous fidgety man who had first entered the chamber into a powerful figure.

Bayne turned to his son. 'Blake, please escort Mr. Enrick to the guest quarters. I want you to supervise this project on my behalf, and report back to me. Under no circumstances are you to make the council aware of your activities. Is that understood?'

Blake nodded, moving alongside the scientist. As they turned to leave, Bayne called out to the scientist. Enrick turned slowly, his confidence seeming to waiver slightly. Starr wondered if perhaps her father had had a last minute change of heart.

'Don't let me down, Enrick.'

The scientist nodded, visibly sighing with relief as he followed Blake out of the room.

Starr shuffled uneasily and glanced at the Necromancer, her friend who she had grown up with for most of her life. He stood silently in the shadows, his Echo glowing a sorrowful sapphire blue.

8

He couldn't see them, but he knew they were practically on top of him.

The demon horde had become nothing more than noise to him as he lay shrouded in the Malice, his other senses deadened as every ounce of effort was focused upon listening to their approach. He did not move. It would have served no purpose anyway; he couldn't see either Haswell or Lottie through the Malice to check on them, and it would only have drawn attention to his position. All he could do was wait and hope.

A foot landed just inches from his head. The fact that it had missed him was a miracle. Madock bit his tongue as he watched the blackened skin sink into the snow, the rotting toenails either curving into the ice like claws or barely hanging on as they swung attached to threads of dead skin. It seemed as though the foot was anchored to the spot beside his head, like the demon it was attached to had frozen beside him. In his mind he could almost picture the creature looking down at him and snarling as it admired its new victim.

Don't be stupid, Madock. He cursed himself silently, remaining rigid. *It can't see you through the Malice. Just keep still.*

It seemed like an eternity passed as he continued to repeat this message reassuringly to himself, but eventually the decayed foot did slowly lift itself from the snow and disappeared into the Malice. Madock knew better than to allow himself to relax, remaining tense and alert for any further sounds. He forced himself to ignore the ice cold snow beneath him and the strangling Malice which swirled around his entire body, focusing only on the sounds of his surroundings.

The noise of the horde seemed to be diminishing, but he was not willing to take any chances. He waited. Even after the last of the groans had long since faded, he waited. He had experienced similar situations before, though never with quite the number of demons that had just passed by. The Death Cheater knew it was far better to be safe than sorry. He hadn't survived this long to be taken out by a lone straggler emerging from behind the horde.

His instincts turned out to be right.

The demon's lumbering feet struck him hard in the side, sending the monster tumbling over his body and pinning him to the ground. The demon growled in a tone of what Madock could swear was confusion, though he knew that was impossible. The demons may have once been human, but now the only emotions they felt were hatred and hunger.

Madock struggled to free himself from beneath the fallen demon, shocked at the surprising weight of the rotting corpse. The monster had spotted him now, its dead eyes narrowing as it opened its mouth and struggled to turn around on top of the old man. Raising his hands to hold the advancing monster above him, Madock wrinkled his nose; even behind his mask, the demon's rotten breath was sickening. Madock held his breath, but found the effort of holding up the snapping demon was proving more challenging than he had expected.

The monster growled as it desperately tried to sink its teeth into Madock's flesh, struggling with the Death Cheater's determined grip. It was salivating wildly, droplets spreading across Madock's mask as he sought a way out of the predicament. It was too risky to call out for help in case any more straggling demons were nearby. Whilst he was confident he could eventually fight his way free of this monster, he highly doubted that he had the strength the take on more than one of them.

Finding a deep reserve of strength, Madock attempted to roll the demon, but the struggle proved pointless. The demon, through sheer desire for flesh, held firm and continued to snap aggressively at his neck. Growing increasingly frustrated, Madock started to blame himself for being unable to fight his way free of this situation. In his youth he could easily have flipped the demon and finished it off, but now his aching muscles and tired bones refused to follow his commands.

Stupid old man, he cursed himself silently. The thought riled him. It made him determined not to allow himself to feel helpless and surrender to the quick release of death the monster could offer him.

Not yet. You're the Death Cheater.

Bracing the demon on one forearm, his right hand shot down to his side. In a blur of movement, he had removed his gun from its holster, placed it against the demon's head and pulled the trigger. The explosion of the shot left his ears ringing, but the demon instantly ceased its desperate movements, instead becoming dead weight which frustratingly seemed to make it even harder to support. Madock grunted as the monster collapsed on top of him, briefly knocking the wind out of the old man. He quickly rolled the monster away before laying there in the snow, slowly recovering as his breathing pattern returned to normal. He lay silently, waiting to see if the horde had heard the gunshot. It had been an act of desperation, but as the minutes ebbed away Madock felt more and more convinced that it had not attracted their attention. That didn't mean there weren't still more nearby.

'Madock?' Haswell's whispered voice cut through his thoughts. He could hear the demon hunter's feet crunching in the snow nearby. It seemed as good an indication as any that they had survived the encounter.

Grunting, he lifted himself from the ground and dusted himself off. Haswell spotted him instantly and started heading towards him, but Madock was already focused on the third member of their group.

'Lottie?' he whispered fiercely, moving around tentatively. He knew better than to raise his voice yet, but the troubling mental image of the thin scarf around the girl's neck made his actions urgent.

She can't stay in the Malice any longer...

Again and again he whispered her name, never losing faith when each call was answered with silence. Haswell joined in the search, as both men scoured the nearby area, treading carefully so as not to trip over her wherever she may have been laying.

What if...? Madock silenced the question before it could fully form itself in his mind. He had seen too many people die in the last few days. He wasn't about to allow it to happen again.

He paused as his boots hit something. Instantly reaching down into the Malice, he felt her lying there before him, every muscle tensed and not making a sound. Crouching down, he gently lifted her up in his arms. She did not respond, her body cold and rigid, but much to his relief Madock could see that she was still breathing.

Madock turned to Haswell, who glanced at the girl with a worried expression.

'Let's get back to Pelera.'

* * *

The outskirts of Pelera emerged through the Malice mercifully quickly. It had been a gamble to push for Mikara from the Bunker, but it had provided them with a much shorter journey to their ultimate destination. Still, Madock had to admit they had been lucky to survive the demon horde. It had been the first of its kind he had ever seen, and he hoped that it would be the only such incident he witnessed.

The girl was surprisingly heavy in his arms as they trudged through the snow, her unconscious body weighing down on him and slowing his progress. Haswell had been patient, but was growing increasingly pensive as they neared his hometown, rubbing his hands together nervously. Madock found it hard to blame the young demon hunter. For all his confidence that they would both be able to say goodbye to Ruskin Broxhart, he knew there was a significant chance the man would be dead long before their arrival. He could only hope that his optimism would pay off.

The outer buildings of old Pelera rose around them, leading to further ruins and the remains of larger buildings which had withstood the force of the elements. Madock knew that soon enough they would reach the chasm within which the new city flourished, blossoming by the edge of the Enki cenote.

'We made good time, considering we nearly didn't make it at all…' joked Haswell, though Madock could sense the young man was covering up his discomfort. The Death Cheater merely nodded and trudged on, carrying the unconscious girl in his arms. He knew there was a significant chance that she had been afflicted with Malice poisoning having hidden in the deadly mist for so long while hiding from the demon horde, but he was not willing to face that outcome just yet.

Reaching the stone steps that led down along the outer wall of the chasm, Haswell took a deep breath as he began the descent. Madock knew better than to question his companion's emotions and simply followed silently. The steps were always steep and slippery, and required careful negotiation to avoid a grisly end by plummeting to the Enki cenote below.

Feeling each step carefully with his weathered boots, the old man descended into the settlement he had not visited for many years. It had been difficult to return, having lived for such a long time within its walls in such a significant role. His departure had been met with speculation and suspicion, but following the Sheol Disaster he had been left with little choice but to pursue the culprit. Initially he had blamed the Necromancers like everybody else, but over time he had come to realise that the blame lay upon other shoulders. The scientists who had constructed the machine in the first place were the architects of destruction. Despite his best efforts, the trail had gone cold many years ago, but the idea of returning to Pelera unfulfilled had not been one he had entertained. He could not rest, and he knew deep down that even this visit was simply to say goodbye to an old friend rather than to bring his journey to an end.

The water below trickled calmly, but already he could see the dancing orbs of light that had become an image of what seemed like a past life to him. He had brought his family here to see them, but Rosa had shied away from the lights. In truth, he could not blame her.

'We're not too late,' he heard himself say to Haswell as the young man descended the steps ahead of him. The demon hunter grunted unconvincingly in response, and Madock found himself unable to offer any further words of comfort.

As they reached the bottom of the steps, they were instantly greeted by guards who recognised the crest upon their Malice Gear. Almost without a word, they were ushered to the Broxhart manor, the grand building which they had both once called home. The cold stone floor echoed their footsteps loudly as they made their way towards Lord Broxhart's chamber. As they approached, Madock glanced down at Lottie. She was still unconscious, though he was thankful to note that there appeared to be no obvious signs of Malice poisoning upon her face.

If she had been poisoned, it would be showing by now, he reassured himself, looking down at her innocent face.

The poor child has been through enough. She doesn't deserve to suffer any further.

The doors to Ruskin Broxhart's chamber were eased open as they were escorted into the quiet room. At first, Madock's heart missed a beat to see the frail figure lying engulfed within the vast bedsheets.

Maybe we are too late, he thought sorrowfully.

The thought was short-lived as Ruskin Broxhart lifted his head and smiled at the pair of them.

'Took you long enough.'

9

'You shot it in *both* legs?'

'I crippled both of it's arms too,' Haswell replied boldly, never shying away from his father's gaze.

'I thought you knew better than to waste bullets,' commented Ruskin, raising an eyebrow in surprise.

Haswell grinned and lowered the mask of his Malice Gear to the floor, placing it with the delicacy of a treasured possession upon the cool stone floor of the bedchamber. Straightening, he ran a gloved hand over his shaved head, the result of his sworn oath to the demon hunter's guild.

'It's only a waste if you miss.'

A moment of silence embraced the room before being shattered by a familiar sound Madock had thought he would never hear again.

Ruskin Broxhart was laughing.

'That's my boy!' boomed the lord of Pelera, the sound almost inconceivable given the frail frame it was emerging from.

They were gathered in Ruskin's bedchamber, his failing body encased within an ocean of sheets and pillows which he tugged at continually in frustration. Somehow the vast room seemed much smaller with the large number of figures packed into it in an effort to maintain the formal arrangements that would have occurred under the stone throne of the Broxhart manor. Marcus Ortiz stood closest to Ruskin, as was his right after so many years of loyal service, ready to offer advice or aid at his lord's whim. To his credit, he had acknowledged Haswell's return with little more than a cursory nod in the demon hunter's direction. In direct contrast, the entire manor seemed to have erupted at the sudden reappearance of Haswell

Broxhart, the twin child and prodigal son of the Broxhart family. In spite of the chaos surrounding Haswell's return, Marcus had remained focused upon his duty at all times.

Beside Lord Broxhart's aide stood the numerous medics (which Madock noted were still mostly Harbingers) and bedside servants who Marcus had insisted remain within the lord's chamber or the adjacent rooms, ready to assist Ruskin at any time, day or night. Madock assumed from previous experience that Ruskin would have dismissed the help as unnecessary, yet he noted that the majority of the medical support team were beautiful young ladies with warm smiles and slender figures.

At the foot of Lord Broxhart's bed stood Haswell. In his hand, he held the butt of his rifle, the long barrel resting over his shoulder. In spite of his largely negative views on egotistical demon hunters, Madock had to admit that the young man had certainly captured the celebrity appearance of his chosen profession. The Malice Gear was a thing of a beauty; sleek black armour encased his entire body, marked only with the Broxhart crest upon the chest, a white tree upon a blue background designed to reflect the tree which was rumoured to have once risen from the Enki cenote around which their great city had been built. The Malice Gear was slender but solid just as his own, created to flow like water whilst being firm as ice. It protected the wearer from the worst effects of the Malice and the fierce elemental impact of the Eternal Storm. The mask Haswell had placed on the floor was equally sleek and durable, masking the wearer's face behind a black visor. Fully assembled, the Malice Gear gave the wearer the unsettling appearance of a shadow.

Ruskin's eyes were upon his son now, his expression a mixture of joy and pride as Haswell regaled them with one of his many stories of his experiences upon the surface.

'Oh, Haswell, I have missed your sense of humour.' Ruskin wiped a stray tear from his eye, slowly suppressing the laughter. 'I'm glad I got to hear your stories one last time.'

As though linked by the same thought, every figure in the room shuffled awkwardly. Even Haswell's grin faded. 'You seem well to me, father,' he offered, clearly uncertain how to respond.

'It would seem life as a demon hunter had dulled your senses, boy. Look at me, Haswell. I know I am destined for Enki cenote soon.'

Their conversation was interrupted as the door was swung open and two familiar figures entered. Madock had seen neither of them for many years, but he instantly recognised the young adults they had grown into.

Calipse pushed through the other people in the room and threw herself into Haswell's arms, burying her face in his chest and wrapping her arms tightly around the demon hunter. He laughed and hugged her back, lifting her off her feet playfully. As he placed her back down, she looked up as though to say something but instead simply stepped back quietly and smiled up at him adoringly.

'So… you're back.' The statement came from the doorway. Madock turned to the other new figure, who had stood his ground stubbornly and refused to join the crowded room.

Kerrin hasn't changed much, mused Madock as he observed the young man. There was still the hint of a physical resemblance to his twin brother, particularly his facial features, but there the similarities ended. Where Haswell was tall and broad, Kerrin was slender and far less physically imposing. Haswell carried himself with confidence, whereas his twin seemed to shy away and looked uncomfortable surrounded by so many people.

'Are you not going to give me a hug too?' joked Haswell, offering his open arms in a mocking gesture. Kerrin scowled and folded his arms stubbornly.

'I'm just surprised you found the time in your busy schedule to visit,' he replied bitterly.

Just like when they were children, thought Madock, struggling to suppress a smile. He could recall countless argument between the boys when he had served under Ruskin. They had always seemed to be in competition, though he knew for a fact that each of them in their own way was simply jealous of the other's strengths. Kerrin had fought hard to keep up with Haswell in physical contests, while Haswell had often struggled to match his brother's intelligence, responding by imposing his physical dominance rather than seeking to gain knowledge himself. Madock had to admit, the experience of becoming a demon hunter seemed to have improved the man's understanding of the world, but he knew that Kerrin was likely to have continued his studies in his absence, though lacking first-hand experience of the things he read in his books.

'Between the demons, the storm and the Malice, it's a little difficult to just casually move around the surface,' retorted Haswell. 'You'd know that if you were ever brave enough to stop hiding down here.'

'That's enough, Haswell,' interrupted Ruskin, lifting himself unsteadily onto his elbows and pushing away Marcus as he attempted to help. Lord Broxhart scanned the room before his eyes fell upon Madock. He smiled at the Death Cheater as his eyes focused, recognition spreading across his face. 'They grow bigger, but they're both still just difficult children.'

Madock nodded and moved closer to Ruskin, resting a reassuring hand upon his shoulder. 'Just like their father,' he joked.

Ruskin laughed, a deep rich booming sound which filled the entire room. As it faded, he stared at Madock, his brow furrowed in concentration. 'You got old.'

'You're not exactly looking spry yourself, Ruskin.'

Ruskin nodded bitterly. 'That seems to be the way these days. Die young or live long enough to see your body crumble and fail.' He paused. 'Still, it's a far greater miracle that you're here than me. Death Cheater... I think Lucky Bastard would have been far more apt.'

'You won't hear any arguments from me,' smiled Madock, though he knew deep down that there was nothing lucky about continuing to survive while those around you continued to become nothing but Echoes.

Even Ruskin now. You'll outlive the Eternal Storm as this rate...

'Father, we need to speak to you about Mikara,' interrupted Haswell, stepping forward to Ruskin's bedside.

'This isn't the right time,' argued Kerrin, 'We can discuss that with father later.'

'No, this needs to be sorted,' responded Ruskin firmly, his voice full of authority and determination. He turned to the various faces stood in his chamber. 'Leave.'

One word from their lord was enough as the room quickly and quietly emptied, leaving just Madock, Marcus, Ruskin and his children in the room. Madock knew that Ruskin commanded great respect, but was still impressed at the obedience which had been demonstrated in response to a single command from the frail old man in the bed.

'Now,' Lord Broxhart croaked as the chamber door was shut. 'Tell me everything.'

Madock and Haswell relayed the story of their experiences in Mikara, telling Ruskin of the scene of devastation which had greeted them and of the girl they had rescued from the settlement.

Ruskin listened to the entire story silently, his face growing ever more concerned with every new detail. 'And where is the girl now?' he asked.

'She's in a room downstairs with the medics,' answered Haswell. 'She was unconscious after we survived the horde, but Madock carried her back here. She was still breathing, but I'm not sure if...'

'She wasn't poisoned,' said Madock quickly. He knew that Ruskin was a practical man, and regardless of the girl's age, if she posed a risk to the people of Pelera he would not allow her to stay within the settlement. Madock cared about the girl's wellbeing too much to see her cast out onto the surface to die. Haswell glanced in Madock's direction, but elected to remain silent.

Ruskin seemed to weigh up everything he had heard before nodding slowly. 'We need to speak to her about what she saw. If what she told you is true, this is deeply disturbing.' He turned to Marcus. 'We need to send some of our men to Mikara to investigate and to lock down the settlement. We don't want anybody else getting in there, especially Raiders.'

Marcus nodded and hurried off to begin making arrangements.

'We should go check on the girl,' suggested Kerrin. 'She may have woken up already. We need to know more.'

'Make sure you find out everything,' said Ruskin firmly, sinking lower into the bed. It was clear that the meeting had drained his energy, and the guests within his chamber all took that as their signal to leave.

Together they descended the steps to the lower rooms of the Broxhart manor in silence. Kerrin led the way whilst Haswell lingered at the back of the group with Calipse. Madock could feel the tension between the brothers, but elected not to involve himself. For now, he was more concerned about the girl, and whether she had regained consciousness. Though he had promised Ruskin that Lottie was not poisoned, he realised that he could not guarantee that fact. The medical examination may well have discovered something.

They slowed as they reached the chamber where Lottie had been taken and Kerrin opened the wooden door.

The room had been wrecked. Shards of glass and splintered wood covered the floor, surrounding the bodies of two Peleran medics who lay lifeless and motionless. With a sense of horror, Madock realised that they both looked exactly like the bodies they had seen in Mikara; no obvious physical sign of injury but devoid of life, as though frozen in the moment of death. But amidst the scene of death and destruction, it was not what Madock could see that worried him the most, but rather what he could not see.

Lottie, whether dead or alive, was not in the room.

Kerrin turned to Haswell, their fraternal rivalry forgotten. 'Lock down the manor.'

10

Chaos engulfed the Broxhart manor. Peleran guards, servants and medics seemed to emerge from every direction as the building was locked down. Cutting their way through the midst of them all were Madock, Haswell and Kerrin. Without saying a word they had known exactly where they all needed to go. Calipse and Marcus had fallen behind, distracted by the tasks of ordering the mass of people to their stations and attempting to maintain an air of calm as panic threatened to take a stranglehold on the situation.

Madock knew that he wasn't serving the Broxharts directly anymore, but his loyalty and duty remained to ensure their safety. At that particular point, there was someone who required protection above all others. Haswell and Kerrin had recognised this too, and together they surged back upstairs towards Ruskin Broxhart's chamber.

As he ran, Madock's mind was a whirlwind of emotion. Not only was there Ruskin's safety to worry about, but also the whereabouts of Lottie. The fact that her body had not been counted among the dead gave him faint cause for hope, but the question remained what had happened to the young girl. He had personally delivered her to that room and lay her unconscious body down upon the bed. Even if she had recovered, he highly doubted that she would have been strong enough to escape the room on her own. Perhaps one of the medics had been able to help her from the room before they had been struck down, or perhaps…

Perhaps whatever killed those people has taken her. There were too many questions and not enough time to discover the answers. Right now, all he could do was force his tired legs to move quicker.

Haswell was leading the way as they arrived at Ruskin's chamber. Madock's heart skipped a beat as he observed the guards slumped helplessly at their posts, confirming his worst fears. There was no time to check on them, and he forced himself to focus on the danger that lay ahead. Haswell threw the doors to the chamber open, already raising his rifle to take out any potential intruders. Madock followed him in, drawing his own trusty weapon and scanning the room with quick, experienced eyes. Kerrin arrived at the back of the group, barging into the room unarmed and desperate.

Silence met them all. The room appeared empty save for Ruskin, who appeared to be lying perfectly still within his bed. Madock thought he could see the old man's chest slowly rising and falling, though he felt himself doubting his own instincts as they all began to cautiously enter the room heading towards the bed.

'Father?' Kerrin called out nervously, ensuring that he kept near Madock and Haswell for security. Though none of them were willing to voice their concerns, each of them felt that something within the room wasn't quite right. Madock could almost taste it in the air; a sense of unease, as though something had changed.

As they finally reached the bed, Madock was relieved to see that his initial assessment had been correct as Ruskin was indeed clearly breathing, though his lack of responsiveness was troubling. He had not responded to the three of them crashing into his chamber, nor had he risen to the sound of Kerrin's voice. Even as the young man now gently shook his father by the shoulders, there was no response from Ruskin. Kerrin looked at Haswell urgently.

'We need to send for the medics. The Harbingers. Anybody.'

'It won't do him any good,' interrupted a mysterious female voice. At the sound, all three men turned back towards the door where a stranger stood clad in Malice Gear. The person had entered without making a sound, catching an experienced demon hunter and Dead Man completely off guard. Haswell seemed to take a moment to gather himself, but instantly his rifle was aimed directly at the stranger's chest.

'Who are you? How did you get in here?' barked Haswell.

The stranger seemed unperturbed at the act of aggression and ignored the questions, instead indicating with a delicate finger towards Ruskin who remained unconscious within the folds of the vast sheets. 'It's beautiful, isn't it?' she commented, 'Life and death in symmetry, locked in a dance that will only end when one surrenders to the other. Such a pity that death is the stronger dancer.'

Madock instinctively took a protective step between the stranger and Ruskin, his weapon now also trained upon the woman who remained in the doorway. The atmosphere seemed to have become dense, as though everything were happening in slow motion. In spite of the chaos they had dashed through earlier, it now felt as though they were the only people in the entire manor.

'These are private chambers, how did you get in here?' repeated Haswell.

The woman giggled and shook her head. 'What makes you believe you have the right to deny access to anybody? We are all born equal upon this land.'

Malice poisoning? An Echo Gazer? Madock searched desperately for some reasoning behind the woman's unusual actions. She had somehow gained access to the Broxhart manor and had now entered the very chamber of the lord of Pelera, but seemed to be addressing them as if they had encountered each other within a tavern or on the streets of the Bunker. *And she's wearing Malice Gear. She's no random Peleran. Perhaps a Raider?*

'I can tell you whether he will recover or not,' continued the woman, placing both her hands on her hips in a confident manner. 'Would you like to know?'

Kerrin and Madock exchanged a quick glance, but Haswell's eyes remained fixed on the woman, his finger poised carefully on the trigger of his rifle. Kerrin was the first to step forward and address the stranger. 'Explain yourself.'

'All in good time,' replied the woman, raising her hands from her hips and removing the mask from her head. As it came away, Madock couldn't be certain which startled him more; the beauty of the young lady or the confidence which burned within her eyes and the smirk that spread across her face. She ran her hand through her strawberry blonde hair, removing a hair clip and allowing it to fall down her back and across her shoulders. She pointed at Haswell's weapon disapprovingly. 'I hope you don't treat all your guests this way! I heard the Broxharts were more hospitable than this…'

She went to take a step forward, but instantly stopped as a bullet surged into the floorboards just in front of her.

'That's far enough,' instructed Haswell firmly, raising the smoking barrel of his weapon to retrain it upon the stranger. 'The next one won't be a warning shot.'

To Madock's surprise, the woman merely laughed.

'Are you sure you're not just a bad shot?' she taunted as she casually leaned against the door frame.

Haswell bristled at the insult and took a step forward towards the woman before recovering his self-control. 'No more games. Get down on the ground.'

The woman instantly stopped laughing, an expression of deadly seriousness covering her face. She sighed dramatically. 'You try and be nice…'

Her speed was startling as she charged towards them, and in many other scenarios it may have been enough for her to get an advantage over her opponents. But Madock and Haswell were experienced, their senses trained and honed by years of dangerous encounters upon the surface.

Both guns fired.

Madock's bullet found its mark as the woman's aggressive surge was brought to an abrupt end, sending her crashing to the floor. For a moment nobody moved, taking the opportunity to try to understand what had just happened and to control their racing heartbeats.

Finally, Madock moved across to check on the fallen woman. His bullet had penetrated deep into the woman's chest, but he was surprised to see that Haswell's shot had not been targeted at the same area. 'You shot her in the shoulder?' he asked inquisitively, turning back to look at Haswell. The demon hunter shrugged and lowered his weapon, though Madock could sense the young man's unease.

'I was trying to stop her, not kill her,' he muttered.

'Madock was right to kill her,' sighed Kerrin, who was clearly shaken by the whole experience. 'And I thought you would have done the same, brother.'

Haswell scowled but remained silent, his eyes focused upon the fallen woman. Madock allowed his gaze to return to the woman who now lay silent and still upon the wooden floor, but already the Death Cheater could tell that something was wrong. It took him a moment to realise the cause of his confusion, but when it dawned upon him it did little to ease the confusion.

There's no blood...

The woman groaned and raised herself weakly to a sitting position. 'I guess you really *are* a bad shot,' she laughed through uneven breaths, clearly weaker for the ordeal but very much alive. 'The old man's steadier than you!'

Madock felt lost for words, and the silence that followed clearly suggested that the twin Broxhart brothers were equally startled. Madock knew that his bullet had penetrated the woman's chest. Whilst there may have been a tiny chance of her surviving, there was no way she should have been able to sit up and talk to them as though all they had done was knock her off her feet and wind her.

'How?' asked Kerrin, barely able to force the words from his lips.

'You can't hurt me, no more than you can save your father.' The woman paused, the confident smirk resurfacing on her face. 'But I can.'

Haswell growled and stepped forward. In one smooth action, he raised his rifle and slammed the butt of the weapon onto the stranger's head. She collapsed, but the self-assured smile remained on her face as she fell unconscious.

The three men seemed unable to tear their eyes away from her body, each of them expecting her to instantly rise again and continue her verbal onslaught as though nothing had happened. This time she remained still, though the rise and fall of her chest indicated that the life she seemed to be clinging to so firmly remained within her.

It was Haswell who spoke first. 'She talks too much.'

Kerrin shot his brother an exasperated look. 'Is this really the time for jokes?'

'Seems as good a time as any,' Haswell shrugged as he set about searching the woman's body for weapons. As Kerrin turned to check on his father once more, Madock knelt beside the mysterious fallen woman. The crest upon her Malice Gear had been torn, presumably during a prior encounter, but there remained enough of it for Madock to recognise the city it belonged to.

He tapped the crest with his gloved finger, drawing Haswell's attention towards it. The young man briefly suspended his search and frowned as he also recognised the crest.

'The Gairen crest?' he asked in confusion.

'Where else would she get Malice Gear from? It's certainly not Peleran.' Madock could see the points in the suit where the bullets had ripped through, but the skin beneath appeared unharmed, as though it had healed itself as quickly as the damage had been done. There was no indication that the bullets had bounced harmlessly off the woman's body, suggesting that somehow the bullets were still inside. He stood and shook his head slowly. 'I've never seen anything like this before.'

'I don't think anybody has,' replied Haswell. He paused as a thought occurred to him. 'Do you think she was behind the deaths in Mikara? The monster that Lottie was talking about?'

Madock considered the question. 'It's possible. She might be behind Lottie's disappearance too. Either way, we need to keep her somewhere secure until we can figure out what's going on.'

'We need to keep her away from our people. We need to keep her away from our father.' Kerrin spoke quietly from his father's bedside as he checked on the old man. Madock joined him and stared down at Ruskin. The Lord of Pelera was still breathing, though he remained as unresponsive as when they had first entered the room. Madock could only hope that his old friend was not slipping away.

'There's only one place we can put her where I'd feel safe,' continued Kerrin. 'Though we haven't had to use them for years now.'

Madock knew the place Kerrin spoke of. *The midnight cells.*

11

The market bustled with activity, noise and scents filling the air and enlivening the senses. Her maids had travelled with her, as both her brother and father had demanded, but as always she had dismissed them once upon the edge of the market. She liked to spend as much time amongst the people as possible, soaking up the atmosphere and greeting those who recognised her. Her maids tended to fuss over her, suffocating her freedom though their intentions were pure. Her brother no doubt knew of her activities through his web of informants, but thus far Blake had deigned to remain silent on the matter.

Though she was the daughter of Lord Airenguarde, Starr never felt threatened walking through the crowds within the walls of the city. She smiled at the thought of the old stone walls surrounding Gair; they were a boundary, full of nostalgia and meaning, but they were no longer the city's protection as they had been in the old days. That honour now belonged to the Shell.

Starr had only to look around her to see it; a shimmering barrier surrounding the entire city, moving gently like running water from horizon to horizon. The Shell protected Gair from the harmful surface conditions, reflecting snow, wind and even Malice away from the ancient stone buildings and the people who dwelt within the walls. It was the sole reason that Gair remained the only living city to exist upon the land's surface.

Yet it had come at a price, one that increased in cost with every passing day it seemed. Starr had been told that the Harbingers had first struck the deal with her grandfather Myren Airenguarde. In return for creating the Shell around the city to allow its restoration, Myren had agreed to allow the Harbingers to construct their temple within the walls of the city. The balance of power had remained favourable to her family, allowing them to restore the city to something of its former glory. Her mother's sickness had shifted the balance more than Starr could bear to accept.

She paused by a market stall, admiring the delicate silver trinkets displayed upon the wooden table. The stall owner was a familiar face to her, and it took her but a moment to recall his name.

'Good morning, Lady Starr,' he greeted her warmly, offering a polite bow.

'Hello Langdar,' she replied, a sad memory resurfacing in her mind as she recalled their previous meeting. Langdar had raised an issue with her regarding his concern over a missing friend of his, a fellow merchant who had vanished whilst within the city walls of Gair. Starr had ordered a number of her house guards to scan the city limits whilst also entreating her brother to use his network of informants to aid her search. Thus far, however, she had heard nothing.

Langdar continued to speak to her eagerly. 'I would be most grateful if you could pass on my humblest gratitude to your brother, Master Blake,' he insisted, his eyes wide and excited. 'It is thanks to his sources that my friend was discovered in a derelict building along the east wall.'

The news surprised Starr. They had been searching for the woman for three days now, yet Blake had not said another word on the matter to her. *My brother spins quite the web of informants*, she considered silently.

'I'm delighted for you both,' she smiled warmly, 'and I will be happy to pass on your gratitude to my brother. What happened to your friend?'

Langdar's smile faded instantly. 'She was robbed of her possessions and of her dignity. She...' He paused for a moment, then shook his head to clear the troubling thought. 'No matter, she is returned to safety thanks to your family's kindness. Please accept anything you see before you as a gift. They are crafted in Tirneth, north of Silverbridge. It is a hard and dangerous place to visit, make no mistake, yet when it provides such beauty as this I find it hard to resist.'

Starr accepted the offer with a grateful smile, picking out a small silver brooch formed into the shape of a dragon. The eyes burned through brilliant tiny rubies, while the creature's tail was so delicately crafted that it seemed possible to count each individual scale adorning it.

As she turned from Langdar's stall her eyes fell upon the Harbinger's temple, a towering structure surging upwards towards the peak of the Shell at the very centre of Gair. The Harbingers certainly knew how to create on a grand scale, yet they insisted their work would be laughable in comparison to that of the angels when they returned to banish the Dark Days.

To Starr's knowledge, the belief in angels had always existed. When the Malice and the Eternal Storm had first struck their lands, this faith in beings of light that would one day drive away the darkness was accepted by many, turning to religion in their desperation. Hope was a powerful weapon, and many believed that the angels would return from the skies above one day to restore the planet to its former glory. It was around this time, as lore and legend recorded it, that the Harbingers of Light had risen to become the dominant religious power.

She was jarred from her thoughts abruptly at the sound of a familiar, unsettling voice.

'Careful, my lady.' The tone made her skin crawl as she turned to face the scientist Merle Enrick. 'You must watch where you are going in this world. There are too many… unwholesome individuals about.'

'Indeed,' replied Starr coldly, forcing herself to maintain eye contact with the man. 'Shouldn't you be helping my brother with your project?' Though the scientist had been in her family's life for only a short time, she found herself mistrusting the man more and more with every encounter. To her frustration, she seemed alone in her concerns. Her father seemed to have forgotten about the entire project, instead returning to his familiar routine of remaining close to his wife at all available opportunities. In direct contrast to this, Blake had formed a close bond with the scientist. In truth, this did not surprise Starr; her brother had always been power hungry and the promise of a machine that could allow their family to command the entire region from coast to coast must have seemed a banquet he could not refuse.

'I am merely passing through to collect some goods from my merchant contact,' replied Enrick, seemingly affronted at her coldness. 'I assure you that I take my work very seriously, especially since your father has been kind enough to support it.' His eyes scanned the crowds around them. 'And where might your maids be? It is not wise for a young lady such as yourself to wander these streets alone.'

Starr smiled. 'You are sweet to concern yourself with my wellbeing,' she said, her voice dripping with sarcasm. 'But I assure you, I am well aware of those whose intentions are pure and those who seek only to corrupt.'

'Then you are wise beyond your years, my lady.' Enrick glanced up at the Eternal Storm, a fresh blizzard attacking the Shell overhead. The magical barrier held strong, as it always did. 'Anyway, you are quite right, I must return to Master Blake and my "project" as you call it. Perhaps when it is complete you will regard me as the honest man I truly am.' With that, Enrick scurried way on his short legs, disappearing into the crowds of the market.

Starr scowled as she watched him leave. *That day will come when the angels themselves return to us.*

The day seemed to have been tarnished by her unfortunate meeting with the scientist, so Starr elected to return to the palace. She found her maids at the pre-arranged meeting point and set off on foot through the streets of Gair towards her home.

In truth, it was a miracle that the palace had still been standing at all when the Harbingers first created the Shell over the city. The surface conditions had battered the walls largely into submission and they had even discovered demons lurking within the walls. Two demon hunters had lost their lives cleansing the area to allow them to return to their home, but those who had returned with the creatures' heads had been richly rewarded for their services. Employing the finest craftsmen and stonemasons from his own people and even the surrounding freeholds, her grandfather had restored the palace and the city itself, allowing their people to return to their rightful home. Gair had always stood in the shadow of the mountains from which it took its name, yet it had only been under the control of the Airenguarde family since they had overthrown the corruptive Marstarn family who had ruled Gair with an iron fist. Starr had accepted that their family's history may not have been as rich and pure as the Broxharts of Pelera, but she was fiercely proud to bear the name Airenguarde.

The stone steps leading to the palace were steep, yet she had travelled them so many times with Blake and Gray as children that she barely even noticed. They had played all manner of games, she recalled, challenging each other to see who could reach the peak first or inventing ingenious and often dangerous means of reaching the bottom. The memories were precious to her, reminding her of a simpler time. Yet even in the memory, her father had been a distant figure, always by their mother's bedside.

A hint of sadness struck her as she remembered the fits of rage Blake had experienced as a child. In the throes of such anger, he had blamed her for their mother's illness, screaming that it was her fault they had lost both of their parents to that bedchamber. Even now the words hurt her, perhaps because she knew that there was an element of truth to them. But she had always found it easy to blame herself. It was important that she kept this secret though. She had been taught from a young age that it was important to maintain a shield of strength and grace in her appearance regardless of what she felt inside. Bitter thoughts and sadness could mingle behind the confident exterior, hidden from public view.

The courtyard was busy with activity as it always was, servants and house guards going about their business with a polite smile of acknowledgement of her arrival. It did not take Starr long to note that one corner of the yard was empty save for one lonely figure. The masses were keeping themselves away from the young man and the orb of light that lingered by his side, burning a sorrowful sapphire blue as it had often done since Enrick's arrival.

It irritated Starr that though Gray was their father's ward, the people of Gair still treated the Necromancer with suspicion and fear. The hatred towards his people for their part in the Sheol Disaster lingered even to this day, long after most of Gray's kind had been executed or fled from the western shore. Some had whispered that he was the last remaining Necromancer on these lands, an idea that Starr found difficult to believe. In the days before the incident, Necromancers had mingled freely amongst the people, even married and bred with others outside their clan. It seemed impossible to believe that Gray could truly be the last of his kind in the entire region.

As she approached Gray, she noted her maids falling behind awkwardly and apprehensively, but she did not break her stride. The Necromancer glanced up at her approach and allowed himself a smile, his Echo altering to a swirling orb of calming gold that lit the dark corner he stood in.

'Lord Airenguarde won't be pleased you wandered off on your own again,' he called out to her as she approached.

'I don't know what you're talking about,' she grinned, attempting to feign confusion. Gray knew her too well, perhaps even better than her own brother. 'My maids were with me all the time. I was never once out of their sights. You can ask them yourself if you don't believe me.'

Gray folded his arms. 'Somehow I doubt they would come close enough, even to lie to me.'

Starr glanced back at her maids who were collectively avoiding eye contact with them. 'You might have a point there...'

Gray sighed, his Echo shifting back to blue. 'I won't say anything, but you should be careful.'

Starr shuddered, remembering her meeting with Enrick at the market. She knew that Gray was still deeply unhappy about the scientist's presence in the city and had become increasingly reclusive. She shared his suspicions about Enrick's true intentions, but they both knew that there was little they could do to stop the project. Her father had authorised it and Blake was already overseeing its progress. The cogs were already in motion, and it seemed nothing could stop them from turning.

Across the courtyard, a door was suddenly flung open as Blake stormed out into the courtyard, his eyes scanning the surroundings quickly before settling upon the pair of them. His expression was one of anger, his intention clear as he paced across the paved surface towards her.

'He looks cross,' whispered Gray playfully, his Echo already switching to a jovial orange. Ever since they had been children, he and Starr had taken great delight in winding up Blake. As a child he had been quick to anger and very little had changed as he had grown into manhood. They had learnt from experience when to hold back though to avoid Blake's wrath. Clearly Gray did not see this as an occasion to be reserved. 'You're in trouble…'

In spite of herself, Starr grinned. Her brother did not look impressed as his voice bellowed out across the courtyard.

'A word, sweet sister…'

12

Madock found them by the water's edge as he had known he would. Since the incident with the intruder a week ago, Calipse had returned to her vigil by the Enki cenote. Now more than ever she seemed convinced it was simply a matter of time before her father's Echo joined the other lights. Ruskin still had not regained consciousness and his breathing was becoming increasingly laboured. Madock himself felt a sense of helplessness regarding the situation as he watched his oldest friend slowly slipping away. He had watched many others become Echoes in the past, but he knew that when the day came for Ruskin's soul to rise, it would be the most difficult to come to terms with.

Haswell had stayed by his sister's side as much as possible, regaling her with stories of his adventures as a demon hunter. Madock had noted that the young man had regained a degree of his former confidence and attitude since returning home, but the Death Cheater believed that this was simply a façade to disguise his insecurity about the impending death of their father. Madock had often seen him staring off into the middle distance, seemingly lost in silent contemplation, and the demon hunter had taken to regularly visiting the Harbingers who were responsible for aiding his father.

Kerrin was not with them. He was coping with the situation in the same way he had since the start, by keeping busy and involving himself in the day to day running of Pelera. Madock respected his decision; since Ruskin had slipped further into ill health, he knew that difficult decisions would need to be made without the guidance of their lord. The Death Cheater put his faith in the idea that Kerrin, with Marcus' support, would cope with the pressure.

Calipse glanced up as she heard Madock approaching. Her eyes shimmered with fresh tears yet she smiled sweetly at him. 'Haze was just telling me about his adventures in Drakewood.' There was immense pride in her voice as she spoke. Haswell attempted to look modest and failed entirely. 'Did he tell you about it? How he was surrounded by three demons with only one bullet left?'

'I can believe you only had one bullet left,' joked Madock, settling himself beside the Broxhart youngsters. 'You always were a little trigger happy.'

Haswell stroked his shaven head. 'The more bullets I fire, the more dead demons there are. That's a good thing, right?' He winked at Calipse who giggled childishly.

Madock smiled, allowing himself a nostalgic moment as memories surfaced in his mind of his time in Pelera as a younger man. He felt confident that he had sat on this very spot with the Broxhart family, watching the children play by the water's edge whilst he and Ruskin discussed some business matter. He had felt honoured that Ruskin had sought his counsel at times, and grateful that his opinion had been listened to and occasionally acted upon. Ruskin had always been a stubborn man, but he also knew when to follow good advice.

His smile faded as his mind once more conjured the image of Lottie. The girl was still missing, despite the Peleran guards searching the entire settlement thoroughly on a regular basis. Madock had spent the first few days joining the search himself, but had increasingly found himself distracted by the task of supporting the Broxhart family during this troubling period. He had only known Lottie for a matter of hours, but he felt responsible for her wellbeing. The mystery of what had happened in the room remained unresolved.

The medics were dead. Should I be thankful that her body wasn't there? Did the monster take her? Is the monster still here? Is the woman in the midnight cells the monster? Did she take Lottie?

He shook his head to end the whirlwind of questions. Reaching into his pocket, Madock's fingers discovered the glass he had found upon the surface. He had almost forgotten about it amidst the chaos of everything else that had happened recently, but now he took the opportunity to remove it and study it closely.

In truth, its greatest value to Madock was the fact that he did not know what it was. He had seen a great many things during his life both underground and on the surface, but this object remained a mystery to him. It was perfectly possible it was simply a piece of jewelry, dropped by a merchant or perhaps even left from the old world, but Madock sensed it was not a crafted object. The curves and smooth edges seemed something which only nature could shape. The mystery intrigued him, and he found himself lost in thought staring at the glass as he carefully turned it in his gloved hand.

He was dragged from his thoughts by a short cough from nearby. As all three of them turned towards the sound, they spotted Kerrin descending towards the Enki cenote.

'Kerrin, Haze is telling me all about Drakewood. Do you want to come listen too?' inquired Calipse earnestly. Madock sensed she was pleased to see her other brother joining them, though her tone was not as openly enthusiastic as it had been when talking to Haswell moments before.

Kerrin sighed and stood formally before them. 'Perhaps you can save your stories for another day. It's time to fetch the intruder from the midnight cells.'

Madock noticed how Calipse shrank back towards Haswell, as though relying on him for safety and security. For his own part, the old man was surprised that a decision had been made on the woman's fate so quickly.

'There's nothing to be worried about,' said Kerrin reassuringly to his little sister, 'We're sending her from this world for her actions.'

Madock was on his feet in an instant. 'Has she said anything about Mikara? Or Lottie?' he questioned urgently.

Kerrin shook his head. 'She broke into the manor and made an attempt on my family's life. Whatever else she might be guilty of, she needs to be punished.' His tone was cold and uncompromising.

Madock paused. He was surprised at Kerrin's blunt tone and wondered if the words were his own, or whether they had been placed there by another. Kerrin had always been the more measured of the twin brothers, so to decide the death penalty without so much as questioning the woman seemed out of character. However, his manner suggested that there would be little room for compromise.

'Let me come with you,' suggested Madock. 'I only need to ask her a few questions, then you can do as you wish with her.'

Kerrin paused as he considered the request before slowly nodding. Calipse was still seeking comfort from Haswell as they all stood ready to return to the manor, keeping close to him at all times. Haswell wrapped a protective arm around her as they began to move away from the Enki cenote.

'You don't need to come down with us, Calli,' he said reassuringly. 'And if she tries anything, I'll put another bullet in her brain this time, see if that does the trick.'

Calipse sniffed and nodded in agreement, but Haswell's words had raised a question in Madock's mind.

'How exactly are you planning to execute her?' he asked Kerrin as they led the way. 'We already know that bullets won't do it.'

Kerrin remained silent, electing not to answer.

This isn't his idea, realised Madock as he chose not to pursue the matter. But this sudden truth revealed another far darker realisation. *The only other person who could have authorised this without Lord Broxhart is Marcus. Is he manipulating Kerrin?*

They continued to make their way through Pelera, crossing the network of bridges which connected the islands of houses and businesses which thrived within the settlement. A small group of house guards joined them as they made their way through the crowds, presumably placed to await their return from the Enki cenote.

Marcus greeted them as they returned to the manor with a somber expression. 'Let's go see what's left of her mind,' he said, ushering them forward. He paused as Calipse walked past him, clinging tightly to Haswell's arm. 'Lady Calipse, perhaps you would be happier staying up here?'

Calipse glanced up at Haswell, then shook her head firmly. 'I'm coming too.'

Marcus clearly seemed unhappy with the idea, but he did not argue and instead silently led the way to the doorway to the cells. The rusty door opened creakily as he turned the key in the lock and pulled with all of his strength. A musty smell of death and decay met their noses, causing them all to turn away momentarily. Calipse hesitated as she glanced down into the darkness.

'Is it safe?' she asked.

Marcus removed a torch from the wall and lit it, the flames barely penetrating the darkness ahead of them. 'For us? Yes,' he replied, before leading them all down the stone steps into the depths of the manor.

The midnight cells were a twisted creation. Located deep in the bowels of the Broxhart manor behind several locked doors, three corridors strayed in different directions, plunging deeper and deeper into the rock. Each corridor culminated in a small cell, basic in nature and easily large enough to contain three or four men. However, they were only designed to allow one individual to be kept in each cell as part of the torturous design, a form of solitary confinement compounded by the pitch black that engulfed these cells. They were named the midnight cells as not a speck of light could enter them, leaving the detained individual completely engulfed by numbing darkness, denying their senses and testing the sanity of those forced to endure confinement for any period of time. In the past, the midnight cells had been used to force confessions from silent tongues and to punish the worst crimes. Even the threat of time in the midnight cells was enough to send chills down the spines of even the most hardened criminals, but it had been some time since they had last been used.

'You're certain… she can't escape?' whispered Calipse, glancing around nervously as the group carefully followed the light of the torch in Marcus' hand.

'Positive,' replied Haswell confidently.

The flames seemed to burn Madock's eyes as he walked at the back of the group. It was not his first descent into the midnight cells, but just as he had every time before, he felt a sense of claustrophobic fear and dread that threatened to overpower him. He could only imagine what being locked in the suffocating darkness could do to a man's mind.

'How is Ruskin's condition?' asked Madock, eager to distract himself from the darkness.

Marcus' voice echoed back from the front of the group. 'No significant change I'm afraid, but we have remained on high alert since the intrusion. There are more people in his chamber than he would feel comfortable with if he were conscious.'

Gate after gate was opened before them, with Marcus sealing each one in turn behind them. The metal clanked loudly as the hinges squeaked and screamed. Madock knew that this was another deliberate choice. "The noise only makes it worse for them," Ruskin had explained, and in truth Madock could understand the reasoning; the noise was unbearable and always set his teeth on edge.

They forked off to the right as they reached the corridors, moving slower now and talking in hushed whispers only when necessary. Prisoners lost their minds down here and it was commonly believed that you could still hear their manic laughter echoing off the rocks. Madock had always done his best to ignore such stories.

Instead, he focused on the questions he would ask the woman. He knew that he would not have much time to interrogate her, but there were answers he had to know before she was silenced. The most pressing issue in his mind remained the fate of Lottie. Despite a thorough search of the city, she had not been discovered either living or dead. The mystery of what had happened in that room remained unsolved, though Madock was certain that whatever had been responsible for the deaths in Mikara was responsible for the deaths in the manor. Unfortunately, that left two worrying questions: what had the monster done with Lottie, and perhaps even more unsettling, was it still here in Pelera? Madock could only hope that the answer to both questions would be provided from the woman in the midnight cell.

'We're here,' announced Marcus. The light of his torch caught the metal bars of the midnight cell. Madock felt himself holding his breath, though he could not say why. The woman clearly possessed unusual powers; that he could say with certainty. But there was also a toxic atmosphere down here, and fear hung heavy in the air.

Marcus rapped his hand against the bars, sending a dull metallic sound echoing around them. 'Your time has come,' he announced, attempting to sound formal and intimidating. Thrusting his torch between the bars, he turned it to light the corners of the cell, his eyes scanning for the prisoner. The action became increasingly urgent as the flames flickered from side to side. Suddenly they stopped, save for the unsteady shaking of Marcus' hand.

Madock pushed his way to the front of the group and shook Marcus firmly, but the aide offered no response. Forcing the torch from his grip, Madock turned the light back into the cell and thoroughly lit every dark corner. It was instantly clear why Marcus was frozen in fear and confusion.

She's not here...

13

They surged back through the darkness towards the manor. There was no time to work out how the woman had escaped from the midnight cell. All that mattered was that she was no longer there.

The flame shook in Madock's hand as he sprinted through the darkness. He couldn't look back to check that the others were following him, but he could hear their rushing footsteps mixed in with his own. He could only assume that they were all thinking the same thing. The woman had confronted them in Ruskin's room the first time they had encountered her, had talked about nothing but whether the lord of Pelera would live or die. There was every chance that she was heading back in that direction.

There are extra guards there, he told himself desperately as they raced up the cold stone steps. *They'll stop her. Or least slow her down.*

He had taken the chain of keys from Marcus as soon as they turned away from the midnight cell, the aide clearly uncertain as to how to proceed and unwilling to take action. Madock assumed he was following at the back of the group, though he knew there was a chance that the man remained in the darkness behind them. There was no time to worry about him at that point though. Right now his destination was the only thing that mattered.

Turning the key in the final lock, he swung the door open and instantly set off for Ruskin's chamber without even turning back to check if the others were following him. Ultimately he did not need to, as first Haswell then Kerrin surged ahead of him, their youthful legs and stamina outmatching his older limbs and shortness of breath.

Keep going. You need to keep going. His mind willed his body to quicken the pace. It seemed to scream in protest, his joints burning and aching with the pressure he was putting them under. Silently he cursed himself. In his youth he had run for miles without a second thought; now it seemed a sprint up some steps was enough to exhaust him. Perhaps this was simply the price he paid for earning his title as the Death Cheater. Few ever lived long enough to see their bodies fail them naturally.

Gritting his teeth, he pressed on. There would be time for melancholic self-reflection later. Right now all that mattered was Ruskin's safety.

As they approached the door to Ruskin's chamber, Madock was relieved to see that the guards posted outside remained alert and focused, though clearly startled to see the group charging towards them.

'Has anybody come through here?' asked Haswell urgently as he skidded to a halt by the door.

The guards exchanged a glance and shook their head, already raising their weapons in alarm. Together they opened the door and entered the chamber, only to find a scene of tranquility. The various medics and guards posted within the room itself looked up in surprise as the group crashed into chamber with weapons drawn.

Madock quickly scanned the room, but nothing seemed out of place. 'Has anybody else been in here?' he asked, glancing around at the confused faces. At first nobody answered, as though confused by the question. 'Has anybody else been in here?' repeated Madock, frustrated at their lack of response.

'Nobody,' answered a medic by Ruskin's bedside. 'Marcus himself checked on Ruskin before he left to take you to the midnight cells. Nobody else has been in here since then.'

Madock allowed himself a silent sigh of relief, though he knew that the opportunity to relax had not yet arrived. The woman was not here, but that did not mean she was not still a threat to Pelera. She may even now be on her way to the chamber as they waited within its walls.

He turned to Kerrin. 'Where are Marcus and Calipse?'

Kerrin turned and glanced around, as if suddenly aware of their absence from the group. 'I thought they were right behind us.' He seemed uncertain as to how to proceed. 'We need to find them.'

More importantly, we need to find the woman, thought Madock, already weighing up the possibilities. *We need to keep the people calm, but we also need to keep them safe. How did she even get out?*

The thought was driven from his mind as Ruskin began to shake uncontrollably within his bed. The medics instantly rushed to his aid, pulling back the sheets and attempting to roll him into a more secure position.

'What's happening?' asked Kerrin desperately as he approached their father's bed. He reeled in shock as blood began to pour from Ruskin's mouth, spluttering out across the crisp white sheets. Lord Broxhart's body continued to fit violently, struggling against the medics as they attempted to clear his airways. Ruskin gasped for air, and just for a moment his eyes opened. Madock could see nothing but terror in those eyes.

Then as suddenly as it had begun, the fit ended. Ruskin was perfectly still and silent. A medic rolled him over and began feeling for a pulse. He seemed to stand there forever, his fingers upon the lord's wrist, desperately seeking a sign of life from the frail body that lay upon the bloody sheets.

His search was answered as Ruskin's Echo slowly emerged from his body.

14

Madock was running. He wasn't even sure where he was running to. He only knew that he had to find Marcus. He hoped his suspicions were wrong, but all of the pieces seemed to be falling into place.

The conversation from moments before circled in his head as he ran.

'What happened?' Haswell's voice seemed to contain such a mixture of emotions that even he hadn't known which to feel. Confusion, anger and sadness seemed to swirl together to create an emotion more powerful than any of them individually.

The medic had examined Ruskin's body as the rest of the room stared helplessly at the Lord of Pelera's Echo, dancing above the frame from which it had just emerged. The shifting colours were both beautiful and tragic in equal measure.

'What happened?' screamed Haswell, pushing through the crowd of stunned onlookers and clutching his father's hand tightly as if he believed that he could still pull him from death's clutches.

Pausing, the medic straightened as the colour drained from his face. Haswell stared at him imploringly, but the man seemed lost for words.

Eventually he discovered his voice. 'Lord Broxhart was poisoned...'

Madock threw open the door to Marcus's chamber. To his frustration, the room was empty. In truth, he hadn't expected to find Ruskin's aide here, but it would have been the lesser of two evils and may even have done something to alleviate the concern that was rising in his chest. He knew now that there was only one other place to go, though he hoped that he was wrong.

Slamming the door shut, he turned and rushed towards the main doors of the Broxhart manor.

'Poisoned?' asked Haswell in disbelief, still clutching his father's hand tightly. *'How is that possible?'*

The medic shook his head uncomfortably. *'I don't know. Nobody's had access to Lord Ruskin except us, and I swear...'* He trailed off, clearly reluctant to even raise the issue.

'Somebody did.' Kerrin's voice was uneven, clearly choking back a great deal of emotion. He had remained silent since Ruskin's Echo had emerged from his body, watching the orb of light as though hypnotised by it. But now he found the strength to speak as Haswell and the medic turned to look at him questioningly. *'Marcus...'*

Madock's feet pounded against the streets of Pelera as he rushed towards the Enki cenote. Ruskin's Echo had probably already made its way there, dancing amidst the other lights. He had always been a ruler who enjoyed mingling among his people, so Madock believed there was a sense of balance and meaning by his Echo now floating equally with those who had lived all manner of different lives. In death there was no superiority, only equality. Death was the great leveller, the one true constant in this world.

He couldn't allow himself time to mourn his friend. Not yet. Not while there was still a risk to the settlement he had once called home.

'Are you crazy Kerrin?' Haswell spat out the words furiously at his brother. *'Why would Marcus do this? He's been father's aide for years!'*

Kerrin withered under the force of his brother's anger, but repeated his argument. *'Marcus was the only other person who's been in here, the only person who could do this...'*

'But why?' asked Haswell desperately.

'He... he was acting strange this morning,' continued Kerrin awkwardly. *'He was the one who wanted to execute the woman without questioning her. He was... very insistent... He wasn't acting like himself at all.'*

Madock suddenly found himself thinking about Lottie's words back in Mikara: "It kept changing what it looked like. It had lots and lots of faces." A monster that could draw the Echoes out of people and could change what it looked like.

The realisation of what may be happening struck him hard. But what alarmed him even more was what might be about to happen next.

He ran from the room without saying another word.

Madock's feet splashed into the water of the Enki cenote as he desperately scanned his surroundings. He wasn't even sure what he was looking for, but he knew that this was where he was likely to find it.

A monster that changes faces. A monster that absorbs Echoes. It's going to be here.

His gun was drawn and ready, his quick eyes darting in all directions. It was only now as he paused that he realised his vision had become blurred by tears. He wiped them distractedly and forced himself to focus.

'Madock?'

He turned at the sound of his name. His eyes settled upon Marcus who was casually approaching him from higher up the bank. The aide seemed confused by the Death Cheater's presence there, but Madock remained alert. It was time to find out the truth.

'Ruskin is dead,' stated Madock coldly. Marcus froze on the spot and silently observed the old man. Madock pressed on. 'He was poisoned.'

Marcus looked shocked, sinking to his knees and staring blankly ahead. 'Poisoned?' he mumbled numbly, as though unable to comprehend the meaning behind the word.

Madock nodded, but made no move to approach or comfort the man. 'They think it was you.'

Marcus stared at him desperately. 'Me? I've been your father's aide for years, I've helped to raise his children... I've been his loyal servant all this time... Why would I have poisoned him?'

Madock raised his weapon and aimed it at Marcus' head. 'Marcus Ortiz didn't poison him. I imagine he died before it happened...'

A tense silence passed between the two men as Marcus' eyes darted between Madock's and the barrel of the gun aimed at his head. 'What's wrong with you?' Marcus eventually gasped. 'Have you gone insane? Is it Malice poisoning?'

Madock observed the man carefully, and just for a second he doubted himself. *Maybe I'm wrong. There may be another possibility.* He paused and steeled himself. Over the years he had taught himself to trust his instincts. They very rarely let him down.

'Marcus is dead. I don't know who you are, or what you are, but I know you killed him. Absorbed his Echo. Took on his form. Just like you did in Mikara.'

He paused and watched the creature that looked like Marcus carefully for a response. When he got one, it was not the response he was expecting.

Marcus laughed.

'Mikara. Yes, that was an interesting experience!' Marcus sighed as the laughter subsided. 'I never expected it to get that out of hand. But you don't see the irony of our situation yet, do you Death Cheater?'

Madock paused, uncertain of how to respond. Marcus stood calmly and began strolling back and forth along the water's edge, seemingly unworried about the weapon trained on him. In his mind, Madock knew that he should fire, attempt to end this insanity right now, but something held his trigger finger at bay.

'You've had so many opportunities to prevent this from happening and you haven't even realised it,' continued Marcus, staring up at the Echoes floating above the surface of the water. 'But I have to know. How did you know I wasn't Marcus?'

'The Marcus I knew would never have pushed for execution,' stated Madock plainly. 'He certainly wouldn't have forced Kerrin to follow his instructions. He would have allowed the boy to make the ultimate decision.'

Marcus sighed. 'Yes, that's true. His memories certainly suggest he wanted Kerrin to be strong and independent. He truly cared about that boy.' He paused, picked up a rock and sent it skimming across the water of the Enki cenote. 'But I had to get you down into the midnight cells *somehow*. Otherwise how else would you have seen my incredible disappearing act?'

Before Madock could respond, his breath was stolen as he saw Marcus' entire body change before his eyes. It shifted like the ripples on the water created by the stone the creature had just skipped across the Enki cenote. Finally it settled on a brand new yet familiar form.

Standing before him was the woman who had confronted them in Ruskin's bedchamber.

'Quite a magic trick, eh?' she smiled, winking at him and placing her hands on her hips. 'You should have seen the look on your faces. I could barely stop myself from laughing! I could have killed you all down there, but that wouldn't have been fun. I owe you a better chance than that. To be honest, I do feel a *bit* bad about poisoning the old man, but I needed his Echo here.'

Madock shook his head in an attempt to clear his thoughts. 'You owe me?' he asked cautiously.

The woman smiled at him mischievously. 'Of course I do! After all…'

She paused as again her features started to swirl like running water, shrinking to a smaller frame. Even before it had finished reforming into the creature's new body, Madock recognised it in horror.

She didn't go missing... she escaped...

The girl waved at him tauntingly. 'You were the one that brought me here.'

Lottie... She was the monster...

The girl began to advance on him slowly, forcing Madock to retrain his weapon on her. His hand was shaking uncontrollably, as though his fingers would not follow his instructions. It took him a moment to understand that this time it wasn't his body that was failing him. His mind would not allow him to pull the trigger.

She looks just like Rosa. A hundred different memories fought for attention, the common theme being his daughter's smiling face, a faded yet eternal part of who he was as a person. He hadn't been able to save her, a fact that had haunted him every day since the Sheol Disaster. And now fate, rather than giving him the opportunity of redemption, was forcing him to kill a ghost with a similar face. In his mind, he couldn't separate the girl's face from the fact that a monster lurked behind it. All he saw was a girl. All he saw was Rosa.

Helplessly, he sank to his knees and stared at the girl, her once innocent features replaced by an ugly sneer.

'Pathetic,' she snarled. 'I expected more of you Madock.' She turned her attention back to the Echoes floating above them.

Opening her arms, Lottie closed her eyes and became very still. Madock watched helplessly as the Echoes seemed to pause in the air, their dance forgotten in an instant as they started to drift towards the girl's body. One by one, they disappeared into her small frame, rushing into her open arms like a child returning to its mother. There seemed to be hundreds of them surging into her, and in the back of his mind, Madock realised that one of them was Ruskin. Yet he felt completely powerless to do anything.

As the final Echo disappeared into Lottie, she gasped as if surfacing for air having been trapped underwater. She paused silently, her eyes remaining closed as she reflected on all of the memories and knowledge she had just absorbed.

A disgusted expression began to spread across her face. 'It's not here…' She clenched her fists and stamped her feet in frustration. 'It's not here!'

Storming over to Madock's slumped frame she grabbed the old man's shoulders and shook him with surprising strength. 'It's not here!' she bellowed at him. 'This is all your fault! It *has* to be here!'

Raising her open palm, she placed it upon Madock's chest. Pain washed over his body, causing him to writhe in agony. Clenching his teeth, he fought to free himself from her power but his strength was sapped almost instantly. The Death Cheater crumpled to the floor, his vision fading as he felt himself slip into darkness.

15

His dreams were dark and confused. Different scenes from his past seemed to rise and mingle to create new surreal landscapes, with various faces, both recognisable and strange to his mind, playing roles like actors on a stage.

At one point he was back in Sheol, breathing in the familiarity of the location. A voice deep within his mind reminded him that it was all gone now, that it no longer existed. But at that point, in that moment, it was as real to him as it had been before the explosion. He could see familiar faces wandering around the settlement, greeting him as he strolled with his family, Rosa in one arm and his wife Elaine holding the other. For a brief, fleeting moment, he allowed himself to relax. He had thought that he would never experience this happiness again, yet here in the darkness of his mind he could stay and relive this moment over and over again until the release of death. It appealed to him more than he dared to admit.

It wasn't to last.

Without warning, the setting suddenly shifted around him. Now he was by the edge of the Enki cenote, watching the Echoes slowly disappear one at a time. As each light faded, the scene became darker and darker. His wife had vanished, and the girl who clutched on to his hand and stared up at him had no face at all.

'I'm not done playing with you yet...' Lottie's voice sounded in his head. 'I don't know what it is about you, but I feel like we have... a connection.' A crooked smile seemed to tear the girl's face open, revealing rows of razor sharp teeth. 'Plus you're just too much fun.'

Madock shut his eyes tightly, attempting to block out the girl's deformed face and mocking voice. He could still hear her laughing as darkness eventually grasped him and pulled him down into dreamless sleep.

* * *

The bed was surprisingly soft beneath him, the room warm and comfortable as he first started to ease his eyes open. He cringed at the light and the sudden awareness of the throbbing pain in his head. Struggling to lift himself from the bed, he felt a firm hand push him back down.

'Easy there, Madock,' a familiar voice insisted as it eased him back to a lying position. 'You need to rest.'

Madock squinted and attempted to focus his vision. He didn't recognise the room he was in, but from the décor he assumed it was one of the many rooms within the Broxhart manor.

'You really are a lucky son of a bitch, you know that?'

'Haswell?'

The demon hunter smiled at him. 'I've no idea how you've managed to stay alive so long, you always seem to be running into trouble.'

The young man's tone was bright, but Madock could sense that he was hiding a great deal of pain behind it.

'Haswell,' he croaked, 'I'm sorry… about your father…'

The demon hunter's smile faded. 'We all need to be strong now. For the people. They're panicking.' He stood and picked up a jug of water, pouring the liquid into a glass for Madock.

'They know Ruskin is gone?' asked Madock, suddenly aware of how dry his throat was. He knew that they had tried to keep Lord Broxhart's ill health private, but he was surprised that news of his death had spread so quickly.

Haswell shook his head and gently tipped some of the water down Madock's grateful throat. 'Not yet. It's the Echoes disappearing that's got them worried.'

The memory of what had happened with the creature came rushing back to him. He spluttered on the water as it threatened to choke him and pushed himself to a sitting position.

'What happened with the creature?' he asked desperately.

Haswell looked at him curiously. 'Creature?'

Madock frowned. 'The creature, the thing that killed everybody in Mikara. It's here in Pelera.'

'Are you sure?' asked Haswell, a concerned look spreading over his face as he set down the glass of water.

Madock quickly tried to recall the events, but found it difficult to discern the reality of what had happened from the mixture of vivid dreams he had experienced. 'Have you found Marcus?'

Haswell folded his arms. 'No. We're still searching but there's no sign of him. I still can't believe that he would be responsible for this.'

'He isn't,' agreed Madock, 'He's dead.'

Haswell watched the old man carefully. Madock sensed that the demon hunter was carefully processing what he had just heard and was perhaps considering fetching a medic. The Death Cheater pressed on, deciding to tell the young man everything he now knew.

'The monster from Mikara, the one that could change faces and absorb Echoes, it was here in Pelera. It killed Marcus and took his form to poison your father. I found it by the Enki cenote. I watched as it changed its face and absorbed all the Echoes.'

Haswell seemed uncertain how to respond. 'It's real? It's here?'

Madock sighed. 'It was Lottie.'

Haswell gritted his teeth, his whole body tensing with anger as he digested the news. He started pacing the room, clearly struggling to cope with the idea that he may have been indirectly responsible for his father's death. Madock knew that he would need to vent that anger, and he was fully prepared to take the brunt of it.

It didn't take long. 'You were the one who said we should bring her here...' he muttered venomously, his hands visibly shaking.

Madock remained calm and silent. He knew that Haswell had to work through this himself.

'You brought her here,' he said through clenched teeth, louder now as the anger began to rise in his voice. 'You brought a monster into my family home, and it killed Marcus and my father. This is all your fault!'

Haswell moved to grab Madock's neck, but the old man remained still and did not flinch. *Just like when he was a boy*, thought the Death Cheater, forcing himself to remain calm in the face of such aggression. *He needs to burn it off.*

'We didn't know,' stated Madock calmly. 'The important thing is what we do now.'

Haswell growled, seemingly torn between taking his frustration out on the old man's face and listening to his advice. Turning sharply, he collected his rifle from where it rested in the corner of the room and aggressively pulled the door to the chamber open.

'Where are you going?' asked Madock.

Haswell glared at him. 'I'm going to clean up your mess. I'm going to kill it.'

As the demon hunter slammed the door behind him, Madock sighed. He had known that Haswell would react negatively to the news, but there was nothing to be gained by keeping it a secret. In truth, Madock was glad that he wouldn't be the only one hunting down the monster now. The powers it had demonstrated so far scared him, leaving him feeling largely helpless and lost for ideas as to how to conquer such a beast. But he knew he had to try.

The thought steeled his resolve and carefully he turned and placed his feet on the cool wooden floor. Pushing himself upwards, his legs initially took his weight but his head began to swim, blurring his vision and forcing him to sit back down. Shaking his head stubbornly, he lifted himself once more, placing a hand against the wall for balance. Again, the room seemed to swirl around him, but this time he held strong and waited till the sensation passed. He felt horrendously weak and the throbbing sensation in his head was getting worse with every passing second, but he knew he couldn't just lie there while the monster could be wandering the streets of Pelera.

Finding his Malice Gear and equipment piled up neatly at the foot of the bed, he dressed himself uneasily and tightened his belt around his waist. Slowly and unsteadily, he opened the door to the chamber and staggered his way into the hallway of the manor.

It took him a while to reach the main doors, occasionally pausing to catch his breath and waving off the concerned faces of those who stopped to check if he was okay. As he finally reached the large wooden doors he paused, his gloved hand securing his balance against the wall. Every muscle in his body screamed for him to stop, but his willpower remained firm. He had to find the monster before it could hurt anybody else.

'What are you doing out of bed?' asked Kerrin curiously, placing a hand on Madock's shoulder. 'You're in no condition...'

'Have you seen Haswell?' interrupted Madock, turning to face the young man. It was important that he found out how much Kerrin knew before he said anything further.

Kerrin blinked, surprised by the question. 'Haze? I haven't seen him today. Why?'

Madock sighed. *Typical of him to charge off into trouble without saying anything*, he thought, tiredness washing over him once more. 'Kerrin, I know what killed your father.'

'The medic said it was poison?' replied Kerrin, looking and sounding increasingly confused.

Madock shook his head. 'No, I mean *what* killed him. It wasn't Marcus. There's a monster, the same monster that killed all those people in Mikara.'

Kerrin's eyes widened. 'How did it get here?'

For a second, Madock considering telling Kerrin the truth. But after seeing how Haswell had reacted, he decided to hide his guilt from the twin brother. Kerrin was likely to be more measured in his response, but he couldn't risk alienating both brothers, especially when he needed Kerrin's help at such an important time.

'I don't know how it got here,' lied Madock, 'But I'm going to go find it. I imagine Haswell is out looking as well.'

Pausing, he observed the young man before him. Kerrin had grown a lot from the child he remembered, but there was still an innocence about him. What he was about to ask of him seemed almost impossible, but he knew there was nobody else. Calipse would help him, he was certain, but the young man was about to have a great deal of responsibility thrust upon his shoulders. He was certain Kerrin would already have considered it, but Haswell's departure had made it a reality. He severely doubted that the demon hunter would return without the situation being resolved one way or the other.

'Kerrin, you need to be there for your people now. You're the one in charge,' said Madock, his tone serious and uncompromising. 'Your father is dead, Marcus is gone and your brother has left to hunt the monster. That leaves you.'

For just a moment panic flooded the young man's face, but to his credit he quickly collected himself and nodded, though Madock noted that his voice sounded shaken as he responded. 'I'll do what I can. Just bring my brother back alive.'

Madock nodded, placed a reassuring hand on the young man's shoulder, then turned and walked out of the Broxhart manor.

As he moved slowly down into the streets of Pelera, he suddenly found himself realising the size of the task ahead of him. He was hunting a monster that could look like anybody. It filled him with a sense of dread that every face he passed as he crossed the bridges over the Enki cenote could be masking the monster behind it.

Don't slip into paranoia just yet, he reminded himself. *The monster is after something. It's already absorbed all of the Echoes here, why would it stay?* He found this thought process more reassuring than the idea that the monster may be wandering the very streets with him and chose to focus his attention on his next plan of action.

As he reached the edge of the Enki cenote, Madock was shocked by just how much darker the area was without the benefit of the light from the Echoes. Devoid of the orbs of light which had always floated above the surface, the very air itself seemed melancholy. He knew that in time new Echoes would gather here, the souls of those departed in recent days which had made their way north, but for now the scene was still and silent.

Madock paused and gazed around, uncertain of how to proceed. Not only did he have to consider where the monster had gone, but also where Haswell was. He suspected that Haswell would already have left the settlement, blindly chasing after it in a red mist. If the demon hunter hadn't left Pelera, there was every chance some Peleran guards would locate him and either help him hunt the monster or return him safely to the manor for his own good. If he *had* left for the surface...

'I hope you're going after him.' The voice was quiet, but it quickly drew Madock from his thoughts as he glanced around him. Calipse had snuck up behind him without a sound, and she now stood nervously gazing up at him. 'Haze seemed really mad... He wouldn't tell me what happened, but he went in there.' She raised a finger and pointed into the distance. Madock turned and looked at what she was pointing at.

Well, I suppose that makes sense...

Branching off from the main body of water that formed the Enki cenote, several smaller rivers and channels spread out in all directions. Some travelled through the settlement itself, but the majority disappeared into fissures, cracks and tunnel in the rock face, flowing through dark tunnels away from Pelera. Madock knew that these rivers ran southwards, feeding the surrounding settlements with water. The tunnels were like a maze within the rock, and whilst it was possible to follow the running water down to the settlements further to the south, it was also worryingly easy to become lost and disorientated in the darkness. It provided an alternative route to the surface with the bonus of being free of demons, but it was no less fraught with dangers. Only desperate travellers took the tunnels, but Madock knew exactly why Haswell had chosen them.

The Echoes from the Enki cenote would eventually make their way down these tunnels, following the flowing waters to the south with the ultimate goal of reaching the Southern Ice Fields. Many believed that this was proof that the mythical settlement of Elysium existed, but Madock remained sceptical.

We're hunting a monster that absorbs Echoes. I guess it makes sense that we follow where the Echoes will be.

'Are you going to bring him back, Madock?' asked Calipse anxiously.

Madock smiled at her reassuringly. 'That's right. Until I get back, I want you to help Kerrin as much as you can, okay?'

'I'll do my best,' replied Calipse quietly.

That will be enough, thought Madock. Checking his equipment, he took a deep breath and began circumnavigating the Enki cenote, heading towards the darkness of the Peleran tunnels.

16

Standing at the entrance to the tunnel, Madock felt a familiar reluctance to enter the darkness. It had been years since he had wandered the Peleran tunnels. It seemed almost a lifetime ago that he had taken the route regularly, preferring the darkness to the risks of the surface far above his head. But that had been before the Sheol Disaster. Now all that awaited him in the darkness was ghosts and memories.

Just remember, keep the river in sight at all times, he reminded himself firmly as he switched on his torch and prepared himself for the journey ahead. The torch was one of the few pieces of technology he kept with him at all times, though he used it sparingly. Energy was increasingly rare and expensive, and he knew that he would struggle to meet the price for a replacement. *If you lose sight of the river, you're in trouble.*

It was a simple rule, but one born of experience. The river seemed to wind in all directions and turn back on itself several times, making the experience of walking through the darkness all the more disorientating. But it was foolish to gamble on the dry tunnels which seemed to offer a more direct route as they inevitably led to nothing but death. Even those who changed their mind and sought to return to the water found their route difficult as the sound of the river echoed through the tunnels, making it hard to locate.

As Madock plunged into the darkness, he held his breath.

The sound of the river running beside him was oddly calming, but Madock knew from experience to be careful with every step. The water was the lifeline he required, but it possessed a darker side. The path alongside the water could be slippery, and in the darkness it was all too easy to drift towards the sound of the rushing water and end up trapped within its icy clutches.

The further Madock continued along through the tunnel, the more convinced he was that both he and Haswell were following the monster in the correct direction. He hadn't seen an Echo since he entered the darkness, and while it had been years since he had last been down here, he knew from experience that he should have encountered at least a few by that point.

He paused as an unfamiliar sound met his ears. Footsteps in the darkness ahead of him. At first he wondered whether it might be Haswell, but it quickly became clear that there was more than one person moving in the darkness. Furthermore, they were moving towards him.

Instinctively, Madock switched off his torch and sank back into the shadows, placing the mask of the Malice Gear over his head and moving a short way down a side tunnel to stay off the path by the riverside. The Peleran tunnels were a notorious hot spot for Raiders, all too eager to relieve unlucky travellers of their possessions. Though there was a chance that the people moving towards him were simple travellers like himself, he was not willing to take that risk.

As he heard the footsteps moving closer, he noted the flickering of a lit torch and began to make out a voice echoing down the tunnels.

'This wasn't one of your better ideas…' said a female voice accusingly. 'Then again, you don't tend to have many good ideas, so I guess I should have expected this.'

There followed a short silence. Clearly the target of the woman's words did not feel like contributing to the discussion. It seemed, however, that she was more than happy to fill the silences.

'I mean, the Peleran tunnels? Nobody comes down here anymore. We could have set up in Sheol and seen more people...'

Madock cringed at the name of his old home, but was grateful that he had chosen to hide rather than confront the strangers. It was clear from the woman's words that they were targeting travellers, so whether they classed themselves as Raiders or not, it was wise to avoid their attention. As they moved closer, he retreated further into the shadows to hide himself from the light of their torch.

The woman continued her one-sided conversation. 'I mean, we met one guy, and that freak nearly shot us! I notice you didn't try and stop him.'

Madock listened intently. *Could they be talking about Haswell?*

As if to answer his question, the second voice spoke for the first time. It was a deep booming voice which startled Madock in the relative quiet of the tunnels. 'Haze Broxhart,' it stated simply.

The footsteps paused. 'Haze Broxhart? Are you serious?' asked the woman incredulously. 'What would he be doing in the tunnels?'

'Malice Gear. Peleran crest,' replied the deeper voice.

The woman fell silent and their footsteps continued to move closer towards the Death Cheater. By now, Madock could see the light eating up the darkness around him and he sought to hide himself even further in the darkness of the side tunnel. As they moved ever closer, he attempted to control his racing heartbeat. He hoped that they would pass quickly, but much to his frustration they paused at the entrance to the side tunnel as the woman stepped in front of her partner and blocked his progress.

'It could have been the Death Cheater!' she said excitedly, 'He wears Malice Gear with a Peleran crest too. I think between us we could have taken one old man.' Now that Madock could get a good view of her from where he was hiding, he saw that she was young with a tall and athletic build. Her fiery red hair was cut to shoulder length, while the scarf around her neck suggested that she had some experience of travelling across the surface.

Her partner grunted in response. 'The rifle,' he pointed out, saying no more than that. The woman was tall, but the man was a giant. Broad shouldered with long jet black hair, he looked immensely intimidating. Madock wondered what the pair could possibly have to bond them into partnership.

The woman stepped back thoughtfully as she considered her partner's logic. 'Yeah, I guess that makes sense...' She paused and turned to consider the path ahead. 'I'm telling you Kye, you better be right about Pelera. We don't have too much left to bargain with.'

She looked back at the giant man to see if he was listening, but was frustrated to see that he was looking down the side tunnel. Madock remained perfectly still, convincing himself that the man couldn't possibly have seen him. The dark Malice Gear covered his entire body, allowing him to blend in completely with the shadows around him. Yet it seemed that the man named Kye was staring directly at him. Madock knew that if he moved now he would certainly give away his position, and forced himself to remain statuesque.

'Am I boring you?' ranted the woman impatiently, punching Kye on the arm. The large man didn't even flinch, but instead started to slowly move down the side tunnel.

Even as the woman continued to shout after the man, Madock blocked out everything apart from the advancing man. He knew he had to make a decision: remain still and hope that the man would stop or move and give away his position. Even if he moved, he then had to decide whether to confront the pair or try and flee.

Although he was outnumbered, Madock knew that he could take out both threats; it was the bloodshed that he wanted to avoid. He had learned from experience that avoiding conflict was always the better option, but fleeing would leave him running into the maze of tunnels. In truth, he wasn't even sure he could outrun them.

Time to decide, he thought as the man came ever closer, the light from the torch rapidly defeating the darkness that was concealing him. *I can take them if I need to*, he reminded himself. He hoped it would not come to that.

'That's close enough,' he commanded, stepping forward with his hands by his side.

The man stopped silently, seemingly unsurprised to discover somebody in the darkness. His partner on the other hand was far more curious about the development.

'What's going on Kye? Who's there?' she called as she rushed up to join her partner. When she set eyes on Madock, her first expression was one of confusion which quickly descended into one of anger. 'You think you can pull a rifle on us and get away with it?' she growled, reaching for the dagger that hung by her side.

Kye shook his head. 'It's not him, Reissa.'

The woman's face quickly shifted back to confusion as Madock continued to stand patient and silent. It was clear to him that they presented a threat, but until it was necessary he would not act. He had learned from his youth that rash actions were likely to get you killed in this world. Instead, he waited and watched.

Understanding eventually dawned on Reissa's face. 'So… we actually *did* find the Death Cheater!' she grinned viciously. 'You know, old man, there's plenty that would pay top price for Malice Gear like that. It's kind of greedy of you to hang on to it for so long, don't you think?'

Madock remained silent, assessing the two threats ahead of him. The woman, Reissa, seemed to be the more aggressive of the two but thus far her tongue seemed more deadly than her dagger. He kept an eye on her, but his main concern was the large man called Kye. He seemed to be scrutinizing the Death Cheater just as carefully as the old man was observing them. His silent emotionless face was difficult to read. In Madock's opinion, that made him the more dangerous.

'So, how about this?' continued Reissa confidently, 'You give us the Malice Gear and anything else you might have, then you can go find a dark corner somewhere down here to curl up and die.' She ran her finger down the edge of her dagger teasingly. 'Of course, if you'd prefer I can just gut you here and now. It'll be like a mercy killing by this point, I'm guessing. I mean, just how old *are* you?'

Madock was no longer listening. Instead, he addressed the giant man who continued to stare at him with an expressionless face. 'This doesn't need to happen,' he said, keeping his voice calm and measured. 'Nobody needs to die today.' His hand twitched instinctively by his weapon, a gesture recognised by Kye who nodded slowly in response. The two men seemed to understand each other.

Reissa was less patient. 'You're right, so stop wasting time and put your weapon down on the floor. We get what we want and you get to keep your life, everybody wins.'

Madock continued to ignore her. She was too volatile to negotiate with, but Kye seemed to be listening to him.

Behind the Raiders, a faint light began to emerge.

17

Madock allowed his gaze to shift from the threatening pair, tensing his body for more trouble. 'Friends of yours?' he asked bitterly, sensing that the dynamic of the situation was about to change dramatically.

Reissa scoffed. 'The old "look behind you" trick? You really must be desperate old man.'

The light was growing bolder with every passing second. Madock had never seen such brightness in the Peleran tunnels before, and knew instantly that it could not be produced by a simple torch.

By now even the Raiders had become aware of the light, and were turning to tentatively glance over their shoulder.

A single Echo floated into view at the end of the tunnel, glowing a warm, comforting golden colour as it danced around in the cool air. It almost seemed to turn and observe the three humans who were now basking in its light, inquisitively moving closer to investigate.

Madock remained tense. *There's no way that one Echo can produce that much light.*

The immense group of Echoes emerged around the corner as a cluster, seemingly following the lone Echo ahead of them like a flock of sheep being led by a shepherd. There were at least thirty of them, huddled together and forming a huge cloud of light which floated carelessly towards them.

Madock tore his eyes away from the light and glanced around. The Raiders were struggling to split their attention between the approaching cluster of Echoes and the Death Cheater.

This is my chance. Madock took a few tentative steps backwards.

'Don't even think about running!' shouted Reissa furiously, her voice loud and fearsome as it bounced off the tunnel walls around them.

The Echoes froze in midair, startled by the loud sound. For a moment, nobody dared to move. Then the Echoes began to advance, their previous warm golden colouring shifting to a deadly burning red hue.

'That's not good...' mumbled Reissa, as she and Kye also began to retreat into the darkness with their eyes locked on the angry burning orbs of light.

Madock glanced desperately around him. The Raiders were no longer his main concern, but he was left with a difficult realisation. It would be all but impossible to get past the Echoes to the river. He had never encountered a cluster of Echoes such as this before, but he had heard of the damage they were capable of inflicting when angered. The idea of turning away from them into the dark, unchartered tunnels behind him presented its own difficulties, but it seemed his only choice.

He was forced into action as the Echoes surged forward.

Madock turned and fled into the tunnel. His route was lit by the light of the pursuing Echoes, though this only served to force his legs to move faster. He could hear the crashing footsteps of the Raiders behind him, but chose not to concern himself with their safety.

His vision blurred as he charged further and further into the twisting darkness of the tunnels. It was clear that he had not fully recovered from the confrontation with the monster in Pelera, and his body was struggling to meet his urgent demands. Scolding himself internally, he forced his body onwards.

The bile rose without warning, spewing from his mouth and knocking him off balance. He attempted to stagger onwards, but his tired limbs failed to respond. He crumpled to the floor, the angry red light of the chasing

Echoes becoming brighter and brighter as they closed in on his prone body.

He heard footsteps charge past him and saw the female Raider surge on into the darkness without so much as a glance in his direction.

With one last final surge of energy, he attempted to lift himself.

Strong arms picked him up forcibly from the ground as he was flung like a ragdoll over Kye's shoulders. The giant Raider continued to rush forward, leaving Madock with no choice but to jolt around helplessly and stare at the ground beneath them.

As more bile threatened to rise in his throat, he blacked out.

* * *

'Wake up, you old git!'

Madock groaned as the voice roused him from his slumber. As his eyes eased open, it took him a moment to comprehend his surroundings.

'Where are we?' he mumbled. His throat was dry and there was still the residual taste of vomit in his mouth.

Reissa was stood over him, arms folded and with a face like thunder. 'We're lost.'

Madock glanced around. They were still in the Peleran tunnels, though clearly the Echoes had chased them into some long neglected side tunnels. He could not even hear the sound of the river, their guide to civilization.

However, the longer Madock took in his surroundings, the more an unnerving sense of familiarity seemed to surface. He had seen these tunnels before.

The realisation hit him hard. *We're near Sheol.*

'Are you happy now, Kye?' spat Reissa furiously, turning her anger on her companion. 'We could have just taken his stuff while he was unconscious. But no, you had to choose this moment to develop a conscience.'

Madock attempted to lift himself to his feet, but his head began to swim again. He knew that he needed time to rest, but he could not stay here in the darkness. Even if he had been able to move, he sensed that the Raiders would not be inclined to allow him to simply wander off.

I could take them out, even in this condition, he convinced himself, resting a hand reassuringly on his weapon in its holster.

An idea occurred to Madock; not one that he was particularly keen on, but it seemed the only alternative to killing the two strangers, possibly getting himself killed in the process. Besides, he needed their help. He hated to admit it, but he knew that travelling to Sheol alone would be foolish. He would need help to navigate the wreckage of the settlement, extra eyes to watch for dangers in the darkness. Deep down, there was also the simple fact that he did not wish to return to Sheol at all. At least by travelling with others, he would be less inclined to turn back.

But seeking the aid of common Raiders? The thought circled bitterly in his head, but he could see few alternatives. The Raiders were not simply going to walk away from this, and it would be far more useful to have their help than their blood on his hands. Besides, Kye had saved him during the escape from the Echoes. Though the reason behind this was unclear, the least he could do was guide them to safety. *That is, if I can convince them to help.*

'I know where we are,' he admitted, instantly gaining the attention of the two Raiders. 'We're near Sheol. If you help me get there, then we can rest and go our separate ways.'

Reissa placed her hands on her hips in frustration. 'I don't think you fully understand the situation you're in. The big guy may not have wanted to rob you while you were taking a nap, but you're awake now. We can just take your stuff and leave you for dead. We'll find our own way out. We don't need you. Just your things.'

Madock sighed. *I hoped it wouldn't come to this.*

Moving his hand from his weapon to his pocket, he reached for the familiar object he knew lay within it. Both Kye and Reissa tensed, assuming a weapon was about to be drawn. Raising his spare hand in a gesture that requested patience, he slowly withdrew the glass from his pocket and held it out in the palm of his hand towards Kye. It glittered as it caught the light from Kye's torch, the large man leaning in to have a closer look at the object. His expression continued to hide whatever emotion he might have been feeling.

He's interested. This might be my only chance. Again Madock briefly considered fighting his way out, desperate to avoid relying on the violent scavengers before him. There was a high chance that he could take out both of them, and it was almost certain that he would take out one of them. But pursuing this course of action would bring his own survival into question, and he wasn't prepared to throw his life away meaninglessly. He was determined to face the monster before his time finally came.

Madock decided to push ahead with his plan. 'I'm going after Haswell Broxhart. I think he's heading for Tirneth.' It was a logical assumption. The Death Cheater did not believe that the young demon hunter would return to Mikara, making Tirneth his logical choice of destination. 'If you help me get to Sheol then on to there, I'll give you this. Nobody gets hurt. Everybody wins.'

'Excuse me?' interrupted Reissa fiercely. '"Everybody wins?" We're not Dead Men like you, we don't do jobs for people. And you want us to go to Sheol? With *you*? You must have Malice poisoning or something. We take what we want. We want that pretty jewel, so we can just take it if we want. Isn't that right, Kye?' She waited patiently for the large man to back her up, but was disappointed to find Kye remaining silent. 'Stop looking at the jewel and focus!' she scolded him, but the man continued to stare at the glass in Madock's hand, seemingly hypnotized by the object.

Finally, he tore his gaze away from the glass and turned to Reissa. 'We're helping him,' he stated in a tone that suggested he did not expect to be argued with. Reissa either did not pick up on the tone or chose to ignore it.

'We're *helping* him?' she spluttered in disbelief.

Kye turned without saying a word and marched past Reissa towards Madock. Offering a strong arm, he helped to lift the Death Cheater from the ground and supported his weight. Together they moved forward slowly, Madock keeping his spare arm against the tunnel wall for extra support. Reissa watched them move off into the darkness, her mouth hanging open in shock. When she realised that her partner was serious and expected her to follow, she moved level with them and shot Madock a look of such venom that he almost wished he hadn't made the deal. When the old man failed to respond, she threw her arms up in frustration and marched angrily ahead of the pair of them.

Madock grimaced, refusing to make eye contact with the giant man by his side and watching the furious woman ahead of them cast aggressive looks over her shoulder.

Well, this should prove interesting…

18

Starr stood nervously outside the door, her hand twitching anxiously by her side. She knew her father would not appreciate the interruption but there were issues that had to be addressed. Namely, the scientist and her brother.

Gray had wanted to come with her, for moral support and to voice his own concerns, but Starr knew that in order to stand any chance of her father listening it had to be her alone that spoke to him. In truth, it was not confronting her father that worried her the most, but rather the reality of facing her mother again.

She had not visited her mother's bedside for a long time now, and whilst she felt a degree of guilt about this she knew that the visits were largely unproductive. Her mother's illness caused her to regard her daughter as a stranger, much as Starr saw the woman in the bed. She wished she could speak to her father in private, but there would be few other opportunities to speak frankly with him and her concerns were growing increasingly urgent by the day.

Steadying herself, she raised a shaking hand and knocked on the door. Initially there was no response. A loud voice in her mind insisted that she walk away, but she knew that this matter had to be resolved. She was about to knock on the door again when her father's voice beckoned her to enter. Gritting her teeth, she turned the handle and entered the room.

Candles flickered in various places, casting light around the room and banishing shadows to the furthest corners. There were plenty of people within the walls as there always had been each time she had entered, mostly Harbingers concocting strange fluids or joining hands in silent prayer. Starr had to admit that the feats achieved by the Harbingers were impressive, most notably the Shell which protected the entire city. She knew that her father distrusted them, but it seemed that his desperation had forced him to seek their constant aid.

A grand four poster bed stood at the far end of the chamber, and Starr knew instantly that that was where she would find her father, sitting beside the bed holding the hand of his wife. She knew that he would stay there all day and night if he could, and that every time he forced himself to leave to attend to other business it practically killed him. There was little doubt in her mind that her father loved his wife more than anything else in the world. He had practically sacrificed Gair to maintain her life.

He didn't look up as she approached, leaving her to stand awkwardly at the foot of the bed and gaze down at her mother. She remembered that during her last visit her mother had been awake, and recalled how the woman had stared at her with wide uncomprehending eyes. She had not appeared panicked, but it was clear that she had not understood anything that was happening around her. There was no recognition in those eyes, only confusion. Thankfully, this time her mother appeared to be in a deep sleep as her husband clutched her hand and stroked her hair gently.

'Father...' Starr began uncomfortably, uncertain as to how to approach the subject. Bayne Airenguarde looked up, as though noticing his daughter for the first time and smiled at her.

'She's resting,' he said softly, 'The Harbingers believe that she is recovering.'

Starr could see no obvious change in her mother's condition from her previous visits but decided not to argue this point. 'Father, I need to speak to you.'

Bayne looked back at his wife, clearly reluctant to leave her side even for a moment. 'Is it important?' he asked distractedly.

Starr nodded. 'Very important.'

Her father sighed, slowly lifted himself from the chair and placed a gentle kiss upon his wife's forehead. Turning, he gestured for Starr to join him in the adjoining room, away from the prying eyes and ears of the Harbingers.

As Starr closed the door behind them, she noticed the impatient look upon her father's face as he waited for her to have her say. She knew that she would have to tread carefully so as not to lose his attention.

'I'm worried about Enrick,' she stated, sensing that her father would appreciate her getting straight to the point. 'So is Gray. We both feel that this project isn't the right decision.' She paused to allow her father to respond.

He sighed and rubbed his eyes, as though nursing a headache. Again, Starr worried about how tired he looked, but remained silent.

'It may not be the right decision,' admitted her father, 'But it's the only decision I can make. Until we possess more power than the Harbingers, we have to remain in their pocket. They think they run this city, but they'll be reminded soon enough that Gair belongs to the Airenguardes.'

Starr could understand her father's logic, but decided to press on regardless. 'But father, this is the same technology that wiped out Sheol. It isn't safe.'

'Enrick says he has modified it. Blake's been working with him, I'm sure if there was any reason to be concerned…'

'Blake's just as bad as Enrick,' interrupted Starr, frustrated by her father's dismissive tone. 'I don't trust either of them.'

She knew instantly that it had been a mistake to say this as Bayne's face instantly hardened. 'Your brother sees that this is the only way to restore our family's power in Gair. I appreciate your concerns, and I can understand

Gray's apprehension, but the project is going to be finished.' As he finished speaking, her father brushed past her and returned to the other room, moving purposefully back towards the bed.

'Father, please...' pleaded Starr as she followed him, but a stern glare from her father silenced her instantly. She stood at the end of the bed and hung her head, frustrated at her inability to resolve the situation but unwilling to leave and admit defeat.

At length, her father sighed. 'You know she loves you...' he stated sadly. Starr looked up at her father, who again was clutching her mother's hand tightly. 'She may not be able to say it anymore, but... I can see it. She was the one that named you.'

Starr had heard the story many times before, but did not have the heart to tell her father. She knew he loved telling the story. In truth, he loved telling any story from the time before her mother had been bedridden with Malice poisoning.

'She was heavily pregnant with you, but not once did she complain,' Bayne started, a faint smile growing on his face. 'She loved Blake with all her heart, but I knew that secretly she wanted a little girl. Somehow she knew. "She's kicking again," she would tell me, "She'll be with us soon." I never even thought to question her, she was just so... confident.' Bayne paused as he allowed himself to slip into nostalgia. 'She's a stubborn woman, your mother. She wanted you to be born with the skies above you. No rocks, no Shell, just the skies. I thought she was just playing games, being an optimist as always...'

The room seemed to fall silent as Bayne approached the end of his story. Starr had heard it all before, but every time it filled her with guilt, though she knew it was in no way her fault.

'She was so stubborn...' continued her father, sighing and stroking his wife's hair. 'I should have known she was planning to do something reckless.' He paused, as if momentarily unwilling to complete the story. 'She got a Harbinger to help her. Went outside the Shell, didn't say a word to anybody. By the time we found them she was barely alive, but she was holding you in her arms so proudly. I still remember her looking up at me. She said that she'd seen the sky behind the storm, that she'd seen a star. That was when she named you.' He paused. 'That was when...'

Starr didn't need to hear the rest. Her mother had only been on the surface for a short while, but even with the aid of a Harbinger she had contracted Malice poisoning. They had brought them both back to the city, though the Harbinger disappeared a day later. Starr didn't need to ask what had become of him.

'Father, we can't let them finish the machine,' she pleaded one last time.

Her father refused to meet her eyes. 'My mind is made up, Starr,' he replied solemnly. 'Now please leave.'

Dejectedly, Starr turned and left the room silently as her father held on tightly to his dying wife's hand.

19

Madock could already feel himself tensing as they neared the outskirts of Sheol. In truth, he had thought never to return to the place he had once called home, and since the explosion, had avoided the settlement at all costs. This had proved easy, as nobody wished to travel to or through the settlement now, with many believing that it was haunted by Echoes which remained there to this day, unwilling to leave their past and accept their fate.

'This is stupid,' complained Reissa, who had not stopped protesting since they had first formed an unlikely and uneasy alliance. 'Why did you agree to this Kye? All this just for a pretty jewel? You want to wear it and feel like a princess?'

Kye, to his credit, did not rise to the taunts and continued to lumber forward at a slower pace to accomodate the Death Cheater. The further they had travelled together, the more Madock had found himself developing a begrudging respect for the giant man. In spite of his superior size, strength and age, he seemed to be constantly on the receiving end of his partner's vicious words, yet he never responded. Instead he allowed the woman to rant at him, patiently waiting for her to end her tirade with an expression of complete disinterest upon his face.

Frustrated at the lack of response, Reissa turned her anger on Madock. 'You better keep your end of the deal once we get to Tirneth, old man. Otherwise I'll slit your wrinkly old neck and take it from you anyway.' She paused and smiled devilishly. 'Maybe I'll slit it anyway, just for fun.'

'Reissa...' said Kye, his tone warning his partner to think about her words. Groaning in exasperation, she dropped further behind the pair, sulking in the darkness as she followed them towards the abandoned settlement.

As they neared Sheol, they started to spot the first signs of what had occurred there years before. Debris littered the edges of the settlement, though most of it had been picked clean by Raiders. There was nothing left here for anybody. Nothing but memories.

Picking their way through the remains of a collapsed building, Madock gasped in horror as he saw the remains of Sheol for the first time. It was evident that something tragic had occurred here, and even now the air seemed to carry the scent of death and decay. None of the buildings were left untouched; most had been reduced to rubble. In his mind he could still picture scenes from his life there, but now they played out as blackened and burnt remains of his past.

He felt his knees go weak but forced himself to remain steady as his eyes drifted upwards to the glowing orbs of light floating above them. *So it's true*, he thought in dismay as he watched the Echoes shift uneasily over the remains of Sheol. *The Echoes of the people who died here. It's all true.* Tears stung his eyes, making him instantly grateful for the mask he was wearing. He couldn't allow himself to look weak in front of the Raiders.

'Ugh, what a dump...' muttered Reissa, kicking out at some nearby debris.

Madock ignored her, focusing his mind away from the memories of his past. 'If we split up, we can explore faster,' he started, but Reissa immediately stepped in front of him.

'No chance, old man. We leave you on your own and you'll crawl off, leaving us in this hell hole with no jewel. Forget it, we stick together.'

Madock shrugged in acceptance. He had to admit that the idea had crossed his mind, and now that he was faced with the reality of Sheol he wanted nothing more than to run away, but he knew that it would be foolish to travel onwards without first recovering. Maybe even the monster would be here too, though Madock sensed that the settlement was full of enough evil anyway without having to confront the shapeshifter.

He still wasn't happy to be in the company of Raiders, but he had to admit they were serving their purpose perfectly. There was safety in numbers and entering the unknown remains of Sheol alone where he may well have encountered the monster would have been foolish. There was the small matter of the end of their agreement to deal with, but Madock assumed he could handle that situation if or when it arose. He had no intention of handing over the glass unless he had no other choice.

As they wandered the streets of Sheol, Madock did his best to ignore the remains of his old life and focus on finding a suitable place to rest. However there really wasn't a lot left of the settlement to explore, and as time passed it became increasingly obvious that there were not many safe places left.

At last they turned a corner the Death Cheater had been hoping to avoid since they entered the settlement, but he kept his reservations to himself as they moved around the remains of a building and he set eyes upon his old home.

It had survived surprisingly well in comparison to the rest of the settlement, perhaps due to its location at the very edge of Sheol. It had clearly been battered by the explosion though, with every window shattered and the entire front of the house ripped open. However, it was largely still standing, revealing the burnt out carcass of rooms that Madock had thought he would only ever see again in memories.

Absently, he freed himself from Kye's support and moved slowly towards the building as the Raiders turned and gazed around them.

'This place is terrible,' mused Kye aloud.

'I told you this was an idiotic idea,' muttered Reissa, keeping a wary eye on her surroundings. 'Now can we please get out of here? This place gives me the creeps.'

Madock ignored them and stepped carefully over the debris to enter his old home. A nostalgic smile grew as he gazed around, drinking in the scenery but seeing it with the benefit of colour and life added by his memories. The floorboards beneath him creaked as he stepped further into the house.

Without warning, one gave way, decayed by years of rot and collapsing under the weight of the Death Cheater. He grunted as he lost his balance and felt the shards of wood cut into his leg as it sank into the foundations of the building. Desperately, he repositioned himself and tried to pull his leg free, but found to his dismay that it was trapped.

'Well, well, well, that is *very* unfortunate.' Reissa was beside him in a second, her gloating tone reflecting her sense of triumph. She crouched down beside him and confidently removed the mask from his face so as to stare into his eyes. 'Seems to me the time has come to renegotiate our little arrangement. Give us the glass, or we leave you here to rot with the rest of this dump of a settlement.'

Without the protection of the mask to conceal his emotions, Madock forced himself to stare back into her deep grey eyes without giving any indication of the pain he was in. He could already feel blood beginning to trickle down his leg, but was determined not to let the woman know just how desperate his situation was.

Before he could respond, Kye pushed his partner out of the way and stared down at the man trapped in the floorboards. For a second, Madock feared that perhaps the giant man would follow his partner's lead, but to his relief instead Kye offered his hand to help him out. Taking it gratefully, Madock allowed himself to be eased carefully out of the hole. His leg was badly cut and bleeding heavily, and as he tried to put weight on it he instantly knew that it wouldn't support him.

Reissa stood with her arms folded, a dark scowl upon her face. 'Looks painful,' she noted bitterly. Madock elected not to dignify the comment with a response and instead lowered himself to the floor. Removing a bandage from his pack, he quickly and expertly tied it around his leg to stop the worst of the bleeding. He knew he would need to seek medical attention, but in many ways that was a minor concern. The leg of the Malice Gear had been torn, an issue which if not remedied would leave him more exposed to the Malice on the surface. However, there was no time to return to Pelera to have it repaired. He would just have to patch it himself until he found Haswell and the monster.

'We stay here tonight,' stated Kye firmly.

Reissa immediately protested. 'Not a chance, Kye! Let's just ditch the old guy and get out of here! This is turning into more trouble than it's worth. Let him keep his stupid piece of glass. There is no way I'm spending the night here.'

Madock had to admit he was less than thrilled at the prospect of resting here, but he knew that Kye was right; they had seen no other suitable locations, leaving them with little option but to make base in the remains of his old house for the time being.

Reissa shot the old man a venomous look. 'I'm really starting to dislike you…' she scowled as she marched out of the house.

* * *

Madock had intended to stay awake so as to not leave himself victim to the actions of the Raiders, but he realised he must have failed when he woke suddenly. It took him a moment to remember where he was, confident that he must have still been dreaming as he glanced around at the burnt carcass of his old home. His leg was throbbing as he shifted into a sitting position on the old sofa. It was a miracle that the furniture had survived at all, so Madock felt it would have been unreasonable to complain about how uncomfortable it was.

'How's the leg?' Kye voice's cut through the silence, though the large man was obviously making an effort to speak softly. Reissa was lying on the floor nearby, and Madock sensed that Kye did not wish to incur any more of her wrath by waking her unnecessarily.

Madock cringed. 'Healing. Thank you again.'

Kye grunted in response, clearly uncomfortable and uncertain at how to receive the gratitude. A short awkward silence followed, with neither man being certain of what to say next.

'Why didn't you just take the glass like Reissa said?' asked Madock cautiously.

'Wouldn't have been honourable,' said Kye, shrugging dismissively.

Raiders have no honour, thought Madock silently, but he felt a grudging respect for Kye. He may have been a Raider, but he had proved himself to be an honest, reasonable man thus far. Which only served to make his choice of partner all the more surprising.

'Why do you let her talk to you like that?' asked Madock, allowing himself to vocalise his train of thought.

Kye turned and briefly considered the young woman sleeping on the floor nearby. 'She's all talk,' he replied calmly. 'We've never killed anybody for anything. We just take what we find lying around or what people are willing to hand over.'

Madock sat back and considered Kye's words. 'You'd have a better life as a Dead Man,' suggested the Death Cheater, 'There's plenty of work out there. Both of you could make a good, honest living off it rather than stealing and scavenging.'

'Honest?' laughed Kye, before quickly checking the volume of his voice as Reissa stirred in her sleep. Both men waited nervously until the soft sound of her steady breathing met their ears. 'There's nothing honest about being another man's servant,' argued Kye, suddenly vocal, as his passion for the argument encouraged his usually still tongue into action. 'We choose our fate, choose our own path. Dead Men blindly follow orders.'

Madock knew the large man was wrong, but in that moment he failed to find the reasons why. It unnerved him to find himself unable to defend the manner in which he had lived his entire life. 'Then why did you agree to my offer?' he asked weakly, hoping it would prove his point.

'You need our help,' replied Kye as if this was the final say in the matter.

Madock shifted uncomfortably and sought to change the topic of the conversation.

'So why her?' he asked quickly, tilting his head towards Reissa. 'She seems like hard work.'

Kye's expression softened. 'I promised her parents,' he answered as he gazed at the sleeping woman.

A promise is a powerful thing, thought Madock as he silently allowed himself to sink back down onto the sofa. Neither man said anything further but simply waited patiently for whatever would happen next, watching through the exposed front of the house as the Echoes continued their reluctant vigil over the remains of their lives.

20

'So my son is to be a Dead Man.' His father spat the words, making no attempt to conceal his anger. He had known this wouldn't be a simple conversation, making every effort to avoid it over the last few days. The only saving grace in his mind was that he knew it couldn't develop into a debate. Hid mind had been made up for days now, ever since the chance meeting with the Dead Man in Pelera.

His father pressed on. 'What's the matter? Tunnel life not good enough for you anymore?'

The room where they stood was small, yet easily the largest of the living areas when compared to the rest of the rooms in their home. He had been sharing a room with his younger brother for as long as he could remember even though there was barely enough room to fit in the two narrow beds. His family had never been distinguished, never held any great claim to fame, but they had been more or less content with their lot in life. They may have just been commoners from Tirneth, but they were satisfied with their position of obscurity within society.

But was it so wrong to want more?

'We're just worried about you Tallec.' His mother's concern was as predictable as his father's anger. In many ways it was harder to deal with; Tallec did his best to avoid the hurt expression on her face. She had always done her best to protect him and his brother from the outside world, and it broke his heart to see the anguish in her eyes as he announced his intention to leave the safety of Tirneth. She hadn't been happy when he began to drift the Peleran tunnels two years ago to transport goods for some of the merchants based in the settlement, but she had grudgingly accepted his decision as he proved himself adept at traversing the dark tunnels safely. In truth, it had been nowhere near as dangerous as he had originally anticipated; Peleran forces often patrolled the tunnels and he knew better than to drift away from the flowing waters of the Enki cenote.

It had been exciting to take his first steps away from Tirneth, to earn a living for himself. But the Peleran tunnels no longer held the promise of fame and fortune. He knew it was time to leave.

'I'll be fine,' he stated absently, avoiding the contrasting expressions of scorn and concern as he continued to pack his meagre possessions. He was due to meet Edwin at the tunnel which led away from Pelera and up towards the surface, a place jokingly referred to by the locals as "World's End". Though he had only met the Dead Man a few days ago in Pelera, he already knew better than to keep him waiting.

His father stood abruptly as Tallec swung his bag onto his shoulders and moved towards the door. In his haste he knocked his chair over, rushing to grab his son by the arm. 'You're throwing your life away!' There was a bitter tone to his voice. Coupled with the fury that burned in his father's eyes, Tallec found that he was forced to confront his father's anger head on. 'I've put up with you drifting the tunnels, trying to turn yourself into some sort of local hero. But this…' He paused, tightening his grip on Tallec's arm as his fingers dug into the young man's sleeves. 'This sudden obsession with becoming a Dead Man, with becoming a Storm Runner, it's too much. This isn't a game. Life on the surface will eat you alive and won't even be considerate enough to spit out your remains.'

Freeing himself from his father's grasp, Tallec stood tall as he faced his parents. In many ways he had inherited the best features of each of them; broad shouldered with eyes the same frozen blue as his father's, partnered with his mother's chestnut brown hair and delicate features. Even now as he entered his mid-twenties he remained eternally youthful, with a wonder and appetite for knowledge and new experiences which had long outlasted his peers. His largely sheltered life had led to him avoiding many of the hardships of the world, his youthful visage a stark contrast to many he encountered both in Tirneth and Pelera who had been withered and aged by a world of death and despair. The last few years of drifting the tunnels had hardened his body and mind, but had done little to quench his thirst for adventure.

'I'll be fine,' Tallec repeated firmly. 'I'll send back money when I can.'

His father scoffed, seemingly accepting defeat. 'You'd be better off sending back a tombstone. At least then your mother will have somewhere to mourn your foolishness.'

Tallec ignored the words, but still felt the pain in his heart. Sensing that there was nothing else to say and unable to face his mother's pained expression for another moment, he kissed her gently on the cheek and silently left his family home. He could hear his mother and father arguing as he closed the door behind him, but steeled himself not to turn back.

Tirneth was a small settlement, larger than its neighbouring settlement Mikara but far smaller than Pelera to the north. However, what it lacked in size, it made up for in resourcefulness. Watermills took advantage of the flowing water of the Enki cenote to provide energy to the settlement whilst Tirneth also boasted the largest amount of livestock of the northern settlements. Providing surplus to Pelera in return for access to the Enki cenote and protection had allowed Tirneth to flourish, but its population had never grown larger than it was capable of sustaining. Many passed through Tirneth on their way to and from Pelera, but few chose to remain there.

As he approached the tunnel known as World's End where he knew Edwin would be waiting for him, he slowed as he noticed a large group of people huddled together chatting excitedly. Intrigued, he veered from his course and moved towards the crowd. As he approached, he was surprised to see Edwin standing on the outer edges of the group, though refusing to get involved in the scrum. Tallec moved alongside him and coughed awkwardly.

'You're late, pup,' he commented without turning to look at the younger man.

'In my defence, you're not where you said you would be,' pointed out Tallec, carefully testing the waters.

Edwin smiled. 'Neither are you.'

Tallec had only met Edwin once before, but already he was in awe of the experienced Dead Man. He was in his late thirties, a ripe old age for a Dead Man to reach (unless of course you happened to be the Death Cheater) and testament to his knowledge and experience. Tallec had been nervous when the merchant he had been delivering to had first introduced him to the Dead Man, the stall owner praising Tallec's enthusiasm and reliability. Edwin had questioned him further before offering to take Tallec under his wing and train him as a Dead Man. Even now, it all seemed like a dream to the young man, but as he now stood beside Edwin ready to leave for the surface for the first time, he realised that it was in fact very real.

'So, what's going on?' asked Tallec, attempting to get a glance through the crowd as his curiosity began to peak.

Edwin smiled and shook his head. 'It would appear we have a celebrity in our midst.'

Tallec looked at him questioningly. In response, Edwin moved forward and gestured for the younger man to follow him. Carefully they carved a way through the crowd until eventually they found some space near the front. Tallec's eyes widened as he saw the figure at the centre of the commotion, dusting off his Malice Gear and waving politely to the crowd.

'Haze Broxhart?' gasped Tallec in shock. There had been some big names to pass through Tirneth in Tallec's lifetime, yet Haze Broxhart had never been one of them. Tallec had heard that since becoming a demon hunter, Haze had avoided the northern settlements surrounding his home and had instead made a name for himself in the south. The stories about his feats and achievements were legendary.

'I'm surprised to see him here,' admitted Edwin, 'I'd heard that he had returned to Pelera, but I can't imagine why he's here.'

Tallec shot Edwin a look. 'Hey, this is my home.'

'And it's lovely,' replied Edwin dryly, the smile upon his face suggesting that his sarcastic tone was not to be taken too seriously. 'Anyway, if we're quite done autograph hunting, we've got work to do.'

Together, they turned and found their way back through the crowd and began to stroll slowly towards World's End. Though Edwin didn't say so, Tallec guessed that the experienced Dead Man had slowed their pace in order to allow the young man to drink in the last views of Tirneth and say goodbye to his home. He didn't know how long it would be until he returned, and he was silently grateful to the Dead Man for the opportunity.

'We're heading for the Bunker first,' explained Edwin as they walked. 'It's the nearest place to find work. From there, we'll work our way southwards.'

'Will we get to see Gair?' asked Tallec eagerly. He had heard stories of the great city protected by a magical barrier, and longed to see it for himself.

Edwin smiled. 'We'll see. It might take…'

They both froze as a gunshot echoed loudly in the air. It was quickly followed by screams, and then another shot was fired. And another. And another.

Edwin turned to Tallec urgently. 'Stay here, find somewhere to hide!' he shouted, already starting to rush towards the sound of the gunfire.

Watching him leave, Tallec glanced around uneasily, uncertain of what to do. In the end, he discovered the answer was simple. Unsheathing his sword, he chased after the Dead Man, rushing straight towards the sound of the gunshots.

21

With a fresh bandage tied tightly around his injured leg, Madock felt that he was able to put enough weight on it to continue his journey. He was glad; the prospect of spending any more time in Sheol was more than he could face. Between hours of restless sleep, he had found himself staring at the Echoes, wondering who they had once been. The idea that his family might be among them had filled him with dread. He could only hope that they had left this place and were finally at peace.

As he moved uneasily to the front of the house, he found Kye and Reissa waiting for him. He hadn't expected them to leave, though he had hoped they would. It would have made the situation far less complicated.

'Ready?' asked Kye as Madock joined them.

The Death Cheater nodded, then glanced back and forth uneasily between the pair. 'I'm sure I can find Hawell on my own now...' he started awkwardly.

Reissa laughed. 'Are you serious old man? You can barely walk. Besides, we're not going anywhere till we get that glass. You've been nothing but trouble, but I'm not walking away empty-handed after all this. You drag us to this graveyard and expect us to just wander off? You owe us, and every day that passes you owe us just that little bit more.'

Madock sighed and shrugged. 'Your choice,' he admitted in defeat.

'This is *not* my choice. If I had things my way, we'd have killed you in your sleep and taken the glass. But for whatever reason, the big guy has your back so...' Reissa raised her arms in exasperation and without another word began to march away from them, back towards where they had first entered the settlement.

The two men watched her leave in silence, neither sure what to say. Eventually Kye gestured that they should follow her and the two men set off, though keeping a safe distance between themselves and the furious woman a short way ahead of them.

As they walked, Kye was the first to speak. 'The house. You knew it.' It wasn't a question, but an observation.

Madock considered remaining silent. He reminded himself that he was talking to a stranger, a Raider, a man who just the day before had tried to rob him. But even as he considered this, he realised that it wasn't entirely true. Kye had not demanded anything of him, hadn't even threatened him directly. Reissa had done both of those things. Thus far, Kye had been guilty of nothing more than helping him.

He decided to tell him the truth. 'It used to be my home.'

Kye nodded but said nothing more, clearly waiting for the Death Cheater to add detail to the admission. Madock surprised himself with how willing he was to provide this. 'I had a wife and a little girl. Lived there for years. They stayed there while I worked in Pelera.'

'You survived the Sheol Disaster?' asked Kye, the interest evident in his voice in spite of his lack of eye contact.

'No,' replied Madock. 'I wasn't here. But they...' He paused unable to finish the sentence.

The two men continued in silence. Eventually, it was Kye who had the final word on the matter. He paused, causing Madock to stop beside him as Reissa continued to march on ahead, oblivious to their discussion.

'I'm sorry for your loss,' he said, his deep voice full of sincerity.

Madock nodded in appreciation at the kind words, uncertain of how to respond. Kye quickly resumed his lumbering pace, leaving Madock on his own.

I guess some Raiders are human after all, thought the Death Cheater. Taking a deep breath, he followed them to the fallen building they had first clambered through.

Picking their way back through the rubble, Madock did not turn back to look at the rest of the settlement. He could not bear to see it in its current condition, and he believed that he had already said goodbye to his home many years before. Instead, he left silently, consigning Sheol to isolation once more.

The journey through the Peleran tunnels towards Tirneth was one completed in silence. Reissa was quietly seething at the situation she had found herself in, while Kye's silence was characteristic of the large man. Madock, for his part, was lost in thought as he walked along uneasily on his injured leg. He had lost time in his pursuit of both Haswell and the monster, and could only hope that Tirneth would improve his fortunes.

I need to stay alert. The monster could look like anybody in Tirneth, he reminded himself solemnly. At one point he had even questioned whether Kye or Reissa could have been the monster, but he had dismissed this as illogical. Only one of them could have been the monster, and neither seemed to be suggesting that the other was acting unusually or out of character. Still, he had always kept one hand ready on his weapon; there was nothing to be gained by making assumptions and becoming too trusting.

Soon they reached the outskirts of Tirneth. Madock had visited the small settlement on countless occasions during his travels, both as a Dead Man and under the service of Ruskin. He paused as his mind drifted back to his friend, recently departed from this world, but he did not allow himself to dwell on it. He needed to focus.

As they entered Tirneth, Madock instantly knew that something was wrong. Sorrow seemed to hang in the air as small groups of people stood huddled together. Some were crying, whilst others seemed to be wandering aimlessly around the settlement with a look of shock and confusion upon their face. It didn't take Madock's trained eyes long to quickly spot the epicentre of the chaos, his stomach turning as he noticed the blood stained bodies lining the streets. Immediately he set off in this direction, not concerning himself with whether the Raiders followed him or not.

Has the monster already been here? he wondered with a feeling of despair rising in his gut. *I could have been here to stop this.* He knew that this wasn't true, but it proved difficult to switch off the feeling of guilt washing over him.

Reaching the scene, Madock crouched beside one of the fallen bodies. In a twisted way, he was relieved to see the bullet wounds and blood pooling beneath the poor man; whilst tragic, it suggested that it was not the work of the monster. All of its victims thus far had been robbed of life without any obvious signs of bodily wounds. It didn't make the situation any less unpleasant, but it eased one of the Death Cheater's concerns.

He became aware of a young man kneeling beside him on the other side of the body. 'His name was Edwin,' said the brown haired youth quietly, clutching at the fallen man's sleeve. 'He... he saved me.'

Madock met the young man's gaze. 'What happened?' he asked gently. The man seemed to be struggling to cope with the reality of the situation, but if he had seen first-hand what happened it was important that Madock got information from him as quickly as possible.

The young man frowned, as though trying to remember the events clearly. 'I don't know why he was here. He just started shooting. He just...'

'Did you know who did this? Did you recognise them?' pressed Madock.

The young man looked up at him nervously, biting his lip as though unwilling to reveal the name. 'Haze Broxhart. It was Haze Broxhart.'

Madock recoiled and stared at the young man as though he were crazy. 'Haze Broxhart?' he questioned incredulously. 'Are you sure?'

'I saw him do it!' shouted the young man, clearly angered by Madock's sceptical tone. 'He was here and he just started shooting people. I don't know why! We ran here to try and stop him. Edwin pushed me into the building to keep me safe. Haze shot him, again and again...'

Madock watched with a mixture of disbelief and pity as the young man curled up over his dead friend's body and began to sob. Standing, the Death Cheater paced back and forth as he attempted to digest the information he had just received.

Haswell did this? But why? It made no sense. Had the demon hunter perhaps suspected somebody of being the monster in disguise? But if so why continue killing others? Madock had seen Haswell reach some deep, troubling levels of anger, but he could not believe that the man would have been capable of such aggression. Yet even as he began to circulate and ask others who had witnessed the massacre, the demon hunter was identified as the perpetrator of the crime by each one of them.

What happened here?

Kye and Reissa appeared alongside him, picking their way carefully through the bodies. To his relief, the woman said nothing, seemingly as disturbed by the scene of death before them as he was.

'Do you believe them?' asked Kye earnestly.

Madock shrugged helplessly. 'They all say it was him.' He had decided not tell the Raiders anything about the monster he was pursuing, but it had crossed his mind that the person responsible may have been the monster wearing Haswell's face. However, he knew that the monster could only take on the form of Echoes that it had absorbed, meaning that this solution was not one he was willing to consider in too much detail. Besides, this didn't match the monster's style.

It must have been Haswell. But why did he do this?

* * *

They sat in silence by the window of the inn, watching the watermills turn through the glass as the Enki cenote continued to flow, oblivious to what had happened beside it. The last of the bodies had been taken away, covered in sheets, further victims of the dark times in which they seemed to be living.

Reissa was remaining uncharacteristically quiet as they sat around the wooden table, the entire atmosphere around them sombre and reflective. Other locals had joined them, but nobody seemed to be talking. It was as if the entire settlement was taking a collective moment to reflect on what had happened, seeking answers that simply were not available.

Madock was still struggling to process everything that he had heard. He continued to doubt that Haswell could have been responsible for such an atrocity, yet everything he had seen and heard seemed to reinforce the opposite. Haswell had been named by so many people that he found it hard to believe it was a conspiracy or a myth. There was such hurt and disbelief in the eyes of those he had spoken to that the Death Cheater had found himself with little choice but to believe their version of events.

Kye lifted his tankard to lips and took a long drink, gulping loudly as the ale poured down his throat. When he had finally had his fill, he placed the tankard down carefully and considered it thoughtfully. 'Did you know?'

Madock looked up in confusion. 'Know what?'

Kye fixed his gaze on the old man. 'You were looking for him. Did you know this would happen?'

The question startled Madock, but he could understand the logic behind it. He had requested their assistance to locate Haswell Broxhart, and during their pursuit of him the demon hunter seemed to have gone on some sort of rampage. It wasn't beyond the realm of possibility that Madock could have been trying to prevent this from happening.

The Death Cheater shook his head vehemently. 'I was just looking to bring him back to Pelera,' he replied firmly.

'Why did he leave?' asked Kye.

At that moment, Madock considered telling them everything; about Ruskin Broxhart's death, the face changing monster which absorbed Echoes, anything that could prove useful in explaining Haswell's behaviour.

But he knew that now was not the right time.

'I'm not sure,' Madock lied, 'But I was asked to bring him back to Pelera. There was no indication that he would do... this.' He paused and looked at the two Raiders. 'I can't ask you to help me anymore. Haswell has clearly become a danger. I'll find him on my own.'

'Are you going to give us the glass now?' asked Reissa impatiently, unable to hold her tongue any longer.

Madock placed a hand inside his pocket, allowing his fingers to grasp the object reassuringly as he shook his head. 'No.'

Reissa scowled and turned to her partner. '*Now* can we leave the old man to die? I really don't think it's worth risking our lives dealing with some psychopath for a pretty jewel.'

Kye turned and stared at her intently. 'He might kill again.'

'All the more reason to get out of this whole thing now! I don't want to end up covered in a sheet, riddled with bullets, just because of your sense of honour and this old fool's sense of duty.'

Saying nothing, Kye continued to stare at her. Reissa did her best to avoid her partner's gaze, but finding it impossible she growled in frustration and slumped over the table.

'Damn it...' she muttered bitterly.

Kye returned to his tankard and took another sip as if nothing had happened.

She might have a mouth on her, but it's obvious who's really in charge here, thought Madock as he took a sip from his own tankard. The ale was warm and sickly, but it was helping to distract him from the alarming questions that were circling in his head.

He looked up as a stranger boldly joined them at the table. As he watched the man questioningly, Madock recognised him as the young brown haired man he had first spoken to at the scene of the tragedy.

'You're the Death Cheater, aren't you?' asked the young man, his eyes alive with focus and desire. When Madock nodded in response, he pressed on with his next question. 'Are you going after Haze Broxhart?'

Madock paused, uncertain as to how much he should reveal to a stranger. 'Possibly,' he replied, remaining as non-committal as possible.

The young man seemed to analyse the response internally. 'I want to go with you.' His voice was eager and passionate. 'I want to help you find him. I'm a Dead Man, I can help you.'

Madock considered the young man before him. His determined expression suggested he believed he was capable of helping, and more importantly, that he was not going to accept no for an answer.

'What's your name?' asked Madock, watching the young man carefully.

'Tallec Silverlight,' replied the young man.

'Why do you want to help us find Haze?'

Tallec's answer was resolute. 'I'm going to kill him.'

22

He didn't want the young man there, but Madock sensed that Tallec was not going to take no for an answer. His refusal had fallen on deaf ears and the young Dead Man had maintained his stubborn stare as Madock explained that he was simply seeking to return Haswell to Pelera. In his heart, he knew that he could not blame Tallec for feeling the way he did; he had been in the same position following the Sheol Disaster, baying for blood and refusing to listen to anything but the fury flowing through his body. But he knew Haswell. He knew that there must be some reason behind the madness, a reason why the demon hunter had killed those people. He could not allow himself to believe it had been motiveless.

Tallec had stormed off, leaving him only with the silent questioning faces of the two Raiders, and though he knew it to be hopelessly optimistic, Madock had allowed himself to believe that that might have been the end of the issue. But sure enough, as they had arrived at World's End a short time later, having stocked up on supplies to continue their journey, they discovered Tallec impatiently awaiting their arrival.

'You're not coming with us,' repeated Madock firmly, his patience also wearing thin as he folded his arms.

Tallec shrugged in response, but said nothing. Sighing, Madock turned to Kye and Reissa to discuss their plans for the next leg of their journey. They had established that the next logical step was to travel to the Bunker. It seemed unlikely that Haswell would return to Mikara, thus making the bustling trading settlement his next likely destination. For now, thoughts of the monster's destination were placed to the back of his mind. Given Haswell's actions here in Tirneth, Madock's only priority was to find the demon hunter and return him safely to Pelera. If he encountered the monster in the process, he would deal with that too.

'We follow the old roads,' he stated, pulling the mask of his Malice Gear over his head. 'It's the quickest and safest route to the Bunker.'

Reissa shot the old man a sarcastic look. 'Wow, really? I never would have known. I also hear it's a bit cold up there, maybe I should bring a jacket?'

Madock scowled beneath his mask. He had never expected the Raiders to follow instructions, but Reissa continued to actively oppose him at every opportunity. She had made no secret of her unwillingness to be involved in the pursuit of Haswell, but it seemed that as long as Kye was aligned with Madock's search, she would follow.

Choosing not to respond to the sarcastic comments, Madock instead turned and beckoned the two Raiders as they began the ascent of the tunnel towards the surface. They had not gone far when Reissa glanced back over her shoulder.

'That creepy kid is still following us,' she commented. Madock had known Tallec would pursue them from the start, but it still frustrated him. In his current state, the young Dead Man was more likely to put them all in danger, blinded by his need for vengeance.

Reissa pressed on as Madock refused to respond. 'He has a point though. Are we really just going to find Haze and bring him back to daddy in Pelera? Seems to me like he probably won't want to come with you.'

'He's needed in Pelera,' responded Madock, unwilling to go into the details of the situation with the Raiders. News may well have started to spread of Ruskin Broxhart's death, possibly even of the disappearance of the Echoes from the Enki cenote, but Madock was determined to address this only when he was forced to.

'That doesn't mean he'll agree to come with you,' pointed out Reissa, unwilling to drop the issue. 'He might even get violent about it. I'm starting to think our stalker has the right idea, we should just kill him.'

'Reissa...' started Kye warningly, but his partner was in no mood to be silenced.

'I'm serious Kye! This guy killed a whole bunch of people for no reason, and now we're just going to find him and ask him nicely to go home? Like it's his dinner time or something? This guy is a killer, he needs to be stopped.'

'He's not a killer,' stated Madock firmly, though even as the words escaped his lips he knew it was a lie. Whatever his reasoning, there could be no denying that Haswell had killed those people in Tirneth. Even if he had suspected them of being the monster, he had been wrong and those innocent people had paid for his mistake with their lives.

But whatever the truth was behind what had happened in Tirneth, Madock knew that he would not kill Haswell. It was not why he was searching for him and would achieve nothing.

The temperature began to drop noticeably as they neared the surface, the Raiders pulling their scarves up over their mouths and wrapping their clothes tighter around their bodies. The Malice Gear provided a great deal of warmth, but once again Madock nervously checked on the damaged leg of the suit. He had wrapped it in fresh bandages both to protect the wound and the flesh around it from the Malice. Its stark white colour stood out against the midnight black of the Malice Gear. Madock knew there was little more he could do to address the damage at this point. The sooner he returned Haswell to Pelera, the sooner he could get it professionally mended.

The driving snow hit them hard as they emerged from the tunnel, the Malice swirling around their ankles like water. With a brief nod to the Raiders to confirm the need to press on quickly, they began to move away from Tirneth, heading south towards the Bunker. Though it had only been a matter of days since he had last been there, it suddenly struck Madock how much had happened, how different his view of the world would be this time when he descended into the bowels of the Bunker.

But first he had to concentrate on getting there safely.

As they trudged through the snow, a wave of apprehension washed over him. Somehow he had always instinctively known when something was wrong, and he was confident that this occasion was no different. As he turned to look back towards Tirneth, his suspicions were proved correct.

Though they had only travelled a short distance, the snow was doing its best to obscure his vision. But even through the storm he could make out the solitary figure of the young Dead Man stood outside the entrance to the tunnel which led to the settlement below. Tallec seemed to be frozen to the spot, his entire body apparently reluctant to venture any further forward.

He's never been on the surface before, realised Madock. It shouldn't have surprised him as much as it did, but he put the emotion to one side as he recognised the benefits of the development. *If he's scared, he won't follow us.*

Confident that his dilemma had been solved, Madock turned and continued to march through the snow, but a familiar sense of guilt tugged at his feet, slowing them more than the deep snow and thick Malice combined. Pausing, he placed his hands on his hips, frustrated at his own sense of duty as he turned back once more to stare at the young man.

You can't leave him there, the voice in his head insisted. *He's scared and alone on the surface for the first time. You know he won't go back, and by the time he moves forward he'll be completely isolated.* He knew the voice well. He despised it sometimes for putting him into dangerous situations, but he knew he had to listen to it. It was the voice that helped him to maintain who he was, the voice that helped him to maintain his humanity.

You can't leave him there.

Shaking his head at his own decision, Madock turned away from their destination and trudged back towards Tirneth, leaving Kye and Reissa staring after him in confusion. It didn't take him long to reach Tallec, but as he neared the boy Madock could already see the distinctive expression of fear upon the young Dead Man's face. Madock imagined he must have looked similar the first time he saw the surface.

As he placed a firm hand upon Tallec's shoulder, the young man jumped as if startled from his trance-like state. Tallec's wide frightened eyes stared at the blank dark mask of the old man's Malice Gear before turning back to the vista surrounding them.

'It's... There's just so much...' Tallec paused, as though searching for the right word to describe the scene. Eventually he found it. 'Nothingness.'

Madock shook his head and tapped the side of his mask. 'You need to think past what you can't see. There are dangers up here, far more than down there. If you don't watch out for them, you'll never survive.' He paused, reluctant to continue but knowing that it needed to be said. 'I'll take you as far as the Bunker, teach you a few things on the way. But then you're on your own. I meant what I said, you are not travelling with us. Do you understand?'

Tallec stared at Madock, and for a moment the old man was convinced that the young Dead Man had not heard a word of his speech. But when Tallec nodded slowly, he knew the young man understood.

'Okay, let's start with the basics,' said Madock, pointing at the faded remains of the old road, barely visible through the snow. 'You see that road? That will be your best friend up here. Never leave the road during the early days. Too many Dead Men try to take shortcuts and pay the price for it. You stick to the roads, understand?'

Again, Tallec nodded. 'Stick to the roads,' he repeated numbly.

'That's right. And there's one more important thing you need to know.'

Tallec looked at Madock, his face still scared but now attentive and quizzical. 'What is it?'

Madock stepped forward into the snow, then paused and turned back to Tallec. 'No matter how many journeys you make across the surface from this point onwards, the first step is always the most important one. Never take that first step lightly. You need to know that you can make it to your destination, or you won't. Are you ready to take that step?'

Tallec paused, and just for a second he glanced over his shoulder back towards the safety and security of his home. When his gaze returned to Madock, the old man could see the determination in his eyes.

'I'm ready.'

'Well then, let's get going.'

Tallec took a deep breath, pulled his scarf higher across his face, and took a single step forward. His boot crunched deep into the snow, disappearing into the Malice. An expression of relief passed across the young man's face as he took the next step with increased determination.

Madock shook his head as he watched Tallec march towards the Raiders, sticking closely to the road as his pace increased with every step.

Don't get too attached, a wary voice in his head reminded him. *Just keep him alive until the Bunker, then it's up to him to fend for himself.*

Marching to catch up with Tallec, Madock drove through the snow and together they joined the Raiders. There was no need to exchange words, though Madock could sense the Raiders' confusion at his decision to bring the young Dead Man along with them having so vehemently fought against it earlier.

Eager to avoid their questioning looks and keen to have this leg of the journey completed as quickly as possible, Madock set off as the others followed in his wake. When he turned back to check on them, he saw the other three members of his party, but the settlement of Tirneth had disappeared behind them, concealed by the driving snow.

What happened there Haswell? What happened to you?

23

The blizzard hit them hard.

They had only travelled a short distance from Tirneth when the Eternal Storm turned its rage upon them, the snow falling thicker and heavier by the second as the wind surged against them aggressively. As if encouraged by the storm's actions, the Malice too seemed to grow increasingly dense to such a point that it had become almost impossible to see the road.

Madock paused, glancing around at his companions as they bitterly trudged forward, holding their arms across their faces to protect themselves from the onslaught of the icy wind.

We can't keep going like this, thought Madock. His Malice Gear may well have provided enough protection to allow him to arrive safely at the Bunker, but he highly doubted that the others would survive the ordeal. Glancing around, he familiarised himself with their surroundings. The storm and the Malice had reduced their visibility, but he had travelled this route enough times in the past to have a good idea of their location. They needed to find somewhere to ride out the worst of the storm, and he knew just the place.

'Follow me!' he shouted, his voice barely audible over the wind. Thankfully all three of his companions heard his voice and unquestioningly turned to follow him as he veered away from their route.

He knew from experience that there was an old village a short distance ahead, left over from the old world and still with some surviving buildings which could provide shelter. Not for one second did he doubt his memory, and sure enough it took only a few minutes for the buildings to begin to emerge through the blizzard. Like empty monuments to the past, they stood firm against the elements and seemed to beckon the group of travellers with open arms.

As they passed each building, Madock's experienced eyes scanned them to find the most suitable for them to rest in. Though the frames may still have been standing, Madock knew all too well that the innards were likely to be dark and dilapidated, posing unique threats of their own.

He paused as they passed a larger building, his interest piqued as he took in the prospect. A dilapidated sign swung helplessly in the blizzard, though Madock could make out the word *hotel* painted in artistic lettering. *At least there should be beds*, he thought as he quickly tested the main door to the building. The handle was frozen solid, but as he pushed his weight against the wooden door Madock felt sure that with enough pressure they could force it open.

Kye made short work of the door's resistance, slamming his significant frame against the weakened lock to grant them access to the dark hallway of the hotel. The blizzard quickly followed them in, spreading snow across the wooden floor of the reception area as the group wandered slowly further into the depths of the old building.

An ancient chandelier swung gently above their head as though being toyed with by the wind, the glass chiming softly and echoing around the empty room. Faded pictures lined the wall, while a dusty wooden desk stood ahead of them. As Madock moved behind the desk to investigate, he found an old guest book hidden on a shelf.

Approaching the desk, Reissa playfully tapped the bell that rested upon it, sending a loud cheerful chiming sound around the room.

Madock instantly placed his hand upon the bell to silence it. 'Don't do that.'

Reissa scowled. 'I'm just drawing out any demons that might be lurking around. Don't want any nasty surprises. Just wait and listen!'

Together the group seemed to collectively hold its breath as they waited, straining their ears to listen out for any movement. When a minute had passed in absolute silence, Reissa grinned triumphantly at Madock. 'I guess nobody's home.'

'Luckily for us,' muttered Madock, placing the guest book upon the desk and opening it up. The pages were full of scribbled writing, recording the names of those who had stayed in the hotel and some comments from the guests. The Death Cheater could barely suppress an ironic smile as he read some of the complaints listed within the pages.

The room was too hot... Not enough bottled water... These people didn't realise how lucky they had it.

'Hey, bookworm, can we get on with finding somewhere to rest?' demanded Reissa impatiently.

'This is history,' explained Madock.

'It's a book.'

'I'm just surprised it hasn't been stolen by Raiders,' pointed out Madock bitterly as he placed it back on the shelf.

'We need to search the building,' said Kye, gazing around at the various possible routes they could take from the main reception area they were currently stood in.

Reissa nodded and moved alongside her partner. 'Me and Kye will take upstairs. You take the rookie with you, just shout if he wets himself again.'

Tallec glared as the two Raiders moved upstairs, but clearly Reissa's harsh words had got to him as he and Madock moved into the first corridor, weapons drawn and following the light of the Death Cheater's torch.

'I'm not a coward, you know?'

Madock chose not to respond, instead focusing on sweeping the narrow beam of torch light around the new room they had entered. It appeared to be a restaurant, with dusty tables covered in ancient faded tablecloths. Drapes hung across the windows, blocking out what little light the outside world could provide. Carefully opening a side door, they found themselves in a long corridor with further doors leading off on either side.

With any luck, we might even find some supplies, assuming this place hasn't been picked clean by Raiders.

Opening the first door on their left, Madock and Tallec entered a small dark room. A single bed stood below a window which revealed the storm outside, the wind battering against the glass. The décor of the room was plain, though tarnished by the peeling wallpaper and rotting, dusty furniture. However, Madock suspected that the poor condition of the room wasn't entirely due to the battering of the surface.

Raiders have been here, he thought as he examined an overturned table. Experience had taught him to recognise where the scavengers had been, and there were definitely signs that they had been in this room. More worryingly, it seemed as though the room had been ravaged fairly recently.

'Do you think I'm a coward?' persisted Tallec, checking underneath the bed for any remaining supplies which may have been missed. Madock sighed and shook his head. Perhaps it was exhaustion catching up with him, or maybe it was simply the frustration of his journey being disrupted, but Madock had had enough.

'I don't think you're a coward,' he stated slowly, as though attempting to restrain himself. It turned out to be a futile attempt, as Madock surrendered to his dark mood. 'I do, however, think you're a bloody fool.'

Tallec straightened in surprise, clearly startled by the old man's words. 'Why do you say that?' he asked awkwardly, unsure as to whether he should be pursuing the matter.

'Where do I start? First of all, you're stupid enough to think you can hunt down and kill Haswell Broxhart when you haven't even been on the surface before. Haswell has years of experience, has killed countless demons and right now seems more than a little unstable. You really think that you stand any chance of killing him? I almost want to see you try.'

As Tallec grimaced under the force of the brutal words, Madock sought to control his tongue. *Enough*, he shouted internally, *He's had enough now*. But it seemed his tirade could not be stopped until he had had his say.

'But the main reason why I think you're a fool? You want to be a Dead Man. You want to throw your life away, and for what? Some extra coins in your pocket? A shot at fame? They're just childish dreams. You're just throwing your life away.'

Tallec quickly seized upon Madock's words. 'But you're a Dead Man! A living legend! You're proof that we can beat the odds.'

Madock scowled. 'I'm not proof of anything. I'm an anomaly. A statistical impossibility. I should have died years ago.'

The old man paused as he took stock of what he had just said. The anger had risen from some hidden depth, hiding in obscurity until the opportunity to announce its presence arrived. Now that he was aware of it, Madock was forced to appreciate the sincerity of his words, as he believed them wholeheartedly.

I should have died years ago, he repeated in his head, measuring the meaning of the words. *I'm not special, just lucky. Luckier than any man deserves to be. And where has that luck got me? I've outlived almost everybody I ever cared about; been forced to cope with a world without them by my side. Even Ruskin's gone now. There's hardly anybody left…*

An uncomfortable silence passed between the two men as they both took stock of what had just been said. They stared at each other awkwardly, neither willing to be the first to break the silence. In the end, neither of them had to, as the sound of a scuffle above them caught their attention. There was the muffled sound of a struggle and voices calling out, and then suddenly there was silence again.

Madock and Tallec didn't need to say anything. Quickly arming themselves, they quietly left the room and headed back towards the main reception area. As they arrived at the base of the stairs, Madock silently gestured for Tallec to pause. Together they listened intently for any further sound from upstairs, but nothing met their ears except the sound of their own nervous breathing.

Taking the lead, Madock began to ascend the stairs, Tallec following close behind. The old man kept his eyes locked upon the top of the stairs, bracing himself for any threat to emerge as they drew closer and closer. He hoped that it would simply be a case that either Reissa or Kye had accidently knocked over some furniture, that the silence was just because they had continued to scout the upper level of the hotel. Madock already knew that wasn't the case, but it didn't hurt to hope for the best whilst preparing for the worst.

A step creaked loudly under the pressure of his boot. Madock grimaced and froze, waiting to see if the sound had drawn any attention. He held his breath as he strained his ears to pick out the slightest noise in the silence. In the end, he didn't need to strain at all.

'Are you armed?' An unfamiliar male voice startled him. Madock stood silently, uncertain as to whether to answer or not. He hoped that there was still a chance of approaching the situation with an element of stealth, but that was quickly dismissed as the male voice spoke again.

'We know you're on the stairs. And we know there's two of you.'

Madock cursed silently. The man's knowledge could only mean one of two things: either they could see him, or they had Kye and Reissa with them providing the information.

'We don't want any trouble,' shouted the Death Cheater, forcing his voice to remain steady.

'Then come up with your arms up,' replied the male voice. After a moment of silence, the owner spoke up once more. 'We have you outnumbered and we have your friends. Don't try anything stupid.'

Well, at least we know they have Kye and Reissa now, thought Madock. Some knowledge of the situation they were entering was better than none at all. Glancing back he could see the concern in Tallec's eyes. No doubt the young Dead Man had encountered Raiders before, but in this unfamiliar setting he clearly felt less confident about how to deal with the situation.

Madock spoke calmly to him, his earlier anger at the young man forgotten. 'Just follow my lead,' he said quietly. 'I'll make sure we all get out of this alive.'

Tallec nodded, reassured by the old man's words and happy to allow him to take control of the situation. The two men raised their arms and slowly continued to the top of the stairs. As they completed their climb, they momentarily paused in confusion. The corridor was abandoned with several doors leading off in different directions, most of them slightly ajar. It was not immediately clear where the voice had emanated from, but as the man spoke again Madock quickly determined the room from which he was speaking.

'Don't keep us waiting,' he growled threateningly.

Moving forward carefully, Madock gently pushed open the room door. As the two Dead Men stepped into the hotel room, Madock's experienced senses were already rapidly analysing the situation and the possible outcomes.

There were four Raiders, most of them armed with simple daggers and bladed weapons. One had a gun, and for this reason alone Madock identified him as the primary threat. Blades were dangerous but slower than a bullet. He would need to neutralise that threat before dealing with the other men. The gun was currently trained on Kye, who knelt protectively over Reissa who lay slumped on the floor. It seemed as though she had been knocked unconscious rather than any worse fate, presumably as a result of the scuffle he and Tallec had heard from the room below.

The room itself offered few options. The only way in or out was through the doorway they had just entered, though in an emergency the window could be smashed to provide an alternative route. It wasn't ideal; the fall to the ground posed its own risks. It was clear that the Raiders had been using the room as a makeshift base of operations for some time now, with old mattresses lying upon the floor and empty food tins scattered around haphazardly. An old lamp burned in the centre of the room, spreading dancing light around the dark room. The fact that Madock and his group had struggled to open the frozen front door of the hotel suggested that perhaps the Raiders were making use of an alternative entrance to the building. It was a fact worth noting if they needed to leave the hotel in a hurry.

'That's far enough,' commanded the owner of the voice who had spoken to them thus far. He was a bearded man with tired eyes, though his attention was fully focused upon the two men who had just entered the room. In his gloved hand he held a sword, clearly rusted but no doubt still dangerous. 'Drop your weapons.'

Madock ignored the command, but spoke calmly and directly to the man. 'We didn't realise this building was occupied. We'll take our things and leave.'

The man seemed confused by Madock's tone. 'I don't think you understand the situation you're in,' he replied.

Madock noted that both his voice and hands were shaking, only slightly but enough to convince the Death Cheater that he could take control of this situation with the correct, measured approach.

'That's Malice Gear,' commented one of the female Raiders from the other side of the room.

'I'm the one in charge here!' shouted the man angrily at the woman. 'I'll do all the talking!'

He's scared, thought Madock. *Good, I can use this to my advantage.*

'Nobody needs to get hurt. We'll take our people and leave.' He paused to see if the man was listening. 'Do the smart thing.'

The man paused to consider the offer, but then shook his head fiercely and raised his weapon to Madock's neck. 'The smart thing is for you to hand over everything you have. We have you outnumbered and if you try anything smart we'll start by killing your friends.'

Friends? The idea that Kye and Reissa could be considered friends made Madock scoff, yet even as he considered it he realised that whilst he certainly had respect for Kye, there was a deeper motive involved here. He didn't want to see anybody else die.

'Now, I'll ask you one more time. Drop your weapons.' The man's tone suggested that his patience was wearing thin.

I need to buy some more time to think, thought Madock in frustration as his hand slowly moved reluctantly to his side to remove his weapon.

The man seemed to sense that the balance of power was shifting in his favour as he turned to the younger Dead Man. 'You too, kid. Drop the sword.'

Tallec glanced at Madock, who nodded his assent for the young man to follow the instruction. The weapon was slowly removed from its sheath, Tallec drawing the blade and holding it shimmering in the light of the lamp.

In a blur, Tallec swung the weapon.

24

The next few actions played out in a matter of seconds, though they seemed to take a lifetime in Madock's eyes. The blade of Tallec's weapon swung through the air silently, barely slowing as it entered the male Raider's head. Flesh and bone crunched and gave way under the pressure of the sharpened edge, sending a splatter of blood arching through the air.

It took everybody in the room a moment to register what had just happened, but Madock knew that he had to be the first to react. Drawing his weapon, he instinctively took aim at the Raider holding the gun, having already identified him as the primary target. The bullet exploded from the barrel and tore through the man's chest, knocking him off his feet with the impact as he fell backwards. Kye was alert to the opportunity. Without the gun trained on Reissa and himself, he threw himself with remarkable speed at the startled female Raider who had commented on the Malice Gear. She barely had a chance to raise her weapon before Kye's giant frame was driving her backward towards the window. The ancient glass shattered instantly upon the impact, the woman screaming as she disappeared from view over the edge and crashed to the snow below.

The final Raider had overcome his initial shock and was now charging with his weapon raised towards Madock, desperation burning in his eyes as he sought to avenge his fallen comrades. The Death Cheater turned and raised his weapon towards the new target, choosing his placement carefully. The second bullet unleashed itself from the gun, rushing towards the threat and ripping through the man's shoulder. The victim roared in pain and instantly ceased his charge, crumpling to the ground and clutching his hand to the wound as he writhed in agony upon the floor.

For a long period of time, the man's howls of pain were the only noise that filled the room as the survivors took stock of what had just happened. Then slowly, inevitably, the Echoes rose from the bodies of the dead Raiders. They drifted, shimmering gently as they seemed to stare down at their previous mortal frames, comprehending their new form and the gravity of what had happened. Then they were gone, floating silently out of the shattered window and out into the storm.

The boy nearly just got us all killed. Madock turned to unleash his fury upon Tallec, but he could instantly see how white the young Dead Man was. Before he could say a word, Tallec doubled over and was violently sick. Madock's anger momentarily subsided as he watched the terrified young man heave, and the Death Cheater allowed himself to place a reassuring hand on Tallec's back, rubbing it gently to reassure the boy.

Kye shook his head in disbelief but said nothing, instead returning to check on Reissa who remained unconscious upon the floor. Madock was certain that Kye could take care of his partner; there was no need for him to involve himself, though he would need answers from them later. If they had been a little more careful, then perhaps this whole ugly situation could have been avoided.

You need to take responsibility too, he reminded himself. *You're the one who brought them here in the first place.*

Tallec seemed to have finally ceased vomiting and was now kneeling down on all fours shaking uncontrollably. He raised his head and stared intently at the Raider he had killed, the deep gash in the victim's face where the sword had entered still oozing blood onto the floor.

He'll need a moment, thought Madock. He knew that he had other business to attend to. Slowly he approached the final Raider he had shot. The man was still whimpering in pain, his weapon abandoned beside him as the wound in his shoulder became his only concern. Madock kicked the weapon away cautiously and stood over the Raider.

'Are there any more of you?' he asked urgently. The last thing he wanted was to be ambushed by any more Raiders. The man did not respond, continuing to whimper and writhe on the floor. Impatiently, Madock raised his boot and applied a little pressure to the man's injured shoulder. It had the desired effect as the man screamed in pain, his eyes alert and focused upon the Dead Man. 'Are there any more of you?'

'No! No, please, there's nobody!' the Raider begged desperately. Madock removed his boot from the man's shoulder, satisfied with the answer.

'We're going to be leaving now,' stated the Death Cheater firmly. 'I suggest that you get yourself to a medic as soon as possible. You'll live... if you choose to.'

The whimpering Raider nodded in compliance, but Madock could see the hatred, the anger the man wished to unleash upon him. *He's not a threat in this condition*, Madock reassured himself. Instead, he turned back to check on Tallec. The young man was still on all fours, focused on the Raider he had killed just moments ago.

'I... I killed him,' stammered Tallec, unable to tear his eyes away. 'I... I've never...' He paused, unable to continue as his body shook uneasily.

'You've never had to kill anybody before,' stated Madock gently, watching the young man with pitying eyes. Sighing, he crouched beside Tallec and spoke to him, confident that the young man was listening in spite of his focus never shifting. 'It never gets any easier. That's why you should only ever kill when you have no other choice.'

The words seemed to register, as Tallec tore his eyes away from the fallen Raider and focused on Madock.

'Did we have a choice?' he asked desperately. 'Did I do the right thing?'

Madock paused, uncertain how to answer Tallec's question. It was a question he had often posed himself in the past. 'Only you can decide that,' he replied honestly. 'Right now, we need to get out of this room.'

Eager to leave the scene as quickly as possible, Tallec nodded and immediately moved into the hallway without so much as a glance backwards. Madock rose unsteadily and moved across to Kye, who was still hunched over Reissa.

'How is she?' asked Madock awkwardly.

Kye glanced up at him, then back down at his partner. 'They hit her hard, but she'll be okay.' Without a further word, he lifted the woman effortlessly and stood to his full height.

Madock turned and moved towards the door, holding it open for Kye to pass through as he carried his partner. As they passed the injured Raider, Kye paused contemplatively. Still carrying Reissa, he turned and stood over the fallen man who stared up at him with a mixture of terror and desperation. Silently, Kye raised his large boot and crashed it down on the man's neck, resulting in a sickening crunch which immediately silenced the victim's whimpering. Madock swallowed hard as Kye silently moved to the door.

'Why did you do that?' he asked the Raider. He had taken care only to shoot the man in the shoulder, unwilling to have any more blood on his hands than necessary. Now it seemed that his charitable action had been in vain.

Kye looked down at him. The Raider's face was normally expressionless, revealing little of what emotion the man may have been feeling. Now though there were tears in his eyes, and a sense of satisfaction in his voice as he spoke. 'He was the one that hit her.'

* * *

Kye refused to leave the hotel until Reissa had recovered. Madock had to admit that the plan made more sense than braving the tail end of the blizzard, and with all the threats now neutralised they could afford to rest in a degree of security. Madock had located the alternative entry point the Raiders had used to gain access to the hotel and sealed it shut, but not before checking on the woman who had crashed through the window during the fracas in the bedroom. In spite of landing on fresh snow, she had not survived the fall. He had taken the time to drag her corpse a short distance away from the main building; the last thing he wanted to contend with was demons who may be drawn towards the corpse.

They now sat silently in one of the bedrooms on the ground floor. Having searched the remainder of the hotel, it had proven itself to be the most comfortable room available. It still had two functioning beds which provided some degree of comfort, and the room itself had been largely undamaged. It seemed different to the other rooms they had explored, leading Madock to believe that it may have belonged to the owners of the hotel.

Tallec was in one bed, curled into a ball of self-reflection and facing towards the wall. It was clear that he was still struggling to come to terms with what he had done. Madock knew that there was little more he could do to help the young man, that this was simply either make or break for Tallec. In a dark twisted way, it had worked out for the Death Cheater; either Tallec would be strong enough to go his own way by the time they reached the Bunker, or he would return home with his tail between his legs. Either way, he was not Madock's burden anymore.

The situation with the Raiders had still played out unfavourably, though Madock knew that his say in the outcome had largely been taken away by Tallec's rash action. He had wanted everybody to walk away from the situation alive, and whilst he was glad that nobody in his party had come to harm, he still felt guilty for what had happened to the Raiders. It was unusual for Madock to feel anything remotely close to remorse for a fallen Raider, but time spent with Kye and Reissa had reminded him that Raiders were simply people too, trying to survive in their own unique way. He may not have agreed with their methods, but he would not have wished them dead.

Sitting on the floor with his back resting against the wall, Madock turned his attention to the other bed upon which Kye had carefully placed Reissa. The woman was blissfully silent, though Madock found himself strangely longing to hear her vicious tongue again. He knew it was simply a matter of time, and had no doubt that he would quickly change his mind when she awoke, but for now he found the silence suffocating.

It dawned upon the old man just how much he had been willing to risk to save the lives of these two Raiders, still relative strangers to him and in many ways forced companions. He could have easily led Tallec away from the hotel, abandoned them to their fate. But he hadn't. He had put his own life at risk to save them.

You always do. It really is a miracle that you've survived this long, you stupid old man, he scolded himself. But as much as he reflected on the stupidity of his actions, he knew that he was bound to repeat them in the future. *If I'm truly the Death Cheater, I should try and help other people to cheat death too.*

As if reading his thoughts, Kye spoke suddenly without turning away from Reissa. 'Thank you.'

Madock squirmed, uneasily accepting the gratitude. 'How is she?' he asked, changing the subject.

'She's fine,' replied Kye.

'And how are you?' Madock paused as Kye seemed to flinch. 'Do you want to talk about what happened back there?'

Kye didn't initially seem willing to discuss it, but when it became clear that Madock was awaiting an answer, he shrugged. 'I was angry.'

'I thought you didn't kill people?' asked Madock, reminding Kye of his words in Sheol.

'She doesn't,' he replied, placing a gentle hand on Reissa's arm. 'I won't let her.'

'And what about you?'

Kye paused reflectively. 'I thought I didn't need to anymore. I guess nobody can escape death...'

The conversation was interrupted as a groan emerged from the bed in which Reissa lay. Kye's focus was instantly upon his partner as she stirred and tentatively held her head.

'What happened?' she groaned through half-open eyes.

'Somebody hurt you, but I took care of them,' explained Kye softly. Reissa smiled, her usually harsh expression softened by gratitude to her partner. She placed another thankful hand on his and squeezed it lightly.

'You should have saved them for me,' she joked, her voice weak but regaining its familiar confidence and bite. 'I'd like to have given them a piece of my mind.'

Madock stood and stretched his tired muscles, before glancing around at the other people in the room; a potentially traumatized Dead Man on his first trip across the surface, a giant Raider who had unveiled the darker side of his personality and his sharp tongued partner who lay weakly in the bed.

How do you get yourself into these situations, Madock?

'We'll stay here and rest for another few hours,' he announced. 'Then we need to get moving again.'

By now Haswell could be miles ahead of us. I have to find him. I have to know the truth.

25

The Dead Men's Guild was a myth. Many believed a location existed, buried somewhere within the sinful layout of The Bunker, where the Dead Men would regularly gather to seek advice and share secrets they had discovered during their travels. As with most rumours, there existed an element of truth albeit vastly exaggerated. Whilst the Dead Men were bound by little more than mutual respect for their companions and their knowledge of surviving the testing conditions of the surface, they often sought each other's help and advice. Their sense of camaraderie had led them to create meeting places in most settlements where work and support could be shared, but the Bunker contained the biggest of these locations. It was common knowledge amongst Dead Men that if you were seeking information, the Bunker was the place to be.

It was with this in mind that Madock approached the inn known as the Silver Bullet.

The remainder of their journey to the Bunker had been thankfully uneventful, though the uneasiness which had surfaced in the hotel remained. Tallec had not spoken a word to anybody and seemed permanently lost in thought, battling with his inner demons. The realisation of what it meant to take the life of another had hit the young man hard. Madock was still uncertain as to whether Tallec would be able to continue on his path once they reached the Bunker. He did his best to remind himself that it was no longer his concern.

Kye had also stirred up a sense of unease within the Death Cheater. He had always regarded the giant Raider as a physical threat, but until the event with the other Raiders that was all it had been; a threat. Now that he had seen what the normally placid man was capable of,

Madock regarded Kye with the same suspicion and distrust which he had experienced upon first meeting him in the Peleran tunnels.

Reissa had recovered quickly from the ordeal, and seemed more than capable of making the journey independently, but Kye had insisted on remaining by her side every step of the way to support her. She had laughed this off and mocked him with her usual brashness, but Madock could see the gratitude behind the words as she had taken his arm.

Upon descending into the familiar sounds and smells of the Bunker, Madock had left the group to their own devices. In some ways, he almost hoped that he would never see any of them again. It seemed a very real possibility; Reissa no longer seemed to care about obtaining the glass he carried in his pocket and would doubtlessly continue to harass her partner into leaving, having made no secret of her distaste for their journey together. As for Tallec, Madock very much doubted that the young man would last long here in the Bunker. He was a lost soul walking among very different types of demons down here.

The Silver Bullet lay isolated from the main hustle and bustle of the settlement, shrouded in relative darkness as it lurked in its own quiet corner, observing the chaos and depravity surrounding it. Madock knew all too well that the walls contained their own unique darker elements, but it was also a veritable font of knowledge for any Dead Man.

The dank tavern consumed him as he stepped through the doorway, his eyes taking a moment to adjust to the gloom, broken only by a single light above the bar. A range of bottles stood on shelves behind the bar, containing all manner of alcoholic beverages; it was an unfortunately popular option for those who couldn't cope with the reality of life. A series of benches of different sizes and colours filled the majority of the tavern, reflecting the diversity of the clientele who frequented the Silver Bullet. Though it may have been a hub for Dead Men, it attracted its fair share of passing travellers and locals from all walks of life. Madock had spent countless days and nights under its wooden timbers, particularly during the early days of his career as a Dead Man. That had been before he had found employment with Ruskin Broxhart, those golden days where he had briefly escaped the rigours of life as a Dead Man. Perhaps that had been the secret to his longevity as much as luck and experience had played their roles.

Madock had made many friends and allies within the walls of the Silver Bullet, and already familiar faces were gazing in his direction, though one burned with more ferocity than the others.

'You've got a lot of nerve coming back here, Leocadia.'

Madock turned to face the woman behind the bar, the familiar stern expression upon her face making the old man smile in spite of her tone. 'Good to see you too Nene. It's nice to see your pretty face again.'

'Don't think you can charm your way out of this one.'

Anybody could tell from looking at her that Nene had once been a very beautiful woman. Madock clearly remembered when he had first met her, a teenager blossoming into womanhood, her youthful curves enticing and exciting. That had been twenty-seven years ago, and even now she still glowed with a sensuality that seemed to warm the heart to behold, although the difficulties of life underground had not been kind to her. Now in her early forties, Nene was as much of a symbolic image of human life underground as you could find. Her eyes retained their sparkle of resistance and beauty, though they now bedded deeply into the pale, tired skin of her face. Her tongue, it seemed, would not be defeated by any element of adversity though. It had been four years since he had last seen her.

He could only hope that this meeting ended better than the last.

Madock settled himself on a rusty stool beside the bar, confronting the full force of Nene's glare. He knew exactly what she was going to say, so he pre-empted her, resuming the argument which had been running for almost twenty years. 'I didn't make your brother go in my place.'

A sarcastic laugh emerged from the landlady as she picked up a cloth and set about cleaning a nearby glass. Madock couldn't help but feel the action was intended to prevent her wringing his neck instead.

'You're still the coward I remember,' she said coldly, the cloth in her hand wiping the glass with intense vigour. 'You accepted the job. I didn't want you to go, but you insisted.' Her voice softened. 'I cried.' She shook her head furiously. 'Then you came strolling back in here, telling us all that you couldn't do it.'

'I know what I did, Nene.'

'Bailey. He took your place. He...' The motion of cleaning the glass slowed slightly. 'He was too young.'

'I need to know if you've seen Haswell Broxhart,' said Madock bluntly, breaking the flow of the story as he ran his finger through the dust upon the surface of the bar.

What little noise that had existed within the bar disappeared. Madock instinctively felt every individual's attention shift towards his conversation with Nene, the landlady's hands having come to a complete stop as she gazed at him.

'You're unbelievable,' she stated, the slight quiver in her voice evident as she turned to place the glass upon the shelf behind her.

'Have you seen Haswell Broxhart in here recently?'

A whisper rushed through the bar like a chilling wind. Madock could only make out vaguely what was being said, but Haswell's name emerged more than once from different tables. Nene remained silent, her back to the

Death Cheater as he patiently waited for her response. She shuddered.

'I'm just glad you're going after him,' she mumbled in the silence, as though attempting to collect her thoughts. 'He was in here earlier, but... something's wrong with him.'

So he was here, and recently too... Madock was alert, sensing that the demon hunter's presence in the Silver Bullet had caused some sort of scene. The entire tavern was silent now, with everybody's attention firmly on the old man's discussion with Nene. 'What happened, Nene?'

Nene turned to look at him, the concern upon her face immediately evident. 'He's been in here before, always strutting about like he's some sort of hero, but it's always been light-hearted. This time, it was different. He was really intense, said he wanted to know if there were any interesting rumours going around the Dead Men's circle.'

He was looking for information? Madock frowned in confusion. 'What did you tell him Nene?'

Nene shrugged innocently. 'Nothing significant, just a few odd snippets here and there. He didn't seem happy with anything I was telling him. He started... shouting at me, telling me I was pathetic and useless...' The landlady paused, as though collecting herself. 'It wasn't like him at all. I thought maybe he was drunk, or worse... maybe Malice poisoning. A couple of the guys in here had the same idea, tried to subdue him. But...'

'Did he kill them?' asked Madock bluntly. It was a question he didn't want to ask, but he knew he needed to find out the answer. Given the events in Tirneth, he needed to know just how much of a threat Haswell had become.

Nene shook her head. 'He was crazy. He aimed his gun at anybody who came near, fired a few shots into the ceiling, but no, he didn't kill them...'

Well, that's something, thought Madock. In a twisted way, it was a relief to know that the demon hunter had retained at least some degree of self-control. 'What happened then?'

'He started ranting and raving about how he had to hunt down some monster. He said... he said it had killed his father. Is that true, Madock?'

For a second, Madock considered denying it, dismissing it as part of Haswell's unstable state of mind, but he realised that if Haswell was spreading word of Ruskin's death then it wouldn't take long for the truth to come out.

He nodded slowly. 'It's true.'

Nene blinked slowly, as though attempting to digest the news, then shook her head sadly. 'That still doesn't excuse what he did here...' she mumbled. 'If you're going after him, I know where you should look next.'

Madock leaned across the bar urgently. 'He said where he was going?'

'He said that if we heard anything about the monster, we should send somebody to find him. He said he was heading for Silverbridge.'

He's heading further south, thought Madock. *If he's going to Silverbridge, that will mean he's heading towards the southern settlements. Border crossing, huh? That could make things difficult...*

'You're going to keep going after him, aren't you?' asked Nene nervously. When Madock nodded, she bit her lip as if reluctant to say anything further. The Death Cheater waited patiently. Though it was in unfortunate circumstances, this was the most open Nene had been with him since she had started blaming him for her brother's death. He couldn't help but relish the moment of peace between them after so many years of conflict.

'I want you to be careful,' mumbled Nene, unable to make eye contact with him as she picked up another class and began to clean it absently with the cloth. 'I don't want you to get hurt...'

Madock smiled and gently reached across the bar to place a gentle hand upon the glass she was cleaning, stopping the distracted motion. At first she made no further movement and remained perfectly still and quiet. Finally she sighed and allowed her eyes to meet his, and for a brief moment there was tranquility between the two of them. Madock was wiser than to think that this would allow Nene to forgive him for what had happened all those years ago, but it was a step in the right direction.

'I'm the Death Cheater, remember? Nothing can stop me,' he joked. Nene rolled her eyes sarcastically, but a smile tugged at the corners of her mouth.

'There's plenty that can stop you, old man. You just haven't met them yet.'

Madock paused and considered her words. Increasingly it seemed as though the world was doing everything it could to bring his days to an end, and with all of the unusual things that were happening he knew that he was confronting the unknown. 'You might have a point there,' he admitted. 'So when I finally do meet it… I'll be careful.'

26

The machine hummed quietly, like a great beast quietly snoring as it lay in slumber. Starr wasn't convinced that she wanted the beast to wake up at all.

It wasn't complete, as Enrick and Blake kept reminding them repeatedly, as if it wasn't plain to see. The innards of the machinery were visible in most places, with dangling wires and exposed circuit boards resembling bones and arteries of the monstrosity. Still, Starr had to admit that she was impressed with how much Enrick and her father's scientific team had achieved in such a short period of time. The beast required flesh, but the basic skeleton was in place.

'Things are running very smoothly, my lord.' Enrick was rubbing his hands together with a mixture of glee and nerves as he showed Bayne Airenguarde the progress of his project thus far. Starr had followed inquisitively, but Gray had refused to set eyes on the machine. In truth, she could understand her friend's decision; this was the same machine that had caused his people to be exiled from these lands. She wasn't convinced that Gray would have been able to restrain himself in its presence.

'How much longer till it is operational?' asked her father, struggling to suppress his marvel at the machine before them. Starr knew that her father was desperate to restore his family's position as the dominant power in Gair, but no doubt he had already realised that if the machine worked to its full potential, he could become the most powerful figure in the whole region. A machine that could not only absorb the Malice, but also convert it into energy would make a true difference to everybody's lives.

Enrick paused, though whether for a sense of drama or because he was genuinely calculating a timescale in his head, Starr could not tell. 'We have achieved a great deal in a very short time,' boasted the scientist. 'If we can maintain this level of work, the machine could well be operational within a week.'

'We *will* maintain this level of work,' said Blake confidently, standing beside the scientist to present a united front to his father. Starr had seen very little of her brother since the project began. He had been angry with her for wandering alone in the market, no doubt tipped off by Enrick or his network of spies, but as the days had gone by he had intervened in her activities less and less. In some ways it was a blessing, allowing her more freedom than she had felt in years, but it also had left her worrying about her brother. She knew he was power-hungry, but she feared that this project was becoming as much an obsession for him as it was for Enrick.

'And you're confident that this machine can transform the Malice into energy?' asked Bayne, fixing the scientist with a questioning gaze.

'Not just confident, my lord. I am *certain* that it will perform as expected. Once we have recalibrated it, it will transform the world as we know it,' replied Enrick.

'And how does it work?' asked Bayne, placing a hand against the humming machine.

Nervously, Enrick went to remove Lord Airenguarde's hand from the machine before catching himself, remembering the power the man held over his future. 'Uh, please my lord, don't concern yourself with such things and please don't touch the machine.'

Her father looked furious, but Blake quickly stepped in to calm things down. 'It's not safe yet, father. Mr Enrick was just concerned for your safety.' The scientist nodded earnestly, latching onto Blake's explanation eagerly. Bayne seemed to accept the reasoning and removed his hand from the machine.

'Will it ever be safe?' asked Starr pointedly. She had not meant to say anything, but following her failure to convince her father to abandon the project, she had become increasingly bitter about the whole affair.

Enrick smiled, though to Starr it looked more like the scientist was sneering at her. 'I can assure you, my lady, it will be perfectly safe once it is complete. You have nothing to fear.'

I highly doubt that, thought Starr, though she bit her tongue to remain silent. Her father seemed so enamoured with the project that she did not wish to irritate him by questioning every last detail.

'It seems you may well deliver on your promise after all,' mused Bayne as he watched the other scientists busily working on the machine. 'You have impressed me, Mr Enrick.'

Enrick bowed low, almost mockingly in Starr's eyes, though she knew the scientist would never have been brave enough to truly mock her father. 'Such kind words, my lord. I am merely here to serve the Airenguarde family and the interests of the people of Gair.'

'And you have not spoken a word of this to the Harbingers?' asked Bayne urgently.

Blake shook his head. 'They know nothing of this project.'

'Make sure it stays that way. I want to see the look on Glenys' face when I tell her we don't need the Shell anymore.'

Starr knew that her father had an uneasy relationship with the Harbingers, infuriated by the amount of control they held over decisions in Gair yet also reliant upon them to keep not only the city running but to maintain his wife's faint hold on life. She knew that her father would love nothing more than to take back power from the Harbingers, but she wondered how much Bayne's concern for his wife would temper his approach. Without the aid of the Harbingers, the Malice would take hold and rip his wife from this world. In some ways, Starr couldn't help but feel that this would actually be a mercy for the poor suffering woman.

Her father must also have been considering the bed-ridden woman, as he suddenly withdrew from the group. 'I need to go now, but I am very impressed Enrick. Keep up the good work.' He was already leaving the room as he said these words, calling them over his shoulder as he disappeared into the tunnel that led back to the palace.

Starr stared awkwardly at her brother and Enrick before turning to look at the machine once more. 'So how *does* it work? I thought it was designed to absorb Echoes using a Necromancer. How have you changed it?'

Enrick and Blake exchanged a look before the scientist suddenly turned and left without saying another word.

'We're missing one key piece to change the machine to absorb the Malice,' admitted Blake, ushering Starr towards the tunnel as well. Clearly he did not wish for her to be there any longer than she needed to. 'My people know where to find it and they're taking steps to bring it here as soon as possible.'

Starr attempted to glance back as her brother escorted her from the room. Enrick was busy making notes by the machine, seemingly lost in thought as he wandered around the metal beast.

No doubt thinking about the best way to wake it up, thought Starr bitterly. She hated feeling powerless, even now as her brother effectively manhandled her to the door. She shook herself free of his grasp and stared at him defiantly.

'This isn't a good idea,' she said angrily as her brother folded his arms in frustration. 'You know father isn't thinking straight at the moment. This machine isn't going to solve our problems, it's only going to make new ones.'

'It doesn't matter what father thinks, *I* think it's a good idea and that's all that counts right now.' Starr was surprised by the bluntness of her brother's words but remained silent as he leaned in threateningly towards her. 'Don't bother trying to do anything to stop it. You should just accept it. It's *going* to happen, no matter what. Besides, don't you want our family to be free of the Harbingers?'

'Of course, but…' stuttered Starr weakly. To her frustration, she discovered she could come up with no new arguments to counter the machine's construction, and instead fell silent in defeat. If her brother and father had not listened to her initial fears and arguments in the first place, it was useless recycling them now.

Blake gripped her shoulder in victory and walked her to the tunnel. 'Stay out of this Starr. There's nothing you can do.'

It was at that point, as her brother pushed her into the tunnel that she realised that there *was* something she could do. It wasn't an idea that particularly appealed to her, and she knew that it was likely to end badly for her regardless of whether the project was completed or not as a result of her action, but she was desperate. She had read about the Sheol Disaster, about the devastation it had caused, the way it had wiped out an entire settlement and led to the execution and exile of an entire race. She couldn't allow that to happen again.

* * *

The Harbinger temple loomed above her as she climbed the stone steps leading to the entrance. Her legs felt weak beneath her and she wanted nothing more than to abandon her plan, if for no other reason than to remove the churning feeling in her stomach. The consequences were weighing heavily on her mind, particularly what would happen to her and her relationship with her family. If she went through with her plan, there was no going back.

This is right. It's the only way to prevent another tragedy, the only way to protect the people of Gair, to protect your family. The thought steeled her resolve and she pressed on further up the stone steps. The Harbinger temple was lined by beautifully crafted pillars and the cool dark air inside carried the air of foreign spices and burning incense. She stepped into the temple nervously, observing the various groups of Harbingers garbed in their traditional robes walking calmly across the cool stone floor or sat in circles around fires which seemed to burn a multitude of different colours. Starr knew that in the recesses of the temple there sat a larger body of Harbingers, lost in prayer and magic creating the Shell which covered the entirety of Gair, protecting it from both the storm and the Malice. In her mind it proved that they truly cared about the future of the city. She convinced herself that they would not allow harm to come to the people of Gair anymore than she herself would have. They were aligned in their intentions, an important factor which allowed her to believe that her plan had every chance of working.

'Lady Airenguarde, what a pleasure it is to see you here!' greeted a nearby Harbinger, hurrying over to her. 'We were not expecting a visit!'

Starr paused, sensing that this was her last opportunity to abandon her plan. She glanced furtively over her shoulder back towards the entrance and the steps that would lead her back down to the streets of Gair. She could return to her old life as if nothing had ever happened. Perhaps Enrick's machine really *would* work without posing a risk to the people of Gair. If that were the case then her family would become very powerful. Furthermore, they would be responsible for removing the

Malice from the surface, for providing a new source of energy which would allow people to rebuild their lives.

Or it could be just like Sheol.

She took a deep breath and fought for control. Starr knew that this was the right choice, and though the road ahead would be difficult for her, she was acting in the best interests of her people. Her family would see that in time. At least, she hoped they would.

'Can I help you, Lady Airenguarde?' asked the Harbinger nervously. He seemed uncertain what to do, tugging apprehensively at his robe as he waited awkwardly for Starr to say anything.

Be brave.

'I need to speak to Glenys Nolwenn,' said Starr with a shaking voice. 'There's something she needs to know.'

27

Tallec was struggling. He stumbled through the streets of the Bunker, dazed by the lights, smells and heat of his new surroundings. Faces passed him in a blur without as much as a glance in his direction. Tallec had never seen so many people in one place before, and the transition from the deserted landscape of the surface to the bustling crowds below the ground was shocking. Though the Bunker was smaller than Pelera, it seemed to contain just as many people within its walls, if not more. He felt himself constantly being jostled and swept along in the crowd, uncertain as to where it was carrying him and doubtful as to whether he could free himself from the torrent.

And then there was the Raider's face, forever burned into his mind with the blood endlessly trickling from the fatal wound that Tallec's blade had inflicted. He could still clearly see the Raider's wide eyes staring at him, conflicting emotions competing for attention in the brief moments before death had wiped them all from the battlefield. But still those eyes seemed to stare at him.

The crowd around him was suffocating, controlling his reluctant progress towards an uncertain destination. Desperately, Tallec fought his way free, ignoring the disgruntled outbursts and the odd insult thrown his way as he launched himself towards the nearest building. He knew he had to get free of the wave of people, had to seek sanctuary away from the streets. Throwing himself against the rough walls of the building, he gasped for breath as the steady stream continued in front of him, seemingly oblivious that he had escaped.

Glancing up, he noticed a sign hanging above the door of the building. *It's a shop*, thought Tallec. Ultimately that was invitation enough for him to enter. He had coins to spend, albeit no intention on parting with them. But the shop offered him something he desperately needed for free: isolation, an opportunity to think without being pushed and pulled from place to place.

Quickly, he entered the shop and closed the door behind him. It was dark and dank inside the shop with very little on display upon the various shelves lining the walls. As such, it was blissfully quiet and calm within, allowing Tallec a chance to take a deep breath and focus on controlling his racing heartbeat. Eager to avoid returning to the streets for as long as possible, Tallec moved slowly around the small shop, examining each item carefully as his footsteps creaked upon the wooden floorboards.

There was very little within the shop in truth, merely a few bottles filled with liquids of varying colour and viscosity. Carefully picking one up, Tallec turned it in his hands, holding it up to the weakly flickering light upon the ceiling. The green liquid within seemed to sparkle slightly, sloshing casually around the bottle as Tallec tilted it from side to side. There was no writing upon the glass suggesting what the contents were, though Tallec felt certain that he had seen something like it before. Uncorking the bottle, he sniffed the contents curiously and immediately reeled back in disgust.

'Quite potent, isn't it?'

Tallec turned, almost dropping the bottle in surprise. He hadn't noticed the shopkeeper emerge from some hidden back room, but the man was now stood watching him with a curious smile upon his face. He was short and balding, with thick glasses sliding halfway down his nose as he peered over the top of them. Dressed in simple dark clothing, Tallec couldn't help but wonder just how long the man had been watching him.

'It's... I didn't...' stuttered Tallec, uncertain as to how to respond. He was saved the trouble as the shopkeeper approached and gently removed the bottle from the young Dead Man's hands.

'This is sanctaint,' explained the shopkeeper softly, turning the bottle gently as he replaced the cork in the glass neck. 'Pungent, but effective. You pour it over a wound which has been subjected to Malice poisoning, and it helps to fight the disease. It stings and smells worse than anything else I can name, but it's a small price to pay I'd say.' He sighed and replaced the bottle on the shelf. 'It can't cure it, obviously, but it certainly gives you a chance to get your affairs in order. We're getting closer to a cure every day, but for now this is the best we can offer.'

'"We"?' asked Tallec dumbly, hypnotised by the shopkeeper's gentle tone.

The shopkeeper smiled patiently. 'Where are my manners? My name is Osane. I am a Harbinger.'

That's where I recognise it from, realised Tallec suddenly. He had met several Harbingers during his travels through the Peleran tunnels, though he knew the majority were based further south in Gair. Tallec had heard many stories about what the Harbingers were capable of, had heard of the skills and knowledge they possessed to help combat the Malice. One in particular had spoken to him at length in Pelera, showing him some of his resources, one of which had been just like the liquid in the bottle.

'I assume you have heard of the Harbingers?' asked Osane, genuinely interested in the young man's response.

Unwilling to appear naïve, Tallec nodded. Maybe the shopkeeper did not believe him, or perhaps he simply wanted to talk about his beliefs. Whatever the reason, Osane began to speak as though repeating a script he had rehearsed endlessly. 'We wait for the angels to free us from the Dark Days, but in the meantime we use the knowledge they imparted upon us to fight for the light. The Harbingers of Light, the servants of the angels.'

'This is all Harbinger resources?' asked Tallec, glancing around at the other bottles on the shelves.

'Oh yes,' replied Osane positively, indicating with his hand around the shelves as he started to name the other colourful liquids. 'There's biotempra, good for drinking before travelling across the surface because it builds your natural immunity to the Malice. And that one is celestros, a very powerful angelic blessing which you can pour on any exposed skin. It creates a tiny barrier that protects the flesh from the Malice for a short time.' He paused and shook his head sadly. 'We would normally have more to offer, but I'm afraid the Dead Man I sent on a supply run to Gair has not returned. I fear some ill fate may have befallen him.'

Tallec swallowed hard as he considered his next words carefully. *Time to prove that I really am a Dead Man.*

'I can collect the supplies for you,' Tallec said, hoping the nerves in his voice were not as evident to the shopkeeper as they were to his own ears.

Osane looked at him carefully, clearly measuring the young man's potential. Tallec straightened himself, attempting to exude confidence. He remembered something that Edwin had told him when he'd first met him in Pelera. *It's all about confidence. Even if you don't feel it, fake it.* Tallec felt a familiar sense of sadness as he remembered the events in Tirneth which had taken Edwin's life, but forced them to the back of his mind. Right now, confidence was key.

'You don't seem like any Dead Man I've seen before,' the shopkeeper commented reluctantly.

'I'm new, but I'm good,' promised Tallec, hoping that his confidence would one day be based on experience and not merely a mask he was wearing to impress his potential client. 'Besides, it looks to me like you need these supplies urgently.'

This argument seemed to sway Osane as his eyes once more sadly swept across the empty shelves of his shop. 'I can't offer you very much for this deal, I'm afraid.'

Tallec shook his head. He had always known that his first few jobs were likely to be low paid given his lack of experience. Instead, this was simply a chance to prove that he had made the right choice to become a Dead Man. He needed to know if he could make it.

In his head, he now heard the Death Cheater's words. *The first step is always the most important one. Never take that first step lightly.* He had told the old man he was ready when he took those first steps from Tirneth. Now it was time to take the first steps on a brand new leg of his journey.

'I'll take whatever you can offer me,' admitted Tallec.

The shopkeeper smiled, peering at Tallec carefully over the top of his glasses. 'A Dead Man who doesn't try to negotiate? I like you already...' He turned and moved into the backroom without saying another word, leaving Tallec standing awkwardly in the quiet, dimly lit shop. The young Dead Man was beginning to wonder whether perhaps he had been shunned and rejected for the job when Osane finally returned, clutching something in his hand.

'I can't offer you any coin for collecting the supplies, but you have been honest and open with me. I respect that, so I would like to offer you something else in exchange for completing the job.' Opening his hand, he revealed a small wooden carving on a twine necklace. 'This is a Harbinger charm. It may not look like much, but it will combat the effects of the Malice as long as you wear it around your neck.'

Tallec accepted the object gratefully. In truth, he had hoped for coin, marking this as his first paid job as a Dead Man, but he sensed from the manner in which the shopkeeper ceremoniously passed the charm to him that it was quite valuable.

'Wouldn't you be better off selling this?' asked Tallec awkwardly. He didn't wish to appear ungrateful, but neither did he wish to appear greedy to his new client.

Osane smiled. 'We both win from this deal. You are more likely to survive to return with my supplies this way. Besides, it will help you when you reach the Harbinger temple in Gair. They will take good care of you if you're wearing that charm.'

Nodding, Tallec placed the charm around his neck. He offered his hand to the shopkeeper to confirm the deal was in place, and smiled confidently when the man shook it firmly.

'Tell me one thing before you leave young man,' said Osane kindly. 'Why do you want to be a Dead Man?'

Tallec paused, slightly startled by the personal question. He had assumed their business was done having agreed the deal, but it seemed instead that the shopkeeper was still measuring his worth. But far more unsettling than that was the fact that Tallec did not immediately know how to answer the question. It was one that had been circling in his mind ever since he had started on this path, and while he had known that he believed he was meant to become a Dead Man, he had never quite grasped the elusive answer as to why. Boredom had certainly played its role, as had his thirst for adventure. But there were easier and safer ways to satisfy both of those needs. Even the legendary Madock Leocadia, the Death Cheater himself, had criticised his decision to become a Dead Man.

Why do I want to be a Dead Man?

'I don't know,' admitted Tallec, 'But I'll tell you when I get back with your supplies.'

The shopkeeper smiled. 'I hope you find the answer.'

Tallec nodded as he approached the door, taking a deep breath as he grasped the handle.

Me too.

'Wait, there is one more thing!' called Osane, stopping Tallec in his tracks. As the Dead Man turned, the shop keeper beamed at him. 'If you're after coin, I know somebody in Gair who needs something delivering.'

Tallec considered the offer. It made sense to accept it, especially as he would be heading to Gair to collect the supplies from the Harbinger temple. That and the promise of financial reward for the delivery made it impossible to turn down the offer.

The shopkeeper smiled as Tallec turned back to hear more details. 'There is just one small issue. There's another Dead Man involved. Luckily, I know where you can find him…'

28

I should have known it wouldn't be simple…

Madock allowed this thought to circle repeatedly in his mind as he surveyed the situation. It seemed ironic that if he had left just a few minutes earlier, he could have avoided this entire conflict. He could easily have been on his way to finding Haswell in Silverbridge.

Instead, here he was with a gun pointed at him.

You should have just walked away old man, he told himself as he and Kye formed a barrier ahead of Reissa. He still wasn't sure why he had agreed to play along with her desperate plan. She held nothing but contempt for him, that much was clear. Yet the pleading look in her eyes had been unlike anything he had seen from the usually brash, outspoken woman he had come to know over the last few days. Whoever the man was who now had his weapon trained on the Death Cheater, Reissa was clearly terrified of him.

'I'm taking her back,' repeated Madock loudly, keeping his hands in the air. He knew it would have been too risky to reach for his own weapon; his wits and experience were his only defence now.

The man with the weapon trained on him scowled. 'Larson never said he was sending anybody else after her…' he growled dubiously.

'He didn't tell me either,' bluffed Madock, 'but I got her first so I'm finishing the job.'

The man gestured towards Kye. 'And the big fella there is alright with that? He's just going to let you take her? I don't think so…'

Madock glanced towards Kye. The huge Raider had given no indication of his consent to go along with Reissa's plan, but Madock assumed that based on previous experience that Kye would do anything necessary to protect his companion.

'It's true, Theron,' shouted Reissa shakily. 'This guy caught me. He caught us both.'

The man Reissa had just addressed as Theron laughed. 'Do you think I'm a fool? That beast there has broken more than one of my bones defending you all these years, and now you expect me to believe that one old man captured you both?'

'He's the Death Cheater,' said Kye, his serious tone finally suggesting his commitment to playing along with the plan.

Theron waivered. 'The Death Cheater?' He paused as he scanned Madock carefully. 'Well, you certainly look the part... But that doesn't change the fact that the girl is coming back with *me*. I've been chasing her for years now. There's no way I'm going to let you swoop in and take my prize, even if you *are* the Death Cheater. Besides, they don't exactly *look* captured. They aren't even restrained.'

'Didn't need to,' replied Madock simply.

A moment of silence washed over the scene. Madock was glad that they were away from the crowds on the very edge of the Bunker. Though the settlement was known for its lawlessness, their seclusion at least reduced the risk of more people becoming embroiled in the standoff.

Again the voice repeated in his mind. *You should have just walked away.* Madock had been stood near the Silver Bullet, weighing up his ability to reach Silverbridge before nightfall when the Raiders had rushed towards him. They must have known that Theron was in hot pursuit, though whether they had come in this direction seeking Madock or simply because they had been trying to flee the settlement Madock was uncertain. Reissa had pleaded with him to pretend he had captured her. It hadn't made sense at the time. Now things were starting to become clearer.

'Well, you may have got her first,' said Theron, finally breaking the silence, 'but it seems to me that you're at a distinct disadvantage, Death Cheater.'

Madock knew that he was right. Theron still had his gun trained on him, and though Madock knew from experience that he was quick on the draw, he doubted he could get a shot off before the man threatening him pulled the trigger.

But before he was forced to consider his options in too much depth, something changed the dynamic of the situation. Spotting the approaching figure over Theron's shoulder, Madock knew that the balance had swung back in his favour. All he had to do was keep Theron distracted.

'Larson won't be impressed,' said Madock, keeping himself tense and focused.

'I couldn't care less what Larson thinks!' shouted Theron angrily. 'All I care about is his money. I've been hunting this half-breed bitch too long to just give up now.' He paused and composed himself. 'Luckily for you, I'm in a good mood. If you hand over the girl now, I'll allow you both to leave with your lives.'

Madock blinked at Theron's words. *Half-breed?* He put the thought to the back of his mind. The figure approaching silently behind Theron was close now. *Just a little longer*.

'I have a counter-proposal,' offered Madock calmly. 'We take them in together. The big guy can be a handful and you'll need help to get them both to Larson.'

For a second, Theron seemed to consider the offer before shaking his head fiercely. 'Not a chance! That reward is mine! I'll be fine on my own. After all, you were going to do it on your own.'

It was time. 'Who says I'm on my own?' asked Madock calmly.

Tallec's sword was at Theron's neck in a flash. 'I suggest you drop the weapon now,' whispered the young

Dead Man fiercely. Theron looked startled, but equally frustrated to have allowed himself to drop his guard. Reluctantly, he lowered his gun and allowed it to drop to the floor. Breathing a sigh of relief, Madock quickly moved forward and picked up the weapon, retraining it on its original owner.

'Very clever, Death Cheater,' sighed Theron as Tallec removed the blade and moved alongside Madock, clearly confident that the experienced Dead Man now had the situation under control. 'I have to admit, I underestimated you. But I guess you don't survive for as long as you have without learning a trick or two.'

'We're leaving now,' stated Madock coldly. 'If you follow us, I *will* kill you.'

Theron laughed and shrugged his shoulders. 'You *know* I'm going to follow you.'

Madock was all too aware of this, but it was something that would have to be dealt with at a later date. Right now it was important that they all leave the Bunker together. There would be time to deal with the fallout of everything that had happened here later.

Together they carefully backed away from Theron, who watched them every step of the way until they turned the corner and rejoined the bustling streets of the Bunker.

'He's going to come after me,' said Reissa nervously as they hurried towards the lift up to the Citadel.

Madock nodded. 'Eventually, but not right now. He's unarmed and he'll know you're on the lookout for him. You need to get as much distance between you and him as you can.' He turned to look at Tallec, the young Dead Man walking quickly alongside him. 'Thank you for helping.'

Tallec nodded in response, but said nothing.

He seems different, thought Madock. *He's carrying himself more confidently. Maybe he'll survive this world after all.*

'I think we all deserve to know what's going on,' said Madock, shooting a look at Reissa.

The female Raider cringed. 'I'll tell you everything, I swear. But right now I just want to get away from here.'

Together they arrived at the lift and squeezed into the small metal confines. Pulling the gate closed across the front, they watched the Bunker disappear beneath their feet as the lift ascended into the darkness. As they climbed towards the surface, Madock focused on slowing his breathing and keeping his head clear. There seemed to be a lot of different events happening at once, and it was important that he sought clarity before he attempted to deal with each of them. His hopes of pursuing Haswell alone had all but vanished, leaving him with nothing but the chaos these strangers had brought into his life.

As the lift clicked into position at the top of its ascent, Madock opened the gate and led the group out into the Citadel. It was thankfully deserted save for a few guards who stood on patrol by the main doors to the building and by the entrance to the lift. Gesturing for the group to follow him, Madock made his way over to a quiet corner of the Citadel and placed himself gently down upon an old wooden pew. The others followed his example and sat in silence.

'What are we doing, meditating?' asked Reissa impatiently, the anxiety clear in her voice. 'We need to get out of here.'

'"We"? There is no we...' stated Madock coldly. His patience for the Raiders was wearing thin, and as he reflected upon all of the problems they had brought into his life he realised that he still had the choice to simply walk away. After he had just saved their lives, he felt confident that he could turn his back on them with their agreement annulled. But he deserved to know the truth before they parted ways. 'You're not going anywhere until we know what's going on,' stated Madock calmly. Reissa looked up at Kye pleadingly.

'Tell them,' said Kye firmly.

Silently, Reissa stared at her partner, seemingly willing him to change his mind. When it became clear that nobody was going to move until she had explained the situation, she sighed.

'My mother… she was a Necromancer.'

Madock's eyes widened at the revelation, but he said nothing. He had of course known that prior to the exile of the Necromancers that some had strayed from their tribes to marry into the general population. But Madock had to admit that he had not heard of many producing offspring.

'Wait, you're a Necromancer?' asked Tallec in confusion. 'But where's your Echo?'

'I'm not a Necromancer,' spat Reissa viciously. 'I just… I guess because my mother was one, that's enough for some people to come after me.'

I guess that explains why Theron called her a half-breed, thought Madock. 'Theron mentioned a man named Larson,' added Madock calmly. 'He's the one who wants you. Do you know who he is?'

Reissa shrugged and shook her head. It was clear that even if she did know who Larson was, she was not about to admit that to the rest of the group.

'He's been hunting me for years now, but he caught us by surprise here,' she continued, rubbing her arm self-consciously. 'He's not going to give up until he gets me. We've been lucky so far, had to fight our way out of a few situations, but mostly we just run…'

'He clearly doesn't want to kill you,' said Madock, thinking back on their encounter. 'Which must mean that this Larson person wants you alive for some reason.'

Reissa stood up and kicked out angrily at the bench she was sat upon. 'I don't know what he wants, but I am *not* going to let him get me.'

Madock stood and placed his mask over his face. He had heard enough. 'Best of luck to you,' he said calmly as he turned and started to walk away from the group.

Reissa watched him carefully as Madock moved towards the door of the Citadel. 'You can't just leave! You owe us...' she started before trailing off as she realised that her words were no longer true.

Keeping his pace steady, Madock was surprised to feel a hand upon his arm. He expected it to be either Reissa or Kye, but as he turned he was surprised to find that it was Tallec that held a firm grip on his sleeve.

'We should stick together,' said the young Dead Man firmly.

Madock freed himself from Tallec's grasp. 'We have no further business together. I don't owe any of you anything.' He was tired of being forced to work with others. Since the Sheol Disaster, he had preferred to work alone. Everything had started going wrong since he had agreed to work with Willow. He wouldn't keep repeating the same mistake.

He continued marching towards the Citadel doors when Tallec's hand once more halted his progress.

'Are you heading south?' asked Tallec earnestly. 'I only ask because I need to get to Gair.'

Madock sighed, placing his hands on his hips. 'You've got to learn to survive on your own. I got you here, that's as much as I promised.'

'You don't understand,' whispered Tallec, glancing over his shoulder to make sure that the Raiders were out of ear shot. 'I'm taking Reissa to Larson. I know where to find him.'

It took Madock a moment to comprehend the young Dead Man's plan. *He wants to collect the bounty on Reissa. The boy's bolder than I gave him credit for.*

'He's based in Gair,' explained Tallec in a hushed voice. 'If you help me get her there, I'll split the reward with you. I've no idea about getting across the border into the southern settlements, but you…' He trailed off, possibly uncertain as to whether he had said too much. Madock realised that if he were to turn around and tell the Raiders of Tallec's plan, the young man would not only lose out on the reward but possibly his life.

But there was something intriguing about the offer. As long as the Raiders remained unaware of their intentions, they would provide safety in numbers. With the deal between them now all but non-existent, the power would firmly be with him. But could he really turn the woman over to the stranger who had been hunting her without knowing the reason behind his interest in her?

This isn't your problem, he reminded himself. *You've got to find Haswell. This is just another complication you don't need.*

Sighing, Madock turned back towards the Raiders. 'I'm heading for Silverbridge. I think that's where I'll find Haswell. Be careful who you trust…'

Casting once last glance at Tallec, who stared back at him with a frustrated expression on his face, Madock opened the Citadel doors and walked back into the storm alone.

29

Tallec watched the Death Cheater disappear through the doors of the Citadel, leaving him alone with the Raiders. He had been convinced that the old man would go along with his plan, and his parting words warning the Raiders to be careful about who they trusted had left him feeling uneasy.

'We're better off without him anyway,' muttered Reissa angrily. 'Come on Kye, we need to get moving.' The two Raiders quickly began organising themselves, leaving Tallec desperately seeking a way to regain control of the situation.

It's not the end of the world if they leave, he reminded himself. *You still have the job of collecting the Harbinger supplies.* But he knew deep down there was another fundamental reason to make sure that his plan to deliver Reissa to Larson went ahead. Without the experience of the Death Cheater, he wasn't convinced that he could make the journey to Gair safely, especially with the added complication of crossing the border. If he could convince the Raiders to travel with him to Gair, he could solve all of his problems.

The Raiders had already begun to move towards the Citadel doors without so much as a parting word to him when the idea occurred to him. It was risky, but right now it seemed his best chance of getting them on his side.

'Wait!' he called out to the pair, jogging over to them.

Reissa turned and impatiently observed the Dead Man. 'Babysitting time is over.'

'There's something I need to tell you,' began Tallec, ignoring the woman's insult. 'I know where this Larson person is.'

Both Raiders instantly froze and gave Tallec their undivided attention.

Got them, thought Tallec confidently. *I just need to phrase this carefully.*

'He's based in Gair. I know exactly where to find him.'

Reissa glanced towards Kye. 'We'd better turn back north then.'

'I've got a better idea,' said Tallec. He knew that what he was about to suggest would initially be dismissed by the Raiders, but if he could convince them that it was actually the safer option, there was a good chance that they would agree to travel with him. 'Let's travel together to Gair.'

The female Raider laughed bitterly. 'You want us to go *towards* the guy who's trying to capture me?'

Tallec nodded. 'It's the last thing he'll be expecting. You don't have to keep running from Theron forever because you can take care of the source of your problem. No more Larson means no more reward, which means no more being hunted.'

Reissa glanced nervously at Kye as she considered the merits of the young Dead Man's plan. 'We haven't crossed the border into the southern settlements for years…' she said, watching her partner carefully. 'Maybe Theron won't expect us to go that way.'

'Look, one of two things will happen,' started Tallec, sensing that he had to push while he had the advantage. 'Theron thinks we're taking you in to Larson, which means he'll head south towards Gair, but if we get to Larson first then he'll have no reason to hunt you anymore. On the other hand, he might think that we *know* he'll head south, so he might turn north instead. If that happens, then our best bet is to head south anyway. Then there's always the chance that *he'll* know that *we* know that heading south is the best option…'

'I think you might be overthinking this,' commented Reissa dryly.

Tallec allowed himself to look embarrassed. It was all part of his plan. 'My point is, heading south is not only our best option, it's the sensible option.'

'Are you sure you want to do this?' asked Kye gently, placing a protective hand upon her shoulder. Reissa paused reflectively, before nodding with renewed determination. Kye looked towards Tallec. 'What's your plan once we get there? We just walk in and kill the guy?'

Shaking his head, Tallec braced himself for the riskiest part of his proposal. 'We carry on with the charade we started with Theron. I act like I'm bringing you two in for the bounty. I'll pretend to tie your arms and disarm you, but you'll be fully prepared. I'll have your weapons with me. The moment he drops his guard, we take him out.' He forced himself to remain calm. If the Raiders were to figure out Tallec's true intentions, they would walk. Or kill him where he stood.

As Kye silently contemplated the plan, Tallec made a final push. 'We can end this. No more running.'

The words seemed to hit their mark and sway the giant Raider. Kye nodded and folded his arms firmly. 'We're coming with you. We might even catch Madock if we leave now.'

Tallec froze. He had managed to convince the Raiders to travel with him to Gair, but Madock knew his true intentions. If they were to join up with the Death Cheater again, there would be the constant risk of the old man revealing Tallec's motive. He knew he had to keep them in the Citadel long enough to allow Madock to gain a good lead on them.

'I don't think we should go chasing after him,' said Tallec slowly, attempting to give his mind an opportunity to formulate an excuse. 'He didn't exactly want our company.'

To his relief, Reissa also seemed reluctant to chase after Madock. 'The kid's right, Kye,' she said to her partner, 'Besides, he's brought us nothing but problems. If the old fool wants to go off on his own and get himself killed chasing after some psychotic murderer, who are we to stop him?'

Kye seemed reluctant to abandon his desire to pursue Madock, but Reissa's firm words and stubbornness was enough to sway him. 'We can't stay here though,' he pointed out. Tallec knew that the giant Raider was right; Theron would no doubt be organising himself right now in the settlement below, getting ready to pursue his target. The Dead Man had known that the threat posed by Theron was an extra complication to his plan, but he felt that he had already demonstrated his ability to outwit his opponent.

That was with the Death Cheater's help. Shaking the thought from his head, he turned towards the giant Raider. 'What if we stayed here for the night?' he offered hopefully.

'You cannot be that stupid…' muttered Reissa.

'Wait, hear me out,' pleaded Tallec, sensing that he was losing control of the situation. 'Theron's going to assume that you've fled. That would be the sensible thing to do. We need to do the unpredictable thing…'

'You mean the stupid thing,' countered Reissa.

Tallec continued, unperturbed. 'The unpredictable thing, which is to stay here in the Bunker. We can lay low, wait till tomorrow and then head to Silverbridge without having to worry about Theron or Madock.'

Reissa still seemed unconvinced. The decision was made as Kye turned and began moving towards the Citadel doors again.

'Hey! Where are you going?' shouted Reissa, her voice echoing around the Citadel.

'We're leaving now,' replied Kye without breaking his stride. 'It's too dangerous to stay here.'

Reissa opened her mouth as if to argue, but then shrugged and turned to Tallec. 'He's right. I'd rather deal with Madock than Theron.'

Frowning, Tallec watched her rush over to her partner as they moved towards the exit. He was frustrated at how close he had come to getting his way, only to see it torn away by the stubbornness of the Raiders. *You're still getting your way though,* he reminded himself, *you're still travelling with them to Gair. You'll just have to do everything you can to avoid bumping into Madock.*

Reluctantly shouldering his bag, Tallec marched after the Raiders.

* * *

With every step that Tallec took through the Malice-covered snow, the Dead Man was convinced that they would spot Madock on the horizon. Every blur he spotted through the falling snow seemed to form the shape of the Death Cheater, the man who had once helped him take his first steps but now held the potential to reveal his dark secret. In his mind, Madock posed a bigger threat to him than the demons at that particular point. The thought terrified him.

Several times he had questioned whether he was doing the right thing. He had no love or respect for the Raiders, and the promise of financial reward would cement his place as an established Dead Man. Yet Madock had rejected the offer of becoming involved in the task. Again and again, Tallec had questioned the old man's reasoning behind this. Perhaps he had secretly grown fond of the Raiders, or maybe he simply respected them enough not to betray them. But Madock's reluctance to help Tallec deliver Reissa to Gair troubled him.

Kye and Reissa were leading the way, for which Tallec was silently thankful. He had remembered Madock's advice to stick to the roads as much as possible, but his sense of direction was still questionable. At least by following the Raiders, Tallec knew that they would definitely reach Silverbridge. He also wasn't sure he could tolerate the mocking he would receive from Reissa if he led them in the wrong direction.

He was torn from his thoughts by the sound of shouting a short distance behind him. The words were muffled by the howling wind which whipped around them, but the tone was clearly distressed. The Raiders ahead of him had also stopped, apparently after hearing the shout themselves. As a trio, they turned and scanned their surroundings. Tallec drew his weapon, knowing that whatever the cause of the shout, it was likely to mean that danger was nearby.

Again, the shout emerged through the wind, though this time the direction was clearer. They all turned towards the source and spotted the figure lunging towards them through the snow. His eyes were wide and desperate, his body in a terrible condition. Tallec squinted through the snow as the figure moved closer to them at high speed. He kept throwing concerned glances over his shoulder, as if watching for some pursuing threat, though Tallec could see nobody else behind the terrified man.

'That's close enough!' shouted Tallec as the man approached, but he either did not hear the instruction or chose to ignore it as he rushed up to the group. Instead he threw his arms around the young Dead Man in a tight embrace.

'Thank the angels I found somebody! You've got to help me! They're coming to get me!' As the man turned to stare wild-eyed in the direction he had come from, Tallec wriggled free awkwardly from the man's arms. He looked startled at the rejection and rushed forward once more with open arms. Tallec braced himself, but before he was forced into action Kye stepped forward and knocked the frantic man back effortlessly. The stranger fell roughly into the snow, but quickly stumbled to his feet and turned to stare back in the direction he had just come from.

'They're coming, they're coming... You've got to help me, please...' he rambled, clearly more worried about the threat that lay hidden behind him than the armed trio. 'They're coming, they're coming...'

Tallec continued to gaze through the snow, but he could see no further figures. Before he could say anything, Kye was already upon the stranger, knocking him back into the snow and placing his heavy foot upon his chest to pin him down.

'No, please, you've got to help me!' the man begged desperately. 'They're coming, you need to help me!'

Tallec looked at Kye questioningly. The man seemed to be in need of help, yet the Raider was treating the poor dishevelled man as though *he* were the danger.

'Malice poisoning,' explained Kye without taking his eyes off the man below his foot.

Shuddering at the words, Tallec turned his attention from the invisible threat the man had fled to the man himself. It didn't take long to spot the signs of Malice poisoning, leaving Tallec feeling ashamed that he hadn't spotted them earlier. There was a deep wound in the man's arm, his skin exposed to the elements where the sleeve of his jacket had clearly been ripped off. Dried blood clung to the man's arm, but the real issue was the dark black veins which were spreading from the wound. They spread all the way up to his shoulder and down his arm, leaving Tallec in no doubt that they had covered far more of his body beneath the remnants of his jacket.

Malice poisoning also explained the man's terror at the invisible threat he seemed desperate to escape. Tallec had heard tales from Storm Runners he had met in the Peleran tunnels about the effects of Malice once it entered the bloodstream. One of the main symptoms they had all talked about was the madness that the victims suffered. They would hallucinate, imagine both terrors and wonders as their grip on reality slowly diminished. Tallec was almost glad that he could not see what the man's Malice poisoned mind had created; whatever it was, it was terrifying him.

'What do we do?' asked Tallec weakly, unable to tear his eyes away from the writhing man beneath Kye's boot. 'Can we help him?'

'There's only one thing we can do,' replied Kye. Tallec instantly knew what the Raider meant, though the realisation made his stomach churn. He waited patiently for Kye to end the poor wretch's life, but the Raider remained still. 'You need to do it.'

Tallec stared at Kye desperately. 'Why me?'

'You need to learn,' stated Kye plainly.

You can do this, Tallec tried to convince himself, but even as he attempted to believe that, he could already see the face of the Raider he had killed in the hotel floating into his vision once more. He could still see the blood dripping across his face and into his dead eyes which stared endlessly without seeing anything.

Stepping forward, Tallec placed the tip of his blade against the man's temple. The man seemed oblivious to this gesture, instead desperately focused on trying to turn his head back towards the invisible threat. He continued to ramble helplessly that the danger was almost upon them.

You've got to do this now, Tallec told himself. He steeled himself, tightening his grip on his blade and taking a deep breath. Placing the weapon back onto the man's wriggling temple, he moved to push the blade down into the brain. It would be quick and merciful. He braced himself.

His hands wouldn't obey. He stood there for what seemed like a lifetime, willing his hands to push the blade into the man's skull. Though he knew that it would be a greater kindness to end the man's suffering, the memory of the events in the hotel room continued to haunt him, holding his hands at bay.

Finally he admitted defeat, turning away from the man in disgust and lowering his head. He could feel Kye's eyes burning into him, but he could not bring himself to meet the stare.

'Pathetic,' muttered Reissa.

Tallec kept his eyes on the snow beneath his feet. In the silence that followed, the crunch of the man's neck breaking under Kye's boot was alarmingly loud. He heard the sound of footsteps moving away, but was startled to feel a heavy hand upon his shoulder. Looking up, he saw Kye looking down at him with a mixture of pity and frustration, but there was a kindness to his voice as he spoke.

'You need to learn.'

Without saying another word, he turned and walked after Reissa. Tallec glanced down at the dead man lying in the snow, before sheathing his weapon and moving quickly to follow the Raiders.

I need to learn...

30

Madock was all too aware that Theron would be in hot pursuit of the Raiders as soon as he had rearmed himself, and weapons were readily available and easily affordable in the Bunker. No doubt Kye and Reissa would have left the settlement by now, though whether they were travelling with Tallec was uncertain. If the young Dead Man had convinced them to follow him to Gair, that meant they would be following him. There was a strong possibility that Theron would head in a different direction, which at least would buy them some time. More importantly it would reduce the likelihood of Madock having to cross paths with Theron again. The Death Cheater made a point of avoiding repeated contact with people who had tried to kill him.

They aren't your concern anymore, he reminded himself as he drove himself onwards through the snow, the Malice swirling around his ankles. *Just focus on getting to Silverbridge.*

The idea of the border crossing worried him. He had moved across the border a handful of times in the past, but largely he had kept himself to the northern settlements. His experiences in the south had been mixed, though he had to admit he longed to see the Shell around the city of Gair once more. He could still remember the sense of awe he had experienced the first time he had seen it, the way it had seemed to shimmer as it cocooned the entire city, protecting so much life within it.

Of course, there was always the possibility that he might find Haswell in Silverbridge, saving him the problem of making the border crossing at all. He would deal with that situation if it happened, but it couldn't hurt to hope for the best possible outcome. After all, his pursuit of Haswell had been far from positive thus far. He felt he deserved a little luck.

He decided to focus on the positives. For the first time in days he was finally working alone again, a fact which brought him much pleasure. He had always preferred to work alone, untethered by concern or wariness for a companion. Dead Men traditionally worked in small groups and often in partnerships, but over time Madock had seen more than his fair share of companions fall to different fates: the storm, the Malice, the demons, even abstract causes such as greed and laziness. If you switched off for a moment on the surface, it could be enough to rob you of your possessions and your life. Madock knew how to take care of himself; others simply proved to be distractions, reducing his own odds of survival. Solitude worked better for him.

Through the snow, Madock could see the Gairen Mountains rising up on either side of him, providing a natural boundary between the northern and southern settlements. They were majestic and daunting in equal measure, disappearing into the storm clouds as though spearing them from the earth below. Whilst it was possible to traverse their peaks, there were few who were brave enough to tackle the mountains, and fewer still who had survived to share the tales of their adventure.

With the mountain path proving so dangerous, the only safe way to travel across the border between the northern and southern settlements was Silverbridge. The bridge had been built before the Dark Days, a steel structure which traversed a mighty chasm in a rare gap between the rising mountains. A small settlement had established itself on either end of the bridge, buried into the ground having constructed high impenetrable walls to prevent travellers from using the bridge without passing through the underground settlement and paying a toll.

Thus Silverbridge had managed to survive, remaining neutral without the support of either Gair or Pelera.

Border crossing had never proven itself to be an easy activity in Madock's experience. The residents of Silverbridge who guarded the bridge were known for their inquisitive nature and inherent greed. They could adjust the price of using the bridge based solely upon your appearance, your background or your attitude. However, there was little choice but to pay the price. Silverbridge had been perfectly placed to gain the monopoly on border crossing. Few people were stubborn or foolhardy enough to choose crossing the Gairen Mountains on foot over a financial penalty.

As Madock closed in on Silverbridge, he could see the wall which had been constructed by the residents of the settlement, preventing him from progressing any further towards the bridge. His only choice was to descend into the settlement and pay for the privilege of using the bridge. However, the matter of payment was something that was playing on his mind. Aside from the glass which he still carried securely in his pocket, he had nothing of real value to trade for access to the bridge. He hoped that perhaps a deal could be struck, but he knew from experience that the residents of Silverbridge were avaricious. He would not pass cheaply.

The entrance to Silverbridge was the remains of an ancient mine lift, housed within an old warehouse, a remnant of the days when Silverbridge had originally been a coal mine before being expanded into the settlement which now existed below the surface. Standing guard at the doorway to the lift were two Silverbridge residents who eyed Madock suspiciously as he approached.

'What business do you have in Silverbridge?' one asked sharply as the Death Cheater paused in front of the lift.

'Crossing to the southern settlements,' explained Madock patiently.

'Where in the south are you heading?' asked the guard, folding his arms in a grand gesture of impatience.

Madock sighed inwardly and bit his tongue. He had experienced this conversation several times in the past and knew from experience that the guards by the lift were likely to be officious in their questioning, when in truth all they could do was allow or deny him access to the lift. However, Madock knew how to play this game. *Answer their questions as far as you need to, show you're not a threat, and they'll let you into the settlement. They can't decide if you cross the bridge or not anyway.*

'Dead Man business,' said Madock vaguely, hoping that that would bring the discussion to an end.

'Dead Man eh? You wouldn't happen to be the Death Cheater would you?' asked the other guard, his eyes growing slightly wider as he eyed up Madock's Malice Gear.

Madock nodded impatiently, frustrated at the delay. There was still a chance that Haswell was in the settlement below, but the longer he spent conversing with the guards the more likely it was that the demon hunter would have crossed the bridge.

'You know there's an extra cost for using Malice Gear on the bridge,' said one of the guards, showing no respect for Madock's status and experience.

'I'm sure there is,' replied Madock bitterly, simply wishing for the conversation to come to an end.

The guard shrugged innocently. 'It's only fair. We charged the other guy who came by wearing Malice Gear.'

The other guy? Madock was immediately alert. 'Was it Haswell Broxhart?'

The guards seemed startled by Madock's sudden intensity, but were determined to maintain their air of control as they scratched their heads and conversed casually with each other.

'Can't say for certain,' started one of the guards. 'He never took his mask off, but it was Malice Gear alright. Plus it had the Peleran crest on it. Kilma here thought it was you, but, well, here you are.' He turned and addressed his partner in a scolding tone. 'I told you it wasn't the Death Cheater Kilma. That guy was far more... youthful.' He paused as he realised that Madock was standing listening to the entire exchange. 'No offence or anything, but you *are* very old, and I told Kilma...'

'I need to get down into Silverbridge immediately,' demanded Madock, maintaining control of his voice in spite of his frustration.

The guards exchanged a further glance, clearly sensing that they might have angered the experienced Dead Man. Without a further word, they stepped aside and opened the gate to the lift. Madock quickly moved inside and as the guard pressed a button on a control panel, the lift began to descend into the darkness.

It was a short journey, the lift picking up quite a deal of speed before slowing suddenly as it reached its destination. The air was damp and stale in spite of the best efforts of the ventilation shafts which lined the walls of the settlement. Electrical lights buzzed all around him, casting light across the scattered buildings and the various people he could see drifting around the streets of Silverbridge. At the far end on the opposite side of the settlement, Madock could already spot the tunnel which would lead back up to the surface and the bridge which connected the north and the south. Blocking anybody from progressing down this tunnel freely were several booths surrounded by further walls, crumbling into disrepair but sturdy enough to prevent trespassers.

Considering how much they must be making from charging for the crossing, they don't seem to be spending a great deal of it. Madock knew that the only thing more famous than the greed of the residents of Silverbridge was their thriftiness. They had a reputation for hoarding their wealth, though why they should choose to do so Madock could never understand. When you lived as a Dead Man, coin was important but only as a means to an end; it could be spent on new equipment, a warm bed to recover in, food and drink, even support from other Dead Men or locals. Coin was only useful when you spent it.

Even as he thought about this, his fingers wrapped themselves around the glass in his pocket. He realised with a degree of surprise and self-loathing that perhaps he could relate to the residents of Silverbridge after all. He had not been willing to part with the glass and those feelings remained strong even now. *It's special*, he reminded himself, attempting to reduce his guilt. *It may prove useful in the future.*

As he descended into the settlement, Madock recognised travellers from all walks of life and backgrounds. There were Dead Men, some with familiar faces but none with names that he could place from his memory. *Most of the Dead Men you know are already dead*, he reminded himself.

Given the settlements proximity to Gair, Madock was not surprised to see several Harbingers walking around in their typical garb, as well as a large number of demon hunters with their shaved heads. Merchants moved past, hauling their goods in large bags and wagons, most of them with the company of a Dead Man or two. Aiding the transport of goods across the surface was a reliable job, readily available at all times of the year and usually associated with low risk, though any journey across the surface carried with it a degree of danger.

However, most distinctive to Madock's ear was the southern accent. It had been a long time since he had heard so many people in one place using the accent which twisted words he was accustomed to into an alien language which required translation. The mixture of familiar and foreign always amused the old man, and he took a moment to stop and drink in the sounds of conversation surrounding him. However, he knew that he could not afford to waste any time, with the possibility of locating Haswell before he crossed into the southern settlements weighing heavily on his mind.

It will probably be easiest if I try to cross the bridge myself, thought Madock as he made his way towards the walls guarding the tunnel back up to the bridge. *If Haswell has passed through, they're more than likely to tell me, especially if they want to levy this absurd Malice Gear charge.*

It didn't take long to wind his way through the streets to the booths. Since Silverbridge was split across either end of the bridge, the settlements on each end were not particularly large on their own. As Madock approached the wall, he slowed his pace. From experience, he knew that although there were five booths allowing access through the wall, in recent years the residents of Silverbridge had resorted to only opening one at a time. As the charges had continued to rise for crossing the bridge, fewer and fewer people were choosing to make the journey, preferring instead to focus their efforts in either the north or the south. Even now as Madock approached there was no sign of anybody queuing to gain access to the bridge. He slowly wandered along the wall, checking each booth as he passed but finding each one to be deserted with the barrier firmly lowered. As he approached the final booth, he prepared to negotiate his passage across the bridge.

The woman in the booth was dead. Madock paused, uncertain as to how to proceed, but even as he entered the booth to investigate he started to feel fear establishing a firm grasp on him. The woman seemed to carry no symptoms of physical injury, and for that in many ways Madock was relieved. A gunshot wound would have suggested that Haswell had been involved, but whilst it reduced the likelihood of the demon hunter's involvement, it carried all the hallmarks of something else he had seen too much of recently.

It's just like the people in Mikara… The monster is here. Madock shuddered as he recalled his exchange with the strange shapeshifting monster in Pelera, the manner in which it had absorbed the Echoes from the Enki cenote, the power it had possessed. Another dangerous thought crossed his mind. *If the monster is here, then where is Haswell?*

Madock glanced around, knowing that he needed to act quickly. Though the bridge crossing was quiet, a traveller could approach at any moment to find him in the booth with a dead body and difficult questions to answer. Emerging quickly from the booth, the Death Cheater realised that the answer was simple. There was really only one option available to him. Leaning back into the booth, he located the button to open the barrier and charged towards the bridge.

31

'You're dead to me.'

She had been convinced that her brother was going to hit her, had braced herself for the physical impact. Though she was relieved when the blow failed to materialise, she felt the poisonous sting of the words even deeper.

They were stood together outside the meeting room in the palace, waiting nervously for their father and Glenys Nolwenn, the head of the Harbingers to emerge. Starr had not wished to anger her brother and father, but it had seemed the only option available to her to stop the construction of the Echo Filter, the machine that Enrick and Blake had become obsessed with. They whole-heartedly believed that it could absorb the Malice and convert it into energy, but Starr knew that the machine was dangerous. No matter how Enrick tried to justify it, in Starr's eyes it was the same machine that caused the Sheol Disaster, wiping out an entire settlement and destroying countless lives. She wasn't willing to allow that to happen to Gair.

It had not been surprising to Starr that her brother had learnt of her betrayal so quickly. He had spies everywhere throughout the city, some of whom were no doubt dedicated to tracking her every movement. An impromptu visit to the Harbinger temple would no doubt have rung alarm bells in his head, and it wouldn't have taken him long to work out her motives.

But now the fate of the project was out of their hands. Glenys had listened carefully to Starr's concerns and had escorted her back to the palace immediately, confronting Bayne Airenguarde on the truth of her words. Starr still shuddered as she remembered the scathing look her father had shot in her direction, but he had carried himself with dignity and agreed to meet with the head of the Harbingers to discuss the project.

Now there was nothing left to do but wait.

She turned at the sound of approaching footsteps, fearing that perhaps Enrick had heard of the meeting and was rushing to intervene, to save his project from being cancelled. But as the figure emerged around the corner, Starr was relieved to recognise the friendly but concerned face of Gray, his Echo burning a deep purple colour as he quickly approached them. Blake growled but said nothing to the Necromancer, biting his tongue and continuing to pace back and forth outside the door to the meeting room.

Gray placed a gentle hand on Starr's arm. 'Can I have a word with you?' he asked quietly. Starr nodded and together they moved around the corner, out of sight and ear shot of Blake. The Necromancer stared at her long and hard, his eyes difficult to read as he seemed to be searching for the right words. Eventually he abandoned the search and instead threw his arms around her and embraced her tightly. She returned the gesture, smiling as she rested her head upon his shoulder peacefully.

When they finally pulled apart, she could see tears were glistening in the corner of Gray's eyes as he shook her playfully. 'That was stupidly risky, you know that right?'

Starr smiled and shrugged innocently. 'I didn't have much choice.'

'Yes, you did,' replied Gray. 'That's why I'm so grateful to you. Hopefully now this madness can stop.'

Starr's smile waivered. 'I hope so, but...' she paused, desperate to make Gray see that there could be further complications ahead. 'There's a chance that the Harbingers might still want the project to go ahead, just with them overseeing it alongside my family. If that happens, then...'

Gray placed his hands on her shoulders, his Echo switching to an intense grey colour, giving it the appearance of liquid metal floating in the air beside him. 'That won't happen. The Harbingers want to retain control of Gair. If the machine is built, then they won't be needed to protect Gair anymore, which hands all of the power back to your father. Trust me, she's not going to agree to support the project.'

Starr could see the logic in Gray's words, but she still felt uneasy about the situation. Perhaps it was simply the fact that no matter what happened today, her relationship with her family would be forever altered. Neither her father nor her brother would ever trust her again, and at worst she may have achieved nothing more than ensuring that her family never controlled Gair again.

Together, they returned to wait outside of the door to the meeting room. Blake barely looked up to acknowledge their presence as he continued to pace about impatiently. Starr knew that the project had meant a great deal to her brother, the prospect of returning their family to a position of complete power a major driving factor behind his fascination with completing the Echo Filter. But she believed that the obsession had blinded him to the dangers of the project. Perhaps in time he would see that, but for now she knew better than to speak to him.

They all turned abruptly as the door to the meeting room opened. Glenys Nolwenn was the first to emerge from the room and she smiled awkwardly at the three faces staring at her. Bayne Airenguarde followed the Harbinger leader from the room and shook her hand. Starr watched the exchange carefully, attempting to understand what had passed between the two important figures in the room. They shared no words, and instead Glenys simply walked past them all and around the corner to where her small entourage of Harbingers awaited her return by the main entrance to the palace.

Starr turned questioningly to her father, but to her distress he refused to make eye contact with her. Instead he directed all of his attention towards Blake. 'We have much to discuss,' he informed his son gravely as he gestured him into the meeting room. Blake moved through the door, shooting one last look of disgust towards his sister before disappearing into the room. Without a word or a look in her direction, her father followed Blake into the room, shutting the door firmly behind him.

Starr stood in the corridor staring at the closed door, uncertain what to do next. It was clear that her father and brother had turned their backs on her. She felt tears begin to sting her eyes as Gray gently put an arm around her.

'They'll forgive you…' he offered sympathetically.

Starr was not convinced, but she also could not be sure exactly what had happened in the meeting room. Had Glenys managed to put a stop to the project? If not then her risk would have backfired on her spectacularly. She had to know the truth, but she was all too aware that neither her father nor her brother were willing to talk to her at that exact moment. Whatever they were discussing in private in the meeting room, she would not be allowed to be involved.

For now, there was nothing she could do but wait.

* * *

Sleep did not come easily to her that night, and when it did, her dreams were dark and twisted creations. She saw the completed Echo Filter before her, a living breathing metallic monster which towered over her with a mouth full of sharp mechanical teeth. Huge claws made of jagged steel and dangling wires lunged around wildly, crashing into the walls of the palace, causing the entire building to shake. It roared deafeningly, throwing anything it could find into its hungry jaws. No matter how hard she tried to evade the monster, it always seemed to be right behind her, snatching at her heels as she fled through endless corridors. Eventually it grasped her firmly and suspended her above its huge mouth, the smell of machinery, blood and death emerging from its innards. Then it would release its grip and she would be falling straight towards those sharp metal teeth and the darkness which lay behind them.

She woke with a start, breathing hard and desperate to free herself from the sheets of her bed which had become tangled around her body.

I won't allow that machine to be built, no matter what happens, she promised herself as she allowed her racing heartbeat to slowly recover. Gently padding barefoot across the cool floor of her bedroom, she gazed out of her bedroom window. The Shell continued to flicker over the city, though through the shimmering colours Starr could see the storm raging overhead, battering down hard against the barrier.

Her attention was quickly captured by a group of Harbingers stood in the main courtyard of the palace, who were locked in discussion with her father and her brother. For a brief moment, she allowed herself to hope. *They've come to stop the project*, she told herself as she quickly got dressed and rushed down to investigate. *They're here to stop the machine being built.*

The palace was a large building, but having spent her entire life growing up within its walls Starr knew how to navigate it quickly, and soon enough she was rushing across the courtyard towards the Harbingers and her father and brother. But even before she had arrived, she could sense that something was wrong. The Harbingers faces were a mixture of sadness, confusion and anger.

'I am truly sorry to hear of this,' she heard her father say as she slowed to a walking pace, not willing to intrude on the conversation but desperate to hear every word. 'I can assure you that we will do everything in our power to find and punish the guilty party.'

'What was the meaning of her business here yesterday?' asked one of the Harbingers, his tone aggressive as he interrogated Bayne Airenguarde.

'She was asked to attend by my daughter Starr. We simply wished to discuss the need to switch the Harbingers currently attending to my wife. I am aware of how hard they have been working for a long time, and I wished to offer them an opportunity to rest.'

Starr felt physically sick as the lies continued to spout from her father's mouth. *What has happened?*

'She parted with her escort in good spirits,' continued her father confidently. 'To think that such a fate befell her just a short while later... I simply cannot understand why such a thing has happened.'

One of the Harbinger group shook his head sadly. 'We appreciate your sympathies at this difficult time, but please refrain from involving yourself in this matter. We will punish the ones responsible for this crime.'

'Of course,' replied Bayne, bowing grandly. 'As you see fit. But should you require any assistance, please do not hesitate to ask.'

The Harbingers nodded and shook hands with Bayne before turning and silently moving away through the courtyard back towards the main city of Gair. Starr stood behind her father and brother as together they watched them leave, but before she could say anything her father had already turned and was walking briskly away from them.

Blake went to follow their father when Starr grabbed him roughly by the wrist. 'What happened? What happened to Glenys Nolwenn?' she asked desperately, though she knew deep down exactly what had happened.

Blake freed himself aggressively from his sister's grasp and confronted her. Starr braced herself, but forced her gaze to remain locked on Blake's eyes. Growling in frustration, he folded his arms.

'Haven't you heard? She's dead.'

Starr's heart seemed to freeze in her chest. 'Dead?' she repeated numbly.

'She was attacked on her way back to the temple yesterday,' explained Blake as he turned away, moving back towards the palace. He paused after a few steps and glanced back over his shoulder towards his sister. 'I guess you never know who you can trust these days.' Without another word, he walked briskly back towards the palace, leaving Starr alone in the courtyard. She was struggling to process all the information she had just received, but one thing was clear to her.

Whether they had been involved directly or not, her father and brother were responsible for the death of Glenys Nolwenn.

32

The bridge crossing the chasm was an incredible structure. Steel beams supported the vast road which connected the northern and southern settlements, the bridge itself easily wide enough to allow huge crowds to cross with ease. Perhaps in the days before the Malice it had done exactly that, supporting the movement of hundreds of people every day upon its mighty back. Now though, it was practically deserted, the surface conditions and the cost of using the bridge deterring the majority of the population from crossing upon the significant structure.

Madock had already drawn his weapon as he made his way slowly across the bridge, the wind pushing him backwards as though deliberately attempting to impede his progress. His senses were heightened as he scanned the horizon, permanently just beyond the edge of his vision thanks to the driving snow and Malice. As he edged forward tentatively, he moved across to the side of the bridge and glanced down into the chasm below. The Malice concealed the bottom of the drop, though through the howling wind Madock was certain that he could make out unusual noises emerging from the depths of the chasm. He shuddered as he remembered some of the stories he had heard about the Malice-engulfed scar in the land. There were rumours that the Malice was thickest at the base of the chasm, creating its own unique malevolent creations far worse than demons. Madock had dismissed this as nothing more than a tale made up to scare travellers, but every time he had crossed the bridge he had found himself wondering if there was some truth to the myth.

Moving away from the edge and continuing onwards, Madock kept his eyes peeled for either the monster or Haswell. He knew that there was a chance that he would find neither, but the dead woman in the booth had convinced him that at the very least the monster couldn't be too far away. The thought both encouraged and terrified him in equal measure as he continued to move carefully forward, leaving a trail of steady footprints in the snow behind him.

The figure appeared before him through the snow and Malice almost without warning. Madock quickly raised his weapon and trained it on the stranger who was staggering slowly away from him, though as Madock closed in on the figure he allowed himself to believe that perhaps luck was on his side after all.

'Hold it there, Haswell!' he shouted out to the Malice Gear clad figure. The figure stopped obediently, but said nothing as Madock continued to slowly move forward. Eventually, the figure reluctantly turned to face the Death Cheater. Even at the distance they stood apart, Madock's suspicions were confirmed as he recognised the Peleran crest upon his chest and the rifle hanging over his shoulder.

Now I can finally find out the truth, thought the Death Cheater as he kept his weapon trained on Haswell. He would never have thought it necessary in the past, but given Haswell's conduct since leaving Pelera it seemed prudent to keep his finger ready upon the trigger.

'Drop your weapon,' he instructed loudly through the wind as he approached. Again, the figure followed his instructions, removing the rifle from his shoulder and laying it carefully down on the ground, his hands visibly shaking as he did so.

Madock was just a few metres in front of Haswell when he came to a stop. He stared long and hard at the demon hunter, waiting for him to say or do anything, but Haswell simply remained still and observed the old man.

'I should have known you would follow,' Haswell eventually commented dryly, his face hidden behind the mask of his Malice Gear.

'What's going on Haswell?' asked Madock, forcing himself to remain calm and vigilant for any signs of danger.

Haswell shook his head sadly. 'You really shouldn't have followed me, Madock. It's not safe for you to be here.'

Madock thought back to the dead woman he had seen in the settlement behind him. He knew that this might be his best opportunity to get Haswell under control again, if the demon hunter would just listen to reason. 'Listen to me Haswell, the monster is near here. We can find him together.'

Haswell nodded and pointed with his right hand at the structure below their feet. 'Oh I know. I believe the monster is still here on this bridge.'

Madock paused, surprised by the demon hunter's words. But before he could respond, everything suddenly clicked into place in his head. Haswell's inexplicable behaviour had a very simple yet devastating explanation.

You're a stupid old fool, he cursed himself. *You should have seen this a long time ago, but you refused to let yourself believe it.*

'I know the truth,' he shouted at Haswell. 'I know that *you're* the monster.'

The demon hunter looked down at the ground, as though lost in thought, before returning his attention back to Madock. 'I almost wish you were right, Madock. But you're not.'

Raising his right hand up to his head, Haswell awkwardly removed the helmet of his Malice Gear. The face he revealed was a familiar one to Madock's eyes, but the old man knew better than to lower his guard. He knew only too well that the monster could take on a false appearance, just as it had in Pelera with Marcus. But the sadness he saw in the young man's eyes caused his confidence to waiver.

'You know that looking like Haswell won't deceive me,' said Madock, keeping his weapon trained on the young man.

'What will it take to convince you?' asked Haswell quietly. 'I can tell you anything you want to know. Ask me something that I would only know if I was the real Haswell.'

Madock shook his head. 'That won't help you. I know the monster can see people's memories.' But Haswell's reluctance to admit to being the monster was beginning to play on Madock's mind. Marcus had only resisted the truth for a short while when confronted, but Haswell continued to deny the allegation.

It will just be another trick. This is the monster.

Haswell did not appear desperate, but rather forlorn as Madock continued to question his identity. 'I promise you Madock, it's me.'

'The Haswell I knew would never kill innocent people,' replied Madock bitterly, remembering the scene of slaughter he had encountered in Tirneth.

Haswell staggered slightly at Madock's words. 'What are you talking about?'

'You know exactly what I'm talking about. What you did in Tirneth.'

The demon hunter's eyes narrowed. 'I didn't kill any innocent people. I made sure I only shot the demons.'

Madock paused. If the figure before him truly was the monster, it was going to great lengths to weave a convoluted web of lies. There seemed to be no logic behind it. 'Demons?' he asked, desperate to allow Haswell the opportunity to either reveal himself as the monster as Madock suspected, or to somehow prove the more disturbing possibility that he was exactly who he said he was.

Seizing upon the opportunity, Haswell nodded desperately and began to pace back and forth across the bridge, seemingly untroubled by the fact that Madock was keeping his weapon trained on him. 'I've never seen them get down into a settlement before,' he began anxiously, gazing around wildly as he paced. 'Demons! In Tirneth! So close to Pelera too. I didn't have time to explain, I just had to take them out. There were so many of them, but I just kept shooting...' He trailed off and glanced at Madock desperately. 'But I didn't kill any of the civilians! I was very careful about that! I swear I did everything I could to keep them safe.'

Shaking his head, Madock spoke calmly and quietly. 'Haswell, there were no demons there. I asked the people who were there... The ones who survived...'

Haswell stared at Madock intently, his hand shaking uncontrollably by his side. 'No... You're wrong, there were demons there. I killed them, chased one of them out of the settlement.' As Madock shook his head, the demon hunter pressed on desperately. 'There *were* demons! I saw them...' He paused awkwardly. 'Didn't I?'

Silence washed across the bridge and over the two men. Neither seemed certain of what to say.

Haswell slowly sank to his knees. 'It's worse than I thought...' He looked up with tears in his eyes, and Madock instantly recognised the boy he had helped to look after all those years ago. 'I swear I thought the effects of the poultice would last longer.'

'Poultice?' Madock asked, struggling to comprehend the truth that was unfolding before him.

Taking a deep breath, Haswell moved his right hand across to his left arm. It was only as the demon hunter began to tug at the useless limb that Madock realised that Haswell had not raised the arm since he had encountered him on the bridge. As the demon hunter slowly removed his glove and rolled up the sleeve of his Malice Gear, Madock understood why.

Malice poisoning. Every inch of skin on his left hand had blackened, the veins coursing and throbbing as the Malice poured through his bloodstream. The infection had spread up his arm and disappeared underneath the upper sleeve of Haswell's Malice Gear. The young man's arm had been entirely corrupted by the poison.

Madock instantly lowered his weapon and approached Haswell. Unable to tear his eyes away from the infected limb, he could only utter one word. 'When?'

Haswell sighed. 'The horde we came across on the way to Pelera. One of the bastards scratched me.' He seemed unable to look at the wound and instead focused steadily on Madock's face, even when the old man was transfixed by the infected limb. 'I didn't want to say anything. Thought it might have put a dampener on our little trip.'

'How have you lasted so long?' asked Madock in awe. To think that Haswell had survived with the effects of Malice poisoning for such a long time was staggering.

'I had the Harbingers in Pelera brew me poultices. I knew they weren't a long term solution, but… I just needed to survive a little bit longer.' He paused and stared up at the storm clouds overhead. 'But after father died, and I heard about the monster, I realised there was still something I could do with the time I had left. So I took the last poultice I had and set off. I didn't think it would take this long…'

Madock paused awkwardly. 'So, what happened in Tirneth…' He didn't need to finish the question, and Haswell's silence indicated that he too knew what had happened. The poultice had been designed to ward off the effects of the Malice poisoning, but clearly it had not been effective enough. The madness had taken Haswell as it had taken so many people before him. It only made it all the more miraculous that Haswell had continued onwards, having created a fantasy in his mind of killing demons rather than innocent civilians.

'Did I do anything else?' asked Haswell weakly. 'I can't trust my own memories anymore...'

'You caused a bit of a scene in the Silver Bullet, but you didn't kill anybody.'

Haswell shook his head. 'I don't even remember going in there. I don't remember a lot of things. Sometimes I lose entire days in my memory. But I'm glad I didn't hurt anybody.' He paused and stared at Madock intently. 'The monster's near though Madock. Did you see the dead woman in the booth? He can't have passed through here too long ago. I know he's still on the bridge. I've got to stop him.'

The Death Cheater placed a firm hand on Haswell's shoulder. 'I'm here to take you back to Pelera.'

Haswell smiled sadly at Madock and shook his head. 'Look at me. I'm not going to make it off this bridge, let alone back to Pelera.' A strange expression appeared on his face. 'Besides, I haven't been back to Pelera in years. I'm not even sure I would be welcome anymore.'

He doesn't even remember going back to Pelera? But he talked about it just moments ago... Madock sensed that the young man was slipping away before his eyes, the Malice poisoning beginning to reassert its hold over his mind. 'Pelera needs you to take over from your father,' pleaded Madock, though he knew that he was already too late. It was a wonder Haswell was still alive at all given the condition he was in.

Haswell tilted his head slightly and looked at Madock questioningly. 'My father rules Pelera. You know that Madock. Besides, even when he dies, Kerrin will be a better leader than I ever could have been,' laughed Haswell. 'Just... don't tell him I said that.'

The madness. It's already taken him. Madock fought back the tears of frustration that were threatening to emerge and forced himself to remain silent. He was too late. The young man he had set out to recover was already gone. All that remained was the muddled Malice infected individual who kneeled before him. *Haswell's already dead.*

Uncertain as to what to say next, Madock stood and offered his hand to the demon hunter, who took it gratefully with his strong hand and allowed the old man to pull him to his feet.

Haswell took the lead, speaking feverishly. 'I don't have much time left, so I'm going to make this quick. We're going to kill the monster, but if I lose my mind or begin to change, you're going to put a bullet through my head. Do you understand?'

Madock tried to nod, but his attention was instantly captured by the figure approaching them from the opposite end of the bridge. He knew who it was even at this distance, but the fact that it had chosen to take that particular form caused the old man to tremble with rage.

Turning, Haswell also noticed the figure and stepped towards it slowly. 'Father?'

'I'm here, my boy,' said Ruskin Broxhart gently, opening his arms in a welcoming gesture. Madock knew perfectly well that it wasn't Ruskin at all. Behind the familiar frame of his old friend lurked the monster that they sought. The Death Cheater forced himself to remain focused, instantly training his weapon on the threat.

'Is... is it really you father?' asked Haswell earnestly, already stumbling forward towards the monster.

'Your father is dead, Haswell!' shouted Madock desperately, torn between grabbing hold of the young man and keeping his weapon aimed at Ruskin. 'That's the monster!'

Haswell paused and glanced back and forth between the Death Cheater and the monster who wore his father's skin. For a moment, Madock hoped that the Malice had eased its grip on Haswell, that the demon hunter would understand the reality of the situation. Eventually the young man turned and smiled at Madock. Before Haswell had even spoken, Madock knew that he had lost him. 'My father? A monster? Are you crazy?' Without another word, he turned and dashed into Ruskin's arms, embracing him tightly.

'Welcome back, my son,' laughed Ruskin, squeezing Haswell tightly. Releasing himself from his son's grip, he smiled at the young man, held up his hand and placed it upon Haswell's chest. The demon hunter shuddered violently, throwing his head back and staring blankly up towards the storm clouds overhead as his Echo was torn from his body. The process took just seconds, then silently he collapsed onto the cold stone bridge. Madock knew instantly that he was dead. The monster wearing Ruskin's face stepped back, allowing the light of Haswell's Echo to surge into his body. He turned with a satisfied smirk to the Death Cheater. 'Poor lost soul. All this time he thought he was hunting me, when in fact he was the prey. Malice can do terrible things to a man. I almost feel sorry for him.'

Madock pulled the trigger before he could stop himself. The bullet surged from the chamber and bedded itself deep in Ruskin's chest, sending the monster stumbling backwards. The second shot was deliberate, as was every shot that followed. Madock pulled the trigger again and again, burying bullet after bullet into the monster until eventually the trigger simply clicked through the empty chambers. With a heavy thud, the monster fell backwards onto the snow-covered bridge, leaving nothing but the sound of Madock's own racing heartbeat and heavy breathing.

Be careful, he reminded himself, *we shot the monster before and it survived.* But that had been just two shots, shared between Haswell and himself. He had emptied every bullet in his weapon into the monster. Surely that would have been enough to kill the beast.

Tentatively he took a step forward to investigate the body of the monster, forcing his eyes not to drift across to Haswell's lifeless corpse.

'That hurts more than you think, you know?'

The voice rose from Ruskin's fallen figure, freezing Madock in his tracks. With barely more than a grunt, Ruskin sat up and dusted himself off, staring up at the Death Cheater with a mocking grin. 'I hope your little tantrum made you feel better.'

I can't kill it. Madock stood watching helplessly, the empty weapon still trained on the monster as it stood and stretched with a sigh. 'What... are you?' Madock managed to ask, forcing the words from his dry throat.

'An interesting question...' replied the monster. 'If I had the answer, I would give it to you freely. I was so certain I would find the answer at the Enki cenote. There were *hundreds* of Echoes there. I was so confident that one of them would be mine.'

Madock blinked. 'You're searching for your Echo?' He felt numb and unable to do little more than allow his tongue to voice the thoughts that popped into his mind.

The monster with Ruskin's face grinned and wagged his finger at the Death Cheater. 'Now, now, Madock, I can't go telling you all my secrets. Although...' Ruskin paused, staring up at the stormy skies above them. 'This Ruskin guy had some *very* interesting secrets. There's one in particular that would really interest you, Mr Leocadia.'

Frowning, Madock finally lowered his useless weapon. The monster had made similar comments about Marcus Ortiz when Madock had first confronted it, and he was all too aware that Echoes carried the memories of the dead. Necromancers utilised this to review the lives of the dead through their Echoes, and since the monster had clearly absorbed Ruskin's Echo it seemed realistic to suggest that he had access to Lord Broxhart's memories.

'Perhaps you'd like to hear the secret?' taunted the monster, strolling back and forth casually on the bridge. 'To be honest, I'm going to tell you no matter what you say. It's just too good not to share!'

Madock grimaced but remained silent. The monster's confidence was insufferable, but perhaps if he allowed the monster to ramble for long enough he may be able to identify a way to destroy it.

Though he hated to admit it, he was also curious about the secret.

Just remember, he's toying with you. Don't believe anything he says.

'It's all to do with the Sheol Disaster,' said the monster, closing his eyes as though picturing Ruskin's memory behind his eyelids. 'Did you know that your old friend Ruskin was the one behind the project?'

Madock froze. *Ruskin ordered the project?*

'He wanted to build this Echo Filter thing, even carried on when some of the scientists started saying it was dangerous. He...' The monster paused, cringing slightly. 'Such a strange memory...' He opened his eyes and snarled at Madock. 'But one thing is clear. He is the one responsible for killing your family, for destroying your home...' With alarming speed, the monster rushed up to the old man and gripped his fingers tightly around Madock's neck, lifting him effortlessly from the floor. 'And now he's going to be the one to kill you. Well, not in a traditional sense, but appearances are everything these days.'

Fight back! You need to fight back! Madock screamed at himself internally, but a sense of helplessness and acceptance was already washing over him. His efforts to loosen the monster's grip around his neck were proving futile, his legs dangling in the air as he was carried over to the edge of the bridge. Already he could feel himself suffocating under the punishing grip, but he forced himself to stay conscious and focused. Terror continuously fought to take over his mind, but Madock fought it back with the last of his fading strength.

The monster paused as they reached the barrier lining the edge of the bridge. 'I always felt there was something special about you Madock,' said the monster with Ruskin's mouth. 'I've never quite been able to put my finger on it. But I guess I was wrong after all. We all make mistakes.'

Lifting Madock higher, the monster moved the old man over the barrier and held him dangling over the Malice-filled chasm. 'Well, it's been fun, but I've got an Echo to find. Any final words?'

Madock attempted to speak, but the fingers around his neck were just too tight, suffocating the last of his air. Already he could sense his vision blurring as consciousness threatened to abandon him.

The monster shrugged at the silence. 'I didn't think so.'

Ruskin released his grip and Madock fell.

33

Darkness. He was so sick of darkness. It engulfed everything, numbed his senses, threatened to drown him. He fought against it feebly, his hands grasping at the cold nothingness around him as he sought a way to free himself from its suffocating grasp.

Perhaps this is it, he thought quietly as he struggled. *Perhaps this is death. Just be glad you've managed to avoid it for such a long time.* The idea was strangely comforting, yet equally alarming. Was this truly all there was to death? Endlessly floating in cold darkness? He couldn't allow himself to believe that. He *wouldn't* allow himself to believe that.

Come on, get up, he shouted at himself angrily. *You're the Death Cheater. Now prove it!* He struggled with all his might, feeling the cold darkness slip beneath his body. On the edge of his vision, a faint light appeared. *That's it! Keep fighting!* Bolder and bolder the light grew as he waved away the darkness surrounding him, pushing for the surface like a swimmer surfacing from the depths. With one final gigantic effort, he pushed for the light.

His eyes shot open, then almost immediately shut again as he cringed at the intense pain radiating throughout his body. He wanted to shout and yell, but his dry throat seemed incapable of producing any sound other than his silent scream of agony. He lay there silently, taking a moment to allow his body to adjust to the pain as he attempted to swallow the bile that was rising in this throat.

Finally, with a great deal of will power, he opened his eyes and forced himself to take in his surroundings, if for no other reason than simply to distract himself from the pain.

It took him a moment to realise where he was, but as the memories came flooding back of his exchange with the monster on the bridge he quickly understood. Lying at the bottom of the chasm, the Malice obscured his view in most directions, but above him there was a clue as to how he had survived the fall. Branches spread across the chasm like fingers, creating dark shadows which criss-crossed repeatedly overhead. They had been hidden by the Malice from the bridge above, but clearly they had at least slowed his descent enough to allow his plummet to not prove deadly as he crashed into the soft snow at the base of the chasm. They had however been far from kind in the process of breaking his fall, and Madock could already sense that his legs were battered and broken having taken the brunt of the damage. There was pain emanating from other places across his body, but his attention was focused primarily upon his legs. They were his priority.

Grimacing, he lifted himself up on to his elbows and attempted to move his legs. It quickly became apparent that they would not obey his instructions, and even attempting to drag himself backward on his wounded arms produced enough pain to almost knock him back into the darkness of unconsciousness. He fell back into the snow, breathing heavily and desperately trying to formulate his next plan of action.

From within the Malice, a low growl met the Death Cheater's ears.

Madock immediately reached for his gun out of instinct, but his fingers found nothing in the holster. *You probably dropped it on the bridge*, he thought furiously, before reminding himself that it was empty and therefore useless anyway. Instead, he focused on remaining perfectly still. The Malice was so thick down here that there was a good chance that whatever was making the sound might pass him by, oblivious of his existence. All he had to do was stay silent.

The creature's red eyes emerged through the Malice, firmly locked on Madock. He watched them approaching, paralysed with fear as the rest of the creature emerged behind it. It was unlike any demon he had seen before, a creature mutated by the Malice into a hideous beast. Black fur covered its entire body as it paced forward on four legs with a barbed tail swishing from side to side threateningly, approaching its prey. Huge, twisted horns rose from the creature's head, spiralling downwards to sit alongside its maw filled with sharp, blackened teeth.

Madock had never seen anything like it before in all his years of travelling the surface. It terrified him, but he forced himself up onto his elbows again in spite of the pain and began slowly retreating from the creature. Without his gun, he felt his best chance of survival was simply to either run or hide. With running very much out of the question, he allowed his gaze to quickly move from the advancing creature to the walls of the chasm on either side of him. He desperately scanned for a crevice or a gap in the rock which he could retreat into, but to his dismay there was nothing but the sheer face of the rocks.

The monster lunged suddenly and without warning. Madock attempted to swing himself out of the way of the beast's jaws but his useless legs slowed down his movement. Teeth ripped into the flesh of his legs, tearing through the Malice Gear and skin. Madock howled in pain, but was forced to remain focused as the beast turned and lunged towards his head. The creature was heavier and stronger than Madock had expected. As the weight of the beast forced him back onto the ground, its front paws pinned the old man's chest, viciously sharp claws tearing into the Malice Gear. It seemed almost to be toying with its prey as it hovered dominantly over the Death Cheater. Digging it's teeth into Madock's Malice Gear, the demon shook the Death Cheater roughly from side to side, attempting to break his spirited resistance.

Madock grimaced and closed his eyes tightly as he was thrown around on the cold snow.

You can't overpower it. Play dead.

As the demon finally released its grip on the Death Cheater, Madock forced himself to remain still. The beast placed it's twisted claws on the old man's chest once more and sniffed at its prey suspiciously. In spite of the weight pushing down on him, Madock forced himself to remain still and silent. Satisfied that the Dead Man had been subdued, the demon returned to Madock's legs and clamped its jaw around one of the broken limbs. Slowly, it began dragging Madock across the snow. The Death Cheater's hands scrambled around desperately in the snow as it passed below his body, seeking some form of rudimental weapon. As his right hand discovered the jagged metal shard, he closed his fingers around it tightly and swung it instantly towards the creature's head. Caught off guard, the creature reeled but quickly recovered and moved towards Madock's head to subdue its prey once more. The Dead Man, however, was quick enough to take advantage of the situation. Again he swung the metal shard towards the beast's head, this time hearing the distinctive crack of the creature's skull as the ragged edges of his weapon found their target. The dark creature's entire body slumped, collapsing to the cold snow below as it fell from Madock's chest, allowing him to breathe freely once more. He did not hesitate. Rolling onto his front, he continued to rain down blows with the improvised weapon until the snow beneath the fallen monster was stained black with its corrupted blood.

Madock fell backwards into the snow, breathing hard but finding it difficult to suppress the laughter that was rising up within him. Accepting defeat, he unleashed it, laughing loud and hard as the sound echoed off the walls of the chasm around him.

The Death Cheater lives on, he thought, his mind becoming increasingly delirious as he struggled over to the rock face and leaned against it in a sitting position. The laughter quickly subsided as he studied his leg where the beast had managed to sink its teeth in. The wound was deep; he could see the bone sticking through the flesh and blood was pouring freely across his leg and onto the snow, tainting the pure white with crimson streams of red. But through the blood, he could see something far worse. It was something he had long known that he would fall victim to eventually, but now that the moment was here he could not quite comprehend it.

Malice poisoning. He watched spellbound as the deep black veins seemed to visibly spread from the wound before his eyes, carrying with it the deadly Malice which would spread through his bloodstream until eventually he became one of them. A demon, feeding on hapless victims until somebody eventually ended his sad existence. The thought filled him with dread. Surviving for as long as he had done had been trying enough whilst he was alive; he did not fancy potentially repeating the sentence as a demon.

He glanced around at his surroundings, desperate to locate a way out. The fresh snow had created a slope leading up one side of the chasm. If he had had full use of his legs, Madock suspected he may well have been able to climb it, but even then it seemed unlikely that it would have carried him high enough to escape. There were rumours of old routes through the base of the Gairen Mountains, but he knew that he could not rely on stories. Besides, even if they were real, he greatly doubted that he would have the strength to complete the journey.

Breathing heavily, Madock lifted his hands and removed the mask from his head. It no longer served any purpose. He had already accepted his fate. *I've lived long enough...* he thought, surprised to discover that he had already made peace with the fact. *Perhaps I've just been waiting for this.* But the acceptance of his imminent death did not resolve his fear of spending years trapped down in this chasm as a demon.

Reaching for his gun, he cursed himself as his fingers again clasped at nothing. It would have been a fitting way to leave this world, using the weapon his father had given him, but it seemed fate intended to deny him even that simple pleasure. He sat still, staring up at the thick Malice floating all around him. It surprised him to think how much of his life had been spent within its grasp, a constant companion on his travels, a lingering spectre reminding him that no matter how many times he evaded death, it would eventually come for him as it came for everybody. He may have attained a legendary status for his longevity, but he was simply holding on tighter than everybody else. Eventually his grip would fail and he would fall just like the others had.

So what now? The question lingered in the air, as potent as the Malice and equally obscure. Madock knew that failing to act would simply secure the outcome that he was desperately seeking to avoid, yet there seemed no action that could prevent it.

His thoughts drifted back to the monster's words on the bridge. *Ruskin was behind the machine that destroyed my home. The machine that killed my family.* He refused to believe it, but there seemed little reason why the monster would lie to him. It was clear that the monster had expected him to die from the fall, so there was nothing to be gained by feeding him lies. *Maybe he just wanted to taunt you? Make you feel even more powerless?* Madock desperately tried to believe these ideas, but the longer he lay there and contemplated the situation, the more he accepted that there must have been at least some degree of truth behind the monster's words.

In truth, Madock wasn't sure what to feel. The revelation had caught him off guard, but in the grand scheme of things it now seemed rather insignificant. Ruskin was dead, and soon Madock would be joining him.

Reaching into his pocket, he removed the glass with shaking fingers and held it in front of his face. Even in the dimly-lit surroundings it seemed to sparkle with light, sending out different colours as the Death Cheater turned it slowly in his hand. In many ways, it frustrated him that he would never know exactly what it was, but at least it would maintain its magical mysticism to the end. As he rotated it, he wondered if perhaps he could have changed his fate if he had simply handed it over to the Raiders when they had first confronted him in the Peleran tunnels. It was an interesting concept, but Madock felt deep down that this was always likely to be his fate, no matter what his actions or choices in the past might have been. It would be far too easy to analyse his entire life, picking at the mistakes and missed opportunities. All that truly mattered was the here and now, and what he chose to do with the last moments of his life.

Through the Malice, a shadow emerged.

34

Starr opened the door to her bedroom and quietly padded out into the hallway. She had been awoken again by the same nightmare, the mechanical monster hunting her down remorselessly and consuming her whole. Even now she could still hear its fearsome roar, the flickering lights and panels which had decorated its entire body like armour. She knew that sleep would only bring life to the metal beast again. Instead, she quietly paced around the palace, offering reassuring smiles to the questioning faces of the guards she passed. To her relief they did not seek to send her back to her room, nor did they offer to accompany her. At that moment, Starr simply wished to be alone with her thoughts.

In truth, she had never felt more alone anyway. She knew that her actions had ostracised her from her family, alienated her forever from their trust and loyalty through her act of betrayal. And ultimately, it seemed the risk had been for nothing. Glenys Nolwenn was dead, the Harbingers seemingly none-the-wiser about the machine that was being constructed within the walls of the palace. At her lowest points, Starr had blamed herself for the death of the Harbinger leader but she knew deep down that her hands were clean in that matter. The blood from that affair was firmly attached to her father and her brother.

Though she had no proof of their involvement and neither would deign to even talk to her, let alone admit their guilt, Starr was still convinced that they had been responsible for the murder of Glenys. It seemed too convenient that the leader of the Harbingers should be murdered following her discovery of the potentially power-shifting machine. She knew that her brother had many men working for him in secret, part of his elaborate network of contacts and mercenaries which he had spread across the whole of Gair. It would have taken very little for Blake to coordinate the attack which had robbed the Harbinger and her entourage of their lives, simply because of the knowledge they possessed.

As she drifted aimlessly, she eventually found herself outside in the courtyard. Her feet crunched into the gravel with each step, her legs seemingly carrying her forward without specific instructions from her brain. She had no idea where to go, nor where she *should* go. The entire palace seemed alien to her now, and not just because of the midnight hour which painted it with darkness. She firmly believed now that the true darkness lay within its walls, perhaps even within her father and brother's hearts.

You need to face your fears, she reminded herself. *You can't run away from life.* It was a lesson which had been taught to her by her father, yet even now she realised that it was a lie. Her father had done nothing but run from his fears, spending all his time and resources on hanging on to his wife when he must have known, must still know, that it was simply a matter of time before she passed away from the Malice poisoning. The merciful thing to do would have been to end the poor woman's suffering years ago.

But it's not too late for you. You can still face your fear.

She glanced around as if waking from a dream. Without being fully aware of her own actions, her legs had carried her to the door which led to the chamber in which the Echo Filter was being housed during its construction. No doubt Enrick would be there, busying himself with calculations and calibrations. But perhaps not? She assumed that he had to sleep just like everybody else.

You can face your fear, she repeated in her mind. *You can take control of this situation.* Her efforts to alert the Harbingers to the machine had failed, but that did not mean she was helpless. There was still something she could do. A few days ago it would have seemed too drastic to even consider, but with everything else that had happened it now seemed not only possible but a prudent idea. Perhaps she would only succeed in delaying its completion, but even that might prove enough to stop this madness.

Gripping the door handle firmly, she opened the door and marched into the darkness towards the chamber. With every step the hum of the machinery grew louder and louder, bringing memories of her nightmare bubbling to the surface. She suppressed them and pressed onwards with clenched fists. She wasn't even sure where she should begin, or what she would do if Enrick was there to greet her with his sneering smile. But she knew that she had to try.

As she entered the chamber she paused briefly, staggered by the progress that had been made on the machine since she had last seen it. It had towered over her then, but now it seemed even more intimidating. More worryingly, it seemed very close to completion; the various wires and circuitry she had observed during her previous visit had disappeared, hidden behind the machine's metal armour. She could almost envision where its mouth would open to reveal the rows of bloodstained mechanical teeth.

Shaking her head, she padded softly further into the chamber. To her relief, it seemed deserted. The scientist and his team had been working around the clock to complete the project, so their absence only served to make Starr certain that the Echo Filter must almost be complete and operational.

Approaching the machine, she nervously placed her hand upon it. She could feel the vibrations as the beast purred softly in slumber. Soon enough though, she knew it would be forced to wake up. Whatever the cost, she could not allow that to happen; she had lost so much already, one further act of rebellion could cost her nothing. She now had little left to lose.

But even as she stared up at the machine, she struggled to comprehend how she could even go about starting her plan. The metal exterior seemed impenetrable, and she did not know enough about the workings of the machinery to target a particular weak spot.

Well just standing here isn't helping, she scolded herself. Glancing around, her eyes fell upon a bag of tools, perhaps abandoned by one of the engineers who had helped to construct the beast. Moving across to it quickly, she picked out a spanner and a screwdriver. She ignored the larger tools, sensing that attacking the exterior with force would achieve very little and perhaps alert others to her actions. However, her chosen tools may well allow her access to the interior, where she could perhaps do some damage which could, if nothing else, delay the completion of the machine.

Walking quietly across to the machine, she identified an easily accessible panel and set about removing the screws. They were tighter than she had expected, and by the time she had removed the final screw she was sweating, though whether through fear or exertion she could not say.

Let's see what damage we can do, she thought as she gazed in at the myriad of different wires and circuit boards which had become exposed by removing the panel. She braced herself, holding the screwdriver tightly in her hand as she prepared to thrust it into the beast's belly.

'I wouldn't do that if I were you.'

Starr turned sharply at the voice to find Enrick standing watching her with his hands in his pockets and a smug look of amusement upon his face. She scowled at the thought of how close she had come to carrying out her plan, her frustration increased by being caught by Enrick of all people.

'Are you going to try and stop me?' she asked aggressively.

Enrick smiled and removed his glasses, cleaning them with his sleeves. 'That was my intention, Lady Starr. You see, I have no desire to see you kill yourself tonight, and your intended course of action would almost certainly electrocute you.'

Starr paused, uncertain as to whether the scientist was telling the truth or simply bluffing to keep her from attacking his precious machine. As she glanced at the exposed hole she had created in the machine's shell, she realised that her knowledge of electronics and machinery was insufficient to be certain either way, but she was not prepared to risk her life on a gamble. In frustration, she dropped the tools to the floor where they clattered loudly beside her feet.

Enrick smirked. 'A wise response. Perhaps the most sensible move you have made for a significant period of time. I heard about your attempt to sabotage my project by informing the Harbingers of our plans.'

Starr was not surprised, but the scientist's tone aggravated her. 'You can't turn this machine on. It's dangerous.'

'Oh, really, this nonsense again?' asked Enrick, rolling his eyes impatiently. 'I can assure you Lady Starr that I am not risking a repeat of the Sheol Disaster. That would result in my own untimely death, and I have no intentions of throwing away my life so meaninglessly.'

'You can't control it,' argued Starr desperately.

Enrick sneered. 'Ah, but I don't need to...' He laughed at the puzzled expression on Starr's face and approached the machine. 'You see, this has been a personal project of mine for several years now. I have endeavoured to modify the Echo Filter, to make it safer and more efficient, and in many ways I have been successful. Yet one aspect continued to elude me, or at least, it did until I happened upon your family and its black sheep.'

Starr stared at the scientist, unable to comprehend his ramblings. 'Black sheep?'

'Yes, the one missing element required to power my new and improved Echo Filter. I must confess, the original technology was ground-breaking, albeit fatally flawed. But I have learned from the mistakes of history, improved upon the technology to create the very machine which will change the nature of the world forever.'

'Malice cannot be turned into energy,' pleaded Starr desperately. 'You must know that? It's too dangerous.'

'Oh, I quite agree.'

Starr paused in shock. 'You agree? Then why are you building this machine?'

'Because I have no intention of using the Malice as the energy source.'

Starr watched in confusion as the scientist placed a hand upon the humming machinery. She wondered if perhaps Enrick had gone mad, been afflicted with Malice poisoning unbeknownst to them prior to his arrival in Gair or maybe even during his time here. Either way, she felt suddenly very uncomfortable being alone in his presence and slowly began to back away.

The scientist continued to ramble, either unaware or unconcerned about Starr's retreat. 'They were right the first time, they really were. If not for a few simple mistakes, they would have changed the world that day. But their misfortune has created my own opportunity to carve my name into the eternal memory of history. I will succeed where they failed.'

Understanding dawned upon Starr, filling her with dread. 'It's the same machine. You're going to use the machine to absorb Echoes.'

Enrick turned to her with a wild smile. 'Don't you see? It's the perfect system! Death is inevitable, but this way we can turn it into something useful. Death can help to maintain life! I just need *him…*'

The scientist's earlier words echoed in Starr's mind. *Black sheep.* She understood everything now. The machine was far more deadly than she had ever believed possible. Enrick had never intended to create a modified Echo Filter, simply an improvement on the old design. And now she knew what the final component was that he required to complete the machine. The same component which had been required to run the original machine. The component which had led to the execution and exile of an entire population.

'I'm going to tell my father. Your project is finished.'

Enrick smiled. 'He already knows.'

Starr felt her heart miss a beat. 'No… You're lying.'

'Even if I am, do you really expect him to trust you after you betrayed him? I'm afraid you've played your hand too soon. You've already lost.'

Turning sharply, she fled from the chamber. She rushed towards the palace, plunging through dimly lit corridors and climbing stairs several steps at a time as she hurried towards his room. As she arrived she opened the door immediately without waiting to knock. Only darkness met her in the empty room.

In desperation, she fled from the room and began searching rooms at random. The palace was immense, but she was determined not to abandon her search until she had found him.

She had read the books on the Sheol Disaster. She knew that the original Echo Filter had used a Necromancer to absorb the Echoes to be processed before being converted into energy. The explosion had been blamed upon the Necromancer, the reports suggesting that he had created a surge in the machinery. Whatever truth there was in that, Starr knew exactly why Enrick had come to their family to propose the project in the first place.

He needs a Necromancer. He needs Gray.

35

The stranger emerging through the Malice was getting closer. Madock attempted to call out to them, but found the words dying in his dry throat, leaving him with no choice but to simply wait and watch. He could not understand what anybody else would be doing down at the bottom of the chasm, but for now that didn't matter; the stranger offered the possibility of salvation.

As it came near enough to become visible through the Malice, Madock's heart immediately sank. It was not the first time his mind had played this trick on him, and he was not prepared to allow himself to believe his eyes like he had the first time. His mad desperation that day had cost Willow his life.

It was his daughter that walked towards him through the Malice, a little older than he remembered her but unmistakably her. Her dark hair flowed down over her shoulders as her eyes sparkled with familiarity. She walked barefoot across the snow, a simple untarnished white dress covering her body as she continued towards him, seemingly unbothered by the snow or the Malice. She slowed as she approached and smiled warmly at him, shaking her head in mock exasperation.

'How do you keep getting yourself into these situations?' she asked, her soft, familiar voice melting Madock's heart. He shook his head, determined not to fall further into the grasp of Malice poisoning.

'You're not really here Rosa,' he mumbled, forcing the words from his throat even as he struggled to tear his eyes away from her. 'It's just the Malice playing tricks on me.'

Sighing, she knelt in the snow beside him and took his hand. Her skin felt so warm against his cold flesh that he chose not to resist. 'Well, I guess that might be true,' she admitted, staring down at him sorrowfully. 'But since I'm here, it would be nice if we could enjoy our time together.'

Madock choked as tears threatened to sting his eyes. He was desperate to maintain control of his senses, but he could not deny the overwhelming urge he felt to accept her presence. 'I guess that would be nice…'

They sat in silence for a moment, Madock struggling to distance himself from what he knew to be simply a figment of his imagination. He had met individuals suffering with Malice poisoning before, had heard their ravings as the madness had set in. Haswell's case had been an extreme one, enhanced due to the fact that he had managed to survive on sheer willpower alone for such a long time, holding back the madness until it had washed over him like a tidal wave. But as much as he did not wish to accept it, he was glad that his psychosis had taken on such a pleasant nature. Many other victims of Malice poisoning were tormented by invisible demons and other dark apparitions just as Haswell had been in Tirneth. All he had to contend with were the sad eyes of his dead daughter.

'We don't blame you for not being there,' said Rosa gently, staring intently into the Death Cheater's eyes. 'We knew you were busy. You didn't know what was going to happen. How could you have known?'

Madock nodded reluctantly. It was a thought which had haunted him ever since the Sheol Disaster had taken his family from him. 'I still should have been there. I wasn't there nearly as much as I should have been.'

Rosa gazed down awkwardly at the snow. 'Maybe, but… it just made me even happier when I *did* get to see you. I know mum felt the same way. We were both massively proud of you.'

Madock shut his eyes, desperate to hide the emotion he knew must be evident in them. He knew that this was simply the Malice torturing him in its own unique way, but to hear his daughter speak such kind words was almost more than he could bear.

Abandoning himself to the fantasy, Madock opened his eyes and smiled warmly at his daughter, allowing the tears to flow freely down his cheeks. 'Tell me something you remember from those days. Anything. Please.'

Rosa smiled and gazed upwards, searching for a fond memory. 'Let's see... I remember you taking us all to Pelera to see where you worked. It was so much bigger than Sheol! I was really scared, but you held onto my hand the entire time, so I knew that it was okay. You introduced me to Uncle Ruskin and all his children, Haswell, Kerrin and Calipse. We played together in their big house.'

The memory was clear in Madock's mind. He could see the children all running around the Broxhart manor playing games together. Ruskin had insisted on being referred to as Uncle Ruskin. "You're part of the family now," he remembered his old friend saying. "Your family is my family." Ruskin Broxhart, his friend whose life had been stolen by the monster. The man who had taken him in and treated him like a brother. The man who had supported the machine which had killed his family. He shook the uncomfortable thought from his head. 'I remember you smiling a lot,' he admitted to his daughter.

She cringed and shook her head. 'I really didn't like all those Echoes though!'

Madock laughed. 'I remember.'

'I just thought it was really sad. All those lives that were finished, leaving nothing but a floating light.'

'But those floating lights were memories, Rosa,' he reminded her gently. 'They were the real people, not just the body they lived in. They'll live on forever as Echoes. Isn't that a nice thought?'

Rosa smiled down at him, but the tears in her eyes were evident now. It broke Madock's heart to see his daughter crying, even if it was just a projection of his Malice-infested mind. 'Is that what's going to happen to you? Are you going to die?' she asked, struggling not to choke on the words.

Madock paused, uncertain as to how to respond. He knew that the girl before him was simply a creation of his own mind, but he could not bring himself to upset his daughter. He had not had the chance to say goodbye to her before she died, but at least now he had the opportunity to part this world on his own terms. 'I've lived a good, long life,' he said softly, squeezing her hand tightly. 'You've had to wait a really long time for me to come home, but I think it's about time…'

His daughter sobbed, looking down at his wounded leg. 'But what if your body becomes one of those things? What if you become a demon?'

Madock refused to look down at his leg, sensing that if he glanced away from his daughter's face she would disappear forever. 'I'm not going to let that happen,' he said, attempting to sound reassuring, though in truth he had no idea how he could keep his word. 'You know there's nothing I can't do. I won't let myself turn into a demon.'

'I don't think you can promise me that,' said Rosa, seeing through his attempt to comfort her. Madock sighed and raised a hand to stroke her hair. He had done the same comforting action countless times when she was upset, back before the Sheol Disaster had ripped her from his life.

'Let me worry about that,' he said softly.

She leant over him and buried her head in his chest, allowing him to continue stroking her hair. Together they lay there in the snow, neither certain of what to say next. Madock could feel his eyelids growing tired as he relaxed, no longer feeling the ice cold snow seeping through his Malice Gear.

Taking a deep breath, he exhaled slowly. 'I'm sorry,' he whispered.

There was no reply.

As he turned to look down at his chest, he saw that there was nobody there. His daughter had vanished, leaving him alone and dying at the base of the chasm. As he rested his head back against the snow he expected the tears to flow, but there was nothing left in him. He felt empty, as though his Echo had already departed his body leaving nothing but a corrupted shell behind.

He closed his eyes, finally at peace with his fate. There was nothing he could do now, and within that knowledge there was a comforting sense of satisfaction. Nothing worried him anymore. The monster, the Malice, the Eternal Storm, none of it was his concern anymore. His tired body had been dragged through enough, and no matter what might happen to it next he was ready to face the next big adventure.

Darkness began to wash over him, dulling his senses as it slowly crept over every inch of his body. He took a deep breath and waited for whatever was about to happen. There was no fight left in him.

As the last of his strength seemed to ebb from his body, he heard a small voice. It was not his voice, nor the voice of somebody standing near his fallen body, but rather an unusual female voice in his head. It was shouting something at him, but it took him a moment to focus in on the words. Eventually he heard it.

'It's not over yet, old man…'

THE STORY WILL CONTINUE…

AZURE SKIES

ECHOES

Printed in Great Britain
by Amazon